**OMNE**

Immortal man, discoverer of the most
powerful weapon in the universe . . .

---

**OMNE**

Dead—and now reborn.
Recreated—a duplicate down to the
last atom and memory impression . . .

---

**OMNE**

Is he the invincible one who will
spell the end of Captain Kirk?

---

### THE FATE
### OF THE PHOENIX

# THE FATE OF THE PHOENIX

**SONDRA MARSHAK
AND MYRNA CULBREATH**

BANTAM BOOKS
TORONTO · NEW YORK · LONDON · SYDNEY

# DEDICATION

For Aliza Tornheim Brown and Rebecca Tornheim Shulkes

Some people deserve immortality. If we had the Phoenix to give in more than words, we would give it to them.

Their lives and the life of their sister, Anna Tornheim Hassan, span the Wright brothers' first flight and man's first step onto the moon. And when their children dream dreams and see visions, and their grandchildren reach for the stars, it will be by their strength and love.

THE FATE OF THE PHOENIX
A Bantam Book / May 1979
2nd printing ..... October 1979
3rd printing ..... October 1981

® Designates a trademark of Paramount Pictures Corporation registered in the United States Patent and Trademark Office.

Published by arrangement with Bantam Books, Inc., under exclusive license from Paramount Pictures Corporation, the trademark owner.

ISBN 0-553-20769-5

Published simultaneously in the United States and Canada

Bantam Books are published by Bantam Books, Inc. Its trademark, consisting of the words "Bantam Books" and the portrayal of a rooster, is Registered in U.S. Patent and Trademark Office and in other countries. Marca Registrada. Bantam Books, Inc., 666 Fifth Avenue, New York, New York 10103.

PRINTED IN THE UNITED STATES OF AMERICA

12 11 10 9 8 7 6 5 4 3

# THE FATE OF
# THE PHOENIX

# PROLOGUE:

## THE NIGHT OF THE PHOENIX

He woke, dying.

Even his iron control wanted to rage against the agony in his chest, where the .45 bullet had blasted away lung and bone, slamming him against the Sickbay wall . . .

Yes, rage against the dying.

Death . . . final . . . this time.

No man could have stood against that fatal blast.

He had smiled the wolf-smile against the night and the opposition and left them his dead-man switch to raise the question, never knowing whether the final irony might not be on him.

Death, the final oblivion, for the man who had beaten death.

Was this merely the last moment before finality?

Or—the first moment after?

Or was this—supreme irony—some other kind of immortality entirely?

The first immortal . . . now to learn that there was no death . . . ?

He was bolt upright. Naked. Alone.

No arms to catch him in that first jolting moment of return, as there had been for the other one . . .

He rejected that thought. He asked for no arms. He never asked . . .

The thought, the memory, seemed to complete some circuit. The whole of the day of the Phoenix was with him . . . and all of his life. He knew who he was and who he had been . . . Omne . . . Omnedon . . . yes, and who he would be again, to the cost of the man who had killed him, and the other four who had fought him today over the fate of the Phoenix . . .

Black Omne . . .

He laughed in his throat, hearing his own words to them: "Never mourn Black Omne."

And yet the man who had killed him had said, "*I shall. The mind. The giant. Not the wolf but the man who defeated death.*"

That man who would mourn him had known bitter defeat at Omne's hands, and Omne had seen in his eyes the tears of a starship captain.

But it had been that captain, beaten and stunned by the shocks of the day, who had devised the plan to draw Omne out. That man had the effrontery to offer Omne amnesty—"Does the wolf accept amnesty from the lambs, Captain?" That man had the nerve to meet him in that moment of elemental confrontation, to meet his naked steel with the Captain's single sword and solitary courage: this time in the primitive clash of gun-on-gun. Or—man-on-man.

In that battle the Captain had won.

It was a victory which should have been final, and was not.

For that there was a price.

Never mourn Black Omne . . .

Omne ran his hands down over his unbroken chest, feeling the smoothly breathing, unbreached lungs, the newly minted, familiar body. It was unhurt, as it had been the first time he rose from the flames this day.

First he had died in the body battered by the titanic, bone-crushing battle with the Vulcan.

Then Omne's hands had marveled for the first time at what seemed even to him the miracle of rebirth. Unbelievingly they had felt the new body and the absence of the agony of the fight, but more, of the blast of that last black moment when Omne had chosen death before defeat.

The Vulcan had been reaching with his mind link to rip out from Omne's mind the memory of the day of the Phoenix, of the original Captain Kirk and his perfect replica, James, whom Omne had created.

But that memory Omne would not yield.

He never surrendered.

The hand which had pulled that first trigger, never knowing whether the Phoenix process would work, had been Omne's own.

For that the Vulcan would also learn the price.

Omne rose.

He padded silently across his impregnable laboratory and flipped a switch . . .

THE COMMANDER said, "James."

His head, more golden now, lifted from beside the Vulcan's dark one at the transporter console.

"Prepare for intra-ship beaming to Romulan flagship," James said into the intercom, in a voice which Dr. McCoy's plastic surgery had made a fraction deeper and more resonant. But the tone of command authority was still the same, and would pass for now. "Kirk out."

"Aye, Captain," Scott said from the bridge.

It was just as well that the Chief Engineer could not see the pointed Romulan ears on the man who had been his captain. Nor the slightly altered face. Nor the faintly Romulan complexion, lightly touched by the fact that bone-marrow cells cloned from the Vulcan gave the Human green blood now.

James turned to the Commander. She faced him directly.

"There is something which you said that I would have to take up with Spock first, James," she said.

James looked startled, as if jolted back past all the hours in which he had become another man. When he had still known himself to be James T. Kirk, even if he and Spock had believed then that the original Jim Kirk was dead, James had thanked the Commander with a kiss for putting her Romulan strength between him and Omne. But James had said that Spock would mind anything more—and that she would have to take that up with Spock first. James had known that neither that kiss nor anything which had happened since had changed what she had felt for Spock. And yet James had supposed that some things had changed, for all practical purposes. "I rather thought we had settled that," James said. "You are beaming me to your quarters."

*"That* has been settled," she said.

"What, then? I have not agreed to your princeling script, you know. Or is even that not far enough 'outside the phalanx' for you?"

"Perhaps not," she said. "We have agreed that you cannot let me leave without you, whatever the public— or private—script. But this must be named."

She turned to Spock. His face wore the glacial look of ice barely sheathing a volcano. It was the look of the primordial Vulcan which had become his during the day of the Phoenix.

"Mr. Spock," she said, "I told Omne you were not my price."

"Yes."

"I lied, Mr. Spock."

The Vulcan face did not alter.

Spock had always known that his path could not lie with hers. But today when he had gone to fight Omne—and they had all known that Spock computed a vanishingly small probability that he would return alive—Spock had given her a trust to keep: James. Spock had seen Kirk die, this day, seen his body, and she knew that Spock had more than once seen doubles for Jim Kirk die. But this one *was* Kirk, to the last molecule and memory. She had seen the Vulcan link minds with the 'replica' while they both believed that Kirk was dead, and, with a generosity of spirit which she would have believed only of the Vulcan, Spock had accepted this first-born of the Phoenix as Kirk. Spock had been prepared to grant him every right which had been Kirk's—even the friendship of the Vulcan, for which they had become legend even as far as the Romulan Empire. But all of the Vulcan's generosity had not been able to conceal from James in the continuing link what it meant to the Vulcan to learn that the original Kirk had not died. In that moment James was born, child of none.

Perhaps it was that, most of all, which made James new, different: Kirk but not-Kirk: more vulnerable, alone. He was displaced, despite anything the Vulcan or any of them could do, from the life which should have been his. And he was only too willing to go against the giant who had created him and his special metaphysical problem.

Against Omne, whose alien strength was born of some unknown race from a destroyed planet where he had once ruled as Omnedon . . . Omne's strength was more than equal to the best of Spock's or her own Vulcanoid species, and it could have destroyed the Human in a moment.

But Spock had foreseen that danger from the beginning and would not permit it—nor permit even James to regard himself as expendable.

And the Commander had kept the trust. If the meaning of her strength had never been clear to the Human, it was clear when she carried James bodily off the field of battle and held him by main force and a will as stubborn as his own.

But it was not merely for the Vulcan that she had done it.

Finally they had all known that there was only one path left which James could walk, or would: by her side.

Spock had concurred in the logic. There was that in him which did not have to like it.

And too much of both Spock's Vulcan and his Human depths had been touched today. He had brought

Kirk's charred body home to Dr. Leonard McCoy, Scott, the *Enterprise*. He had gone down into the labyrinthine hell of Omne's Black Hole planet to challenge its owner for the murder of Jim Kirk, in which Spock had even suspected the Commander of complicity. But he had arrived to find that less than murder had been done, or worse. For the crime of creating a man with no place, there was no name. For the first time in the galaxy two men and those who were their friends, or their most dangerous enemy, faced the fact of absolute identity: two Kirks each fully as real and as valuable. Which had the right to everything which had always been his?

James had only his memories of the day of the Phoenix to call his own, and what the Commander had become to him.

No. She saw now that he still had one more thing which had always been his, and always would.

Spock looked at the Commander stonily and withdrew, as if behind a wall, without moving. "There is James now," he said flatly.

"Indeed," the Commander said. "That does not alter an exchange which was permanent."

Spock looked at her bleakly out of the burning eyes. "No. It does not."

He started to turn away.

She reached up, asking no permission, making no concession now to the customs of the ancient, common heritage they shared, by which they had first touched on her starship. They lived between the stars. And they lived in a universe which had become new today. There was immortality now. There would be time enough for love, and for all things. If they lived . . .

She pulled the Vulcan's head down into a kiss.

It was not goodbye.

For a long moment he was stiff. There was Vulcan logic. And there was James.

But she had walked through fire with the Vulcan this day, and she had kept the trust.

Now he must let her go, and she knew now that it was with the one man to whom he would have allowed it. And there was that in him which still did not have to like it.

Finally the Vulcan crushed her to him with that strength of a male of her own species, which he knew she would not get from James.

They had had perhaps an excess of nobility for one day. And she had told him how tired she was of respecting him. This was the Vulcan she had seen from the beginning. Nothing had altered that, or him.

He took her breath—then wrenched her away.

"There will be time for us, Mr. Spock," she said.

"There will be *no* time," Spock said with sudden ferocity. "Do you not understand? Once you leave my sight, I am your worst enemy. Omne has a transporter scan of my body, and he has my memories from the moment when we were linked as he killed himself. He can come against you in my body. *You* might detect it with the mind link. James cannot. Jim cannot. And Omne has tried to take both of them as hostages against us for a thousand years."

"I know that, Mr. Spock," the Commander said.

"None of us know it fully. We have named a few dozen permutations of the danger of the Phoenix process. There are hundreds. There is no one who cannot be bought at the price of the Phoenix. And you are going off into the Romulan Empire with the first fighting commander of half a galaxy—who now cannot raise his hand without being revealed as a Human, and getting his more delicate bones broken against Romulan strength. If you do not grasp that fully—there is zero chance that you will be able to keep the trust and to keep him alive."

"My capacity to keep that trust has been established, Spock," she said. "I kept it today. How will you keep yours? And what will you do when Omne takes Jim?"

"I do not know," the Vulcan said bleakly. Then he pulled his shoulders back. "But I will keep that trust, as you will yours."

"Yes," she said, seeing now the full cost of this day to the Vulcan. He now gave more hostages to fortune—

perhaps even herself—and he could protect none of them from the deadliest threat they had ever faced.

Least of all could Spock protect them from himself. She saw him look down the long vista of his efforts to guard against an Omne who had been, in himself, perhaps the most formidable man in the galaxy. Now he was the first immortal: first truly to come back from the finality of death. But he was not merely the Phoenix from the flame. Omne had spoken of the legend of the Fire Dragon, and she knew it from obscure areas of Romulan space. It was the legend of two who were reborn as one.

Omne was not merely Omne now—if he lived again. His first death had given him Spock's mind, entwined with his own—all of the Vulcan's knowledge and all his Vulcan telepathic powers and mental disciplines to add to Omne's own powers.

He had always been a superlatively dangerous enemy. Now he was menace, squared. There was no secret which they had from him or could keep. And now he could come to Jim or James using the body and mind of Spock.

The Commander saw now that after such knowledge and at the end of the whole of this day, the Vulcan was not entirely logical, perhaps not entirely sane.

It was still an open question whether even now Spock would stand and see James go.

But neither she nor the Vulcan had fully reckoned with the man who had still been Captain James T. Kirk.

She did not see James begin the move, but suddenly he was close and his hand reached for the Vulcan's shoulder as if to renew that contact, perhaps even the mind link, by which they had seen each other through this day—through the gates of hell, and back.

Then she saw James realize that the last of the terrible Vulcan control could crack entirely.

With that years-deep knowledge of the Vulcan which was still his, James drew the hand back, with an effort which looked as if it broke something . . . perhaps his heart.

But he was steady, as if to steady the Vulcan with his eyes.

The moment when only their eyes met was the seal on everything they had been, with the ending of it.

Whatever would be their future it could never be the same, and from this road there was no turning, and no return.

"Gates of hell, Spock," James murmured, not finding much breath for it, in the phrase which had become their watchword today.

" . . . shall not prevail against us," the Vulcan completed. "I will not say goodbye."

Some ghost of the Human's old hell-bent smile found its way to the mouth which was still much the same. "We've still broken out of worse places, Spock. No goodbye."

Then Spock turned as if to put James into her hands, not trusting himself to move to do it. "Keep the trust," he said to her and turned abruptly to the transporter console.

James moved with her to the transporter platform, while he still could. She doubted that he could see, but she did not have to guide him as she had once today when James' eyes had filled with Jim's tears.

James knew this place by his heart. He took her hand and his step onto the platform was firm, but she could feel the tie to his whole life stretched taut behind him.

For a moment she wondered whether the slender bond they had forged this day could stand against that. Would he always be a displaced person, bereft of his ship, his friends, his place, even his name? Or could he really find a new life with her?

Would there be time—for him, for her, for Spock— while they stood under the shadow of the Phoenix—and the Fire Dragon?

"Energize," James said for the last time in the command tone.

And the Vulcan, without a word, since there were no words, sent them off with his own hand . . .

KIRK looked up into the Vulcan face.

Spock must have come into Sickbay quietly after seeing James and the Commander off.

Kirk had sent Dr. McCoy, under protest, to have Dr. M'Benga take care of the wrist Omne had broken when McCoy went against the giant with a spray-hypo.

Kirk must have let his eyes close.

He caught the Vulcan watching him sleep.

But Spock's face was the face of prehistoric Vulcan, carved in flame.

The veneer of Vulcan's thousand years of peace and logic had been burned away in the fires of the Phoenix.

Kirk understood, too well. James had said that Spock would need to retreat behind the wall of Vulcan emotional control, after this day. But perhaps even that was to be denied to Spock. He had seen Kirk dead, seen him defeated, beaten, and had just sent James off into the impenetrable Romulan Empire.

Nor could Spock defend either one of them from what he must expect: the return of Omne.

Spock saw that Kirk was awake, and the Vulcan turned with great precision and put his fist through the intercom. Omne had tapped into it before—with a technology which they could not match.

Then the Vulcan came and put his hands on Kirk's face in the position of the Vulcan mind link.

"Spock?"

Kirk felt the sudden wrench of a terrible doubt. This was no Vulcan he knew. Spock would have made certain of permission—

Spock's mouth went tight. "Do you begin to understand?" he said. *"I have been out of your sight."*

Kirk felt the world reel. They had *said* that Omne could come to them in the form of Spock . . .

"Go ahead," Kirk said steadily. "You *are* Spock."

He saw the look on Spock's face of acknowledging that trust. "It will be the deep link," the Vulcan said gravely. "The kind of special mind link I had with James until Omne broke it by my own power. The directional tracing link. Omne will come to take you hostage, and I would have no way to find you."

"I know," Kirk said, "do it."

Kirk set himself and tried to open his mind completely, to answer only in his mind. 'Yes, here I am. Spock. It *is* Spock?'

He did not know how to reach out to the Vulcan, and at some level Kirk sensed his own resistance, without quite knowing the nature of it. There would be a safety for both of them in the tracing link, and a kind of communication which they had shared for only moments, but which had spanned a gulf between stars. Spock was no alien to him.

And yet—and yet, would it somehow tie his hands, make him more cautious, cut off that lone freedom of action which a commander must have—?

And—was it *Spock?*

The last thought caught at his heart with the icy hand of pure terror. If it were *not,* and he opened to this kind of link . . .

Nevertheless, if it were Spock and he did *not* open—
. . . He tried again, in one leap of faith. " '*Spock!*' " he called aloud, and silently.

'I will do the one thing I cannot do,' the Vulcan's mind voice said in Kirk's mind, and Kirk caught some hint of the cost of that kind of link to the Vulcan.

And in the same moment Kirk felt the full mental contact—but it was flame.

Kirk screamed—somewhere in his mind, he thought, but could not be sure.

Something was wrong with the Vulcan, and something was wrong with him, and the meeting of their minds was one sheet of blind, incandescent flame which sent searing tendrils down into Kirk's mind, burning out—God knew what.

He writhed in agony and called " 'Spock!' "

But the Vulcan seemed caught in it, too. Spock must be hurt, psionically. He had used the deep link today for a purpose it was not to serve, and Omne had torn out Spock's link with James by the roots.

If this flame was the result of psionic shock—

But Kirk could not maintain coherent thought. The agony was beyond anything he had known. From somewhere it was as if he could feel his mind putting up defenses, beyond his will, and for his life—shutting off, shutting out, closing down. Perhaps it was for the Vulcan's life, too—their last line of defense.

Or perhaps that flame in the other mind was another kind of psychic shock from the mingling of Omne and Spock.

No. That thought led to utter chaos.

Kirk felt the walls closing down, locking him away from the Vulcan—if it *was* the Vulcan—locking down tight, clanging like all emergency doors closing. *No— not alone—*

But Kirk could not stop it, and he was falling down into oblivion—and nightmare . . .

The nightmare was filled with the searing fragments and images of the day of the Phoenix, above all with the brooding, terrible presence of Omne. Then the nightmare went on, into the night of the Phoenix, and Omne wore the face and the flesh of Spock . . .

THE COMMANDER emerged to hear intruder alarm sounding and the green-alert level of battle-engage.

She collected James by an arm, propelled him into a corner not covered by the cameras, and moved for the intercom.

The screen flared into life with the face of her Sub-Commander S'Tal on the bridge. He was sounding search and destroy against the intruder and hailing the *Enterprise* with the demand to deliver his Commander immediately or be destroyed.

"Cancel battle-engage," she ordered. "I am the intruder."

S'Tal whirled and stared into the view screen which showed her face. For a moment she saw the relief. Then his expression was correct again. "Commander." He inclined his head, but his eyes narrowed. "Doyen to Princeling grid three."

"Tribute in two moves," she answered with satisfaction.

S'Tal had not been unduly awed by her script performance with Jim Kirk. S'Tal knew that the reports of Kirk's death might not have been greatly exaggerated. And if there were a question of one identity, there might be a question of hers. That the code would be of no help against the Phoenix S'Tal could not know.

On completion of the code S'Tal's hand slashed down to cut off the battle-engage. He opened a hailing frequency. *"Enterprise,* the promptness of your return of our Commander is satisfactory. S'Tal out."

S'Tal stood up and looked at her. "Permission to come to your quarters," he said.

It was a request not to be denied.

She stood a trifle straighter. "Not now, S'Tal. Triple security on all ships. Use phase-two shielding and attempt to strengthen it against nonstandard transporter penetration. Assume all intercoms are being tapped at all times, even when off, and disable critical units by removing main viode. Important messages by runner. Warp Eight on course for previous mission. Meet me in one minute at lift GQ1. Out."

She switched off and turned to James.

She had watched him from the corner of her eye, catching on his face the look of seeing her in her element. She liked what she saw—and what she liked most was that so did he.

But she had no time for that.

She gathered him up and moved him to the connecting door. "You'll find what you need here," she said. "Don't be long. Don't come out without my permission."

He was half through the door as she said that, and he turned and looked at her, startled.

She stepped through the door for an instant and crumpled the intercom console with the edge of her hand. There was a time for patience . . .

Then she stepped back through the door and it closed in his face.

She scooped up a handweapon to replace her own, and made record time to the rendezvous with S'Tal.

Without preamble and before he could speak she said: "You are to assume that we are on undeclared war alert. Assume maximum technological assault, including tapping of all electromagnetic systems, penetration of shields by transporter, possible infiltration by intruders and imposters. Assume a massive, well-organized opposition of extreme sophistication—"

"The Federation?" S'Tal said.

"No," she said. "The Federation is as always. However, for practical purposes you will on no account fire on the *Enterprise,* nor any Federation ship without my direct order, nor permit anyone to do so."

S'Tal's eyes were hard with puzzlement—and with anger.

She was not obliged to explain, nor did she care to. But she understood that she had been playing a lone hand—while he waited, alone and uninformed. He had been her arm. It was not his fault if she had found her heart.

She inclined her head to him in acknowledgment. "S'Tal. Consider for practical purposes that the opposition is from Omne's organization and his conference of disaffected delegates, which narrowly failed to vote secession from the Federation."

"Narrowly—by the margin of your joint speech with the Federation Starship Captain who was your arch-enemy," S'Tal said pointedly. "Secession of many planets from the Federation would have strengthened our Empire—particularly the War Party."

She nodded. "No one chooses my enemies for me, S'Tal. Nor—my friends. Do you stand with me?"

His eyes narrowed. He understood that it was an invitation to treason. At least, so the War Party would judge her actions of this day. Worse, what she had done went against S'Tal's own grain, too.

Nevertheless, he did not hesitate.

"Where else?" he said.

For a moment she held his eyes. "Nowhere," she said gravely.

Then she broke it. "Proceed, S'Tal. Take every precaution. You have the con until further notice."

She turned, feeling his eyes on her back.

When she rounded the corner she broke almost into a run and was back to her quarters seconds later.

The lock on the connecting door was undisturbed.

She took another moment to shed her uniform and step into the flasher to emerge clean and glowing, feeling as if she wore a new skin—which was virtually the case.

For a moment she stood still, stopped by a sudden cold chill.

What would that Romulan process, one micro-second of which flashed away unwanted debris and a cell-deep layer of skin unprotected by the hair and eyebrow shield, do to Human skin?

She felt the silken texture of that skin in the memory of her hands and knew that his skin was far more delicate than Romulan skin.

For a long moment she was stopped, appalled—seeing a sudden vista of the daily death traps which would open for James among Romulans. His strength would be as a child's, his delicacy like a newborn. Could he use the flasher at all? Or the water-fresher without scalding himself? Could he turn it on—or off? Could he work the catch on the door? They had considered the problems which would make him an alpha male who could not raise his hand to fight against Romulan strength. But could he open a vehicle door?

She felt the sudden rise of something that was almost panic.

She put it down. She was not given to panic, nor did she give herself to it.

Nevertheless she knew that the cause for panic was there. Bad enough the cold panic of the danger of Omne to the man who was his first creation. But the danger of her world, her way, to James could be quite as deadly, and less obvious. This was the last man in the galaxy who would take to finding his easy strength balked and his toughness turned to delicacy. This was a starship captain, *the* Captain who had been a legend in his own service, the most nerveless of a fearless breed. That fine courage had been the cause of this day and it was the reason for his being here. But it had also driven a Vulcan to distraction and to the state she had seen this day.

She did not propose to be driven. Nor did she intend to see the day when she would stand over the results of this one's recklessness and know that his death was final and that immortality would be of no use to her.

She would keep him safe.

She did not much care whether he liked it or not.

She slammed into the white gown.

She went through the door without knocking ⋅ ⋅ ⋅

She found him trying to open the closet.

He was using something to pry at the ordinary thumb catch. The catch gave just as she entered to open on the guest wardrobe of a Fleet Commander. There were robes and uniforms or civilian clothing for males and females of a variety of Romulan and other cultures.

James had removed the telltale Star Fleet uniform and had evidently managed the water shower. The new gold hair was damp, the skin glowing with the faint new color of Romulan pigmentation and blood.

He was all but naked and wearing a strip-towel wound around him.

Both her rear view and several front angles in the mirrored doors showed that the narrow towel did not quite cover the territory.

He saw her first in the mirrors, and for a long moment merely looked at her, stunned.

Finally he turned with fire in his eyes, incredulous. "You came in without knocking?" he said tightly.

She felt an eyebrow rise. In truth it had not occurred to her.

"Yes," she said. "Of course."

"Where I come from," he said, "the custom is to ask permission to enter."

"Where you *are*, it is not," she said.

"But even Vulcans—"

"Romulans are not Vulcans. And if they were it still would not be the custom to ask permission to enter the presence of a male who is mine."

"Yours?" He was a little surprised—but he had never quite been certain whether she was kidding about regarding him as the property of the victor. He was not certain now, but he was beginning to look interested again. She had, after all, fought for him. "Did we establish what would happen if I needed to own *you?*" he said.

"No. Merely that you could not let me leave without you. And that I would not. But we did establish that you would manage even the 'princeling' script, if necessary."

"There remains the working out of the private script," he said, moving toward her and reminding her a little of his own power.

"Yes."

For a moment his eyes flickered toward the closet full of clothes, the guest cabin, and she thought that he thought also of the Vulcan. "New script," he said. "I doubt you will have time to spare."

He reached for her, but she laughed silently and took his face in her hands. "*I* decide on scripts here," she said, but she let the beginning of the mind touch flow— that tingling, exotic current which had taken his breath on the *Enterprise* when she had first claimed him with a kiss.

It caught at his breathing now, and for a moment he wanted nothing more than to crush her in that claiming of his own which he had not been able to permit himself—with Spock linked to his mind and Jim linked by the strange resonance to every nerve of James' body.

Suddenly he did do it, putting the argument aside— or as if it were an answer to the argument.

His arms locked around her and molded their bodies together with that confident control which was his and which transcended lines of strength. His mouth found hers with that same strength and subtlety of control, the practiced expertise controlling the elemental fire and, for that moment, her, with that essence of maleness which commanded worship across any line.

She answered and felt his body answer with a worship of its own.

Her innocent princeling . . .

'As innocent as any virgin,' she said in his mind, in the words which Omne had used, 'and more than most. A grown man—and without sin.'

He laughed back within her mind. 'Less than anyone. I am still—'

She felt the ancient fires rise to a solid column within her, searing and urgent, and she reached for the depths of his mind. . . . Yes, . . . the bonding link, deep and not to be broken . . .—to make him hers forever and lead her to him even into fire . . . She reached down into those levels of link which were not to be touched for less, and which were raw now with the agonies of the day . . . Gently now—

He recoiled suddenly and flung her away—out of his mind, away from his body, his whole being becoming one essence of negation: "No!" he said in his throat.

She was unprepared and caught herself only as she crashed against a wall.

For a moment she was open, vulnerable at the deep levels of the link. Then she turned the flame to the white heat of anger.

She came back at him—and stopped just short, suddenly remembering his vulnerable Human bones.

And then she felt the chill in her own bones, and knew that it was terror. He had provoked her, not counting cost or risk—and what other Romulan would he provoke tomorrow to court his death?

She pinned him against the mirrored wall and locked her hand into his face again.

She let him feel the rage, and her strength, and drove

for the deep link again. She could not let him out of her sight, out of her mind. He would try his alpha-maleness on some Romulan and be killed. Omne would come and James would try some hare-brained defense intended to protect her—and die, or be taken away where she would never find him without the directional tracing link . . .

'Parted from me and never parted,' she said in the ancient tongue and words which her race shared with Vulcan. The formula from the time of the beginning translated in his mind and he knew it for the words of forever. But he was not ready.

He was struggling, but he had to focus on the mental struggle now—and untrained though he was, his mind was startlingly powerful.

Somehow he was finding the ways to block the deep levels. She could have forced her way through. She wanted to. She wanted to press down through to that last layer where there could be no secrets from her, no innocence and nothing which did not belong to her.

It was not civilized, and she did not care. This was how mates had been taken in some ancient time by Romulans and Vulcans, and by Vulcans still. Her bones held some memory of it, and some longing.

And the part of her mind which knew only this day also raged for it, demanded it, knowing that in the next moment, any moment, Omne could come and take his handiwork—this man—leaving her alone and with no way in the galaxy to find James.

She pressed in, but his resistance was now total.

He mustered some strength and heaved her away from the wall, but could not lose her. She brought him down on the sleeping platform and caught an armlock which he could not break.

But neither could she break his mental resistance—except at the cost of such agony for him that now she pulled back a little.

"No," he whispered.

And then silently in the upper level of the link: 'No—I don't want it. I can't. Not—yet.' He could not breathe or move and his own anger flared high. He would have liked to be able, as with other women he had known, to play the game in teasing or in earnest of his easy male power—to pin her with muscle and hold her with his strength. And some part of him would have liked to surrender to hers—just to let it happen and to feel that exquisite caress at the deepest levels of mind which he could sense but had never known.

But he could not do it, and would not, and he doubted that he could stand against her mentally, but would, to the last of his strength—and hate her forever.

And still—he would be alive . . . stay alive . . .

'Don't do this to—us,' he sent. 'God damn it—don't do it to me, I am *not* your "princeling." '

He strained against her again. He was powerful for a Human. Active. Determined. But no match for her Ito mulan strength.

'Of course you are. The property of the victor.'

He shook his head. 'I've given you my life. I can't give more. Stop it, before I can't give that.'

There was an urgency and a strength to the open plea which touched her. And the raw nerve ends and sense of loss where Omne had torn out the roots of the link with Spock moved her. The loss of all this man's roots touched her profoundly—and the real strength of this man, who had chosen that loss with all it meant, to put his life in her hands.

She saw the long view open before her. She would never know where he was or what he was doing. He would be taken one day, and she would not know whether he was in the dungeons of Empire, or with Omne, or held for ransom by someone else who knew what James was to her.

Then she let him see it, too, in the link: the search. The terror. The bitter rage at herself for knowing that she could have prevented it at this moment.

She opened her eyes from the inner focus and saw James' face, his lips, register her terror and understand. His lip trembled and he tried to hold it steady. Some-

thing in his mind shifted and he almost opened to her.
But he could not.

She brought her mouth down on his, and this time it
was she who kissed him, to the depths of his soul.

She had not let up on the mind touch, but neither did
she press deeper. Still, he was stiff and his mouth was
cold.

Then for just a moment she touched into the deep
level to show him what it could mean, what he denied
them both—the level of intensity, the point beyond endurance.

He gasped, but still he could not reach for it.

She withdrew then, slowly, trailing fire along his
nerve ends.

He gasped and twisted under her, and suddenly he
knew that he had won—or that she had.

She was leaving him his privacy, and his pain.

She felt him flood with relief, and then his mouth was
warm under hers again and answered her again, silently.

She lifted her head and looked down at him.

"We shall both live to regret this day," she said. "I,
most of all."

# CHAPTER I

KIRK woke to find Spock keeping sleepless Vulcan vigil over him.

That was normal.

But Kirk sensed instantly that something was terribly wrong. With the ship? He reached out to test the subliminal "feel" of the *Enterprise*. No. She flew straight and true. The fault was in *him*.

He felt—alone. Alone in some way in which he had not been alone for years . . .

"Spock?"

The Vulcan rose stiffly, formally. "Captain."

That prehistoric look which Spock had worn the night before was gone as if it had never existed. He wore a mask—that Vulcan mask which he had not worn in that form for years. It no longer seemed to fit his face.

"Mr. Spock . . ." Kirk said.

"Ship's functions are normal, sir."

"*Spock,* report on *your* functions."

The mask threatened to slip for a moment. "Not normal, Captain."

But Kirk was way ahead of him on that count. He had realized that the Vulcan's "carrier hum" was gone—that psychic awareness which made most humans bask in the Vulcan's presence, and made a few acutely uncomfortable. Its absence made Kirk uncomfortable to the point of pain. He felt locked in his own skull, alone.

"You're not *there,* Spock," Kirk said.

"No. Nor are *you.*"

"*I* don't have psychic powers—"

"Whatever you have—call it intuition, hunch, luck—it is closed down now. I have done that to you. I am unable to estimate the effect on your command. It was a psionic 'burnout.' My fault. I should have known the capacity could not be strained in that way. We are both now virtually psi-null."

"How long?" Kirk said.

"Unknown. There has been no such case."

"Perhaps forever?" Kirk asked.

"Unknown. Any attempt to test the hypothesis would only worsen the effect, and cause great distress, especially to you."

"Try it, Spock. A moment. We can't function like this. Not at our best. And—not against Omne."

The Vulcan's manner indicated a foregone conclusion. But he touched Kirk's temple.

Nothing.

And then there was a flash of excruciating contact.

Kirk almost blacked out again. And as he did the thought came unbidden: How convenient for Omne, if he wanted to be here in the shape of Spock . . .

"All right, Mr. Spock, let's mind the store."

"Very well, Captain."

Kirk almost groaned. Spock or not, it was as James had predicted. The real Spock would have to retreat behind the great wall of Vulcan to rebuild his defenses after the day of the Phoenix—and now after its night.

Double-Vulcan, McCoy would call it—and they would all suffer and grouse to each other until it blew over and Spock was himself again.

And Kirk would be glad enough to suffer, as long as it *was* the Vulcan.

If it was *not*—

No. No point in thinking of it. He could only treat this man as Spock.

And perhaps Omne was not here. Kirk *had* killed
him. And even if he lived, Omne would have many other
things to do to pursue his galactic purpose, and ultimately to spring some trap on them.

What would Omne be doing, loose in the galaxy?

"Mr. Spock," Kirk said. "It is time for us to become
flamespotters."

"Indeed," Spock said, and helped him across to the
door without flickering an eyebrow.

"Where, Spock?"

"Everywhere."

ROBLEIN put the office in order, touching but not
seeing the familiar symbols of his authority, oblivious to
his view of the great flagwall to the courtyard of the
United Federation of Planets Centroplex.

His successor should have an orderly, scrupulous
transition, be aware of the crucial matters, as Roblein
had always tried to be.

He was not abdicating responsibility. He merely
knew that he was not fit for it.

He kept seeing the flames. He had seen the aircar go
down in flames. He saw nothing else except her face.

He was fit for no high office. Certainly not this one.

And from his body came the warning signals.

He had been well, only yesterday. He did not expect
to live out the year—perhaps not the week.

It did not matter.

There were those who loved not wisely, but too well.
And there were those who loved wisely. And once.

He signed his letter of resignation with the same firm
hand which had charted the course of much of Federation policy for decades.

In a moment he would call the President.

In just a moment . . .

"Roblein."

It was not a question.

Roblein looked up to see the dark giant who seemed
to have appeared silently out of the gloom of the office.

Roblein had not come up the hard way for nothing.

His hand filled with the hand phaser which rested in the arm of his chair.

"Who are you?"

For an answer the dark figure stepped forward—the most powerful man Roblein had ever seen—and placed a golden shape on the desk.

It was a curious flattened shape, like a medallion, yet almost reminiscent of a face.

"Touch it," the man said.

There was a compelling aura about him. Roblein did not take to being compelled.

"Maia," the giant said.

Roblein's hand fell on the shape to smash it toward the giant's skull.

The hand froze. He saw her . . . laid out as if dead, but breathing. Somehow he saw the whole picture:

The offer. The price.

"No," he said.

Then he saw the alternative. The woman lying quiet and vulnerable, undefended. The giant entering the room . . .

The giant made no threatening motion, said nothing. It was all graphically simple and absolutely plain.

The mental projection left no possibility of doubt or argument. In the projection the giant touched her face.

Roblein's hand tightened on the phaser. But he sensed in the projection that even the giant's death would not stop him from that inexorable progression. The giant would rise again, as Roblein's wife Maia had.

She lived. Roblein had seen her charred body, and she *lived* . . .

Then the projection filled with her thoughts, her living thoughts.

Roblein put the phaser to his head.

Then he put it down.

He crumpled the resignation . . .

KIRK turned in the command chair to take the intelligence summary printout from Uhura as it came into her communications station on the bridge. "Priority one, Captain," she said.

Kirk murmured his thanks, scanned the report, and after a long moment handed the printout on to the stone-faced Vulcan. "A fire alarm, Mr. Spock."

Kirk and his First Officer had lived with the mental silence between them for more than two weeks, and the bridge crew, finally the whole ship, had become uneasily aware of it, in spite of all the efforts of the two of them to maintain that everything was business as usual.

Nor had the *Enterprise* crew really recovered from the finality of believing Kirk to be dead. Crew-people found excuses to be close to him, almost to touch him. He tried not to show quite how much that did touch him.

Kirk, Spock, and McCoy watched for the evidence in the galaxy of what might be Omne's work. And they had found it—in too many places. But not on the scale which this report indicated—until now.

The Vulcan scanned the report without a flicker of expression. But no psychic aura was required to project or to read his reaction. The intelligence summary spoke for itself:

INTELLIGENCE SUMMARY. STARDATE 9722.4 FEDERATION DIRECTOR OF INTERWORLD AFFAIRS R. A. ROBLEIN ANNOUNCED TODAY AN OPEN DEBATE ON THE MATTER OF THE PRIME DIRECTIVE OF NONINTERFERENCE. HEARINGS SLATED WILL CONSIDER NOT MERELY INTERSTELLAR ACCUSATIONS OF FEDERATION VIOLATION OF ITS OWN DIRECTIVE BUT THE PHILOSOPHICAL VALIDITY OF THE POLICY ITSELF. "DO WE PLAY GOD AS MUCH OR MORE BY NONINTERFERENCE AS BY JUDICIOUS INTERVENTION?" ROBLEIN SAID IN A SURPRISE SPEECH TO A CONFERENCE OF INTERWORLD DELEGATES. "CERTAINLY WE CONDEMN BILLIONS TO DEATH WHOM OUR MEDICINE COULD SAVE, BILLIONS MORE WE CONDEMN TO SLAVERY OR OPPRESSION, AND TRILLIONS TO CON-

FINEMENT ON THEIR SINGLE WORLDS, WITH-
OUT THE STARS. HAVE WE THE RIGHT?"

THE STATEMENT IS EXPECTED TO CAUSE
REPERCUSSIONS AS FAR AS THE ROMULAN AND
KLINGON EMPIRES, AND UPHEAVALS WITHIN
THE FEDERATION. ROBLEIN WAS FORMERLY
REGARDED AS A CHAMPION OF PROPER AP-
PLICATION OF THE PRIME DIRECTIVE.

ANY FEDERATION MOVE TO ALTER ITS POSI-
TION ON THE PRIME DIRECTIVE WOULD BE
TAKEN AS CAUSE FOR WAR OR SECESSION BY
NUMEROUS DISAFFECTED MEMBERS OF THE
FEDERATION. SOME OF THEM MET RECENTLY
AT THE BLACK HOLE CONFERENCE WHICH
DISBANDED WITHOUT ACTION ON THE DEATH
OF ITS HOST, OMNE.

A FOLLOWUP CONFERENCE HAS NOW BEEN
SCHEDULED FOR THE ORIGIN WORLD OF
THE VORAN DYNASTY HEGEMONY, NEAR THE
BORDER OF THE ROMULAN NEUTRAL ZONE.

ROBLEIN HAS AGREED TO APPOINT AN
AMBASSADOR PLENIPOTENTIARY FROM THE
FEDERATION WITH FULL POWERS TO DEAL
WITH THE DYNASTY AND ITS THREAT TO SE-
CEDE FROM THE FEDERATION, TAKING THE
VORAN HEGEMONY'S MANY MEMBER WORLDS
AND ALLIES WITH IT.

ROBLEIN'S MOVE WAS UNEXPECTED. HE HAD
BEEN EXPECTED TO RESIGN FOLLOWING THE
DEATH IN AN AIRCAR CRASH OF HIS WIFE.
HOWEVER IN THE FREAK ACCIDENT ANOTHER
UNIDENTIFIED WOMAN RIDING IN THE AIR-
CAR WAS KILLED. MAIA ROBLEIN WAS AP-
PARENTLY THROWN CLEAR AND WAS FOUND
24 HOURS LATER SUFFERING NOTHING WORSE
THAN AMNESIA. SHE WAS RESTORED TO HER
HUSBAND SHORTLY BEFORE HIS SURPRISE
ACTION.

"The Voran Dynasty Hegemony," Kirk said when
they had done some checking and had received a sealed

order in code which caused Kirk to call the Vulcan off the bridge to a private conference. "The Hegemony has scheduled an inauguration to coincide with the delegate conference. They will recognize a new regent. The Regent, in fact, will rule. It is the ordained wish of the old Hegarch, who is dying. His grandson, the young Hegarch, is not mentally competent. The new Regent is known to favor secession from the Federation. Nothing else is known of him. We are ordered on a diplomatic mission to pay our respects, and prevent secession."

"In that order?" Spock said stiffly, but rather sourly.

Kirk grinned on about the same note. "Not necessarily. The Voran group of planets is the largest in the Federation, and as it goes, so goes half or more of the Federation. It would be crippling, at best. At worst, if they allied with Romulans or Klingons it would be civil war—perhaps the end of the Federation as a civilizing power."

"The fruition of Omne's political dream," Spock said. "The dismantling of the wall-to-wall super-empires. Especially ours."

"Except that we are not an empire. Damn it, Spock. Those planets have the right to secede, if it comes to that. What more does he want?"

Spock shrugged. "Everything. An end to 'smothering benevolence,' to the Federation's 'creeping do-goodism,' to its bending of the Prime Directive."

"That's Omne's argument," Kirk said.

"Yes."

For a moment Kirk felt the chill again. Spock? He almost wanted to ask.

The Vulcan had been so strange these last two weeks . . .

Kirk pulled himself back to the moment. No. He was not "all right" himself. He had nightmares, and they were of Omne and Spock and Omne as Spock.

They left Kirk exhausted and almost physically ill.

And in the morning he had to face the silent Vulcan, and the reports from the galaxy.

Flamespotters?

It was as if somebody were running loose through the galaxy with a torch . . .

Or as if some ghost ship sailed at impossible speeds, some legendary Flying Dutchman, doomed to sail and dooming all they defended.

There was no way Omne could have been in all of the trouble spots—and yet the trouble seemed to bear the marks of his hand.

A dictator toppled. A do-gooder went home. A planet changed the policy of generations. A man changed the convictions of a lifetime. The Klingons were restless. The Romulans were probing the Neutral Zone, testing the Federation again. The disaffection within the Federation and from both its members and its loosely affiliated allies was growing. Even the planet Vulcan was affected, and Spock's father, Ambassador Sarek, was fighting a close political battle to prevent the disaffection over the Prime Directive from swaying Vulcan. As Vulcan goes, so goes the galaxy.

It was the reason Omne had named for aiming his test of the Phoenix at Spock.

At whom were the tests of the Flying Dutchman—or the Fire Dragon—aimed? Kirk? Or was Omne truly dead, and all of this merely Kirk's imagination—perhaps even his own reaction to having killed Omne?

Perhaps many of the crises were merely coincidence. Perhaps all of them were. Perhaps Omne did not live—or perhaps he was *here*—and everything else was merely imagination.

If one had read a newspaper or intelligence summary on any day for the last few centuries—would it not have seemed that some dark force was running loose, raising havoc?

Kirk drew himself up and handed the sealed order to the Vulcan.

"You might want to look at this, Mr. Spock," he said. "I have been appointed Ambassador Plenipotentiary to the Voran Dynasty Hegemony Conference."

For the first time since the day of the Phoenix, Kirk saw a flicker of emotion touch the Vulcan's face.

"By the custom of the Hegemony," Spock said, "an ambassador plenipotentiary is required to have full powers to decide war and peace—and to settle the question, if necessary, by personal challenge. He answers for his mission with his life."

Kirk sighed and indicated the order. "So I am informed, Mr. Spock." Then he tried one more time. "Spock—?"

"Yes, Captain," the Vulcan said in the tone of restraint.

"Nothing, Mr. Spock." Kirk turned to go. "Warp Seven for the conference," he ordered.

CHAPTER II

THE COMMANDER turned to James.

His Romulan was doubtless not quite up to the sheaf of reports which she held, despite the fact that he was a very quick study and could speak Romulan with her now without the implant-translator.

But in this case what he would chiefly lack would be the knowledge of the Romulan Empire needed to make the inferences which she was making, and which raised the fine hairs at the back of her neck.

Nevertheless, she handed him the reports. He deserved that respect.

He read them with some difficulty, but eagerly, rising to pace her cabin like an old war-horse eager to get back into action. It had been very difficult for him to be caged here in her cabin and the adjoining one—whatever the pleasures of the cage. They had had an interesting time—not without the problems of two stiff-necked old campaigners trying to work out who was more stiff-necked. She knew the answer. She doubted that he did. In deference to that gallantry with which he bore his loss, she was more gentle with him than she had any right to be.

The matter of the link remained a source of constant fear to her. No moment passed when she did not know that she should have done it, whatever the cost. Nevertheless, she had not. Nor had she let him out of her sight for more than a moment. It was doubtless the first

31

and only time she would have him entirely to herself and in that state of innocence and vulnerability which made him trust himself to her entirely.

Of his pain and loss he did not complain, but neither did he try to deny it.

That had met its fate on the night when she woke to find him alone and unmoving, torn by grief for the life and people he had left, but trying not to disturb her.

That she could not allow and she had pulled him to her and made him share it. He had not, quite, reached the release of tears, and she thought that Omne had burned that release out for both Jim and James.

Nevertheless, what he found with her was sufficient.

With every day that passed she understood more completely Omne's warning that they would have to "snatch happiness from the teeth of terror."

Now with the intelligence printfax S'Tal had sent down from the bridge, she felt the cold breath of that terror on the back of her neck.

James looked up from the report and she saw that the chill touched him, too.

"Some of this may be Greek to me," he said, "but even in Greek I would read only one fine hand in this."

She nodded. "In any language: Omne."

"It's too soon," he said. "Even if we assume that he had everything mapped to roll before Day One, he could not physically cover the territory. It's barely more than a couple of weeks."

The Commander nodded.

The illusion of omnipresence was overwhelming. Omne seemed to be everywhere.

"Is it possible that we are reading into this?" she said. "A tyrant deposed on a fringe planet . . . A political scandal on the second heartworld, with accusations of a complete shift of policy by the first Triumvir, following the death of his son . . . The Korlon of Veda missing for twelve hours, appearing confused on his return . . . A street crowd chanting for war with the Federation, denouncing any peaceful contact with the Federation as treason—led by the daughter of the founder of the Peace Party—on the day after his burial pyre . . ."

The Commander stopped, not saying that she had known both father and daughter.

"Friends?" James said.

She smiled ruefully. There was not much this one missed, even without benefit of telepathy. "I had thought so," she said.

He glanced down at the report. "*Bruchón*—it is 'traitor,' isn't it?"

She nodded.

" 'Traitor, come home,' " he translated. "The crowd chanted it." He looked into her eyes. "They meant you."

"Yes."

His eyes smoldered with a heat which might have been Romulan. He came and took her by the shoulders and she saw how he would have faced down that crowd, or fallen with her. There was a fierce protectiveness about him which took no account of his actual strength here. It would get him killed.

"The treason is theirs," he said flatly. "We will show them what kind of loyalty is yours."

She took his face in her hands. "My loyalty *is* my treason," she said.

His gold-flecked eyes clouded. "I should never have let you bring me."

She let her eyes laugh. "You had a great deal less choice about that than you supposed. I had not yet begun to pack you off."

His face caught up the challenge. "I trust I am not going to hear about the 'princeling' again," he said.

She kissed him and slipped out of his hands.

When she turned to face him, it was as the Fleet Commander. "The path I chose *was* treason, by the standards of most of my military command and civil government. It would have been comparable in your history with an English or American fleet admiral making a joint statement with the commander of a German U-Boat—and in a way which would turn the tide of war and peace, perhaps decisively. I have, in fact, a great deal to answer for."

His lips pursed. He had not thought of it in that light. But he shook his head. "We are not twentieth century. More like eighteenth—when a far-ranging captain or commander frequently *did* make decisions of war or peace, and rightly so. The Federation will back my— will back Jim's play—and your command, if it gave you the weight, must back yours."

She smiled. "On this side of the Neutral Zone, it is rather earlier than *that*. I am expected to return with my shield, or on it."

She withdrew the single stat-fax from where she had tucked it into her belt. "I have, essentially, been ordered to do so."

She handed him the fax.

It was an order to report by a certain date to show cause why she should not be court-martialed for consorting with the enemy, rendering aid and comfort, and, possibly, treason. Specification: that she knowingly betrayed the clear interests of the Empire in making a joint speech with a Federation spokesman which undercut the then-forming anti-Federation alliance.

The order was signed by the Romulan Commander-in-Chief, Rovan.

James looked up and his eyes blazed again, but now they were afraid for her. "Don't go. It is a large galaxy. You do not have to answer to a system which gives you responsibility without authority, and claims your life if you act outside the phalanx."

She shook her head. "A few weeks ago the galaxy was large, James—although I would not have run even then, and never have. Today the sea of stars is— Omne's lake. The whole of the Romulan Empire may not be sufficient to protect you, but nothing less will."

"Then don't—" He started to protest, but she cut him off.

"Nor anything less than my success in the Empire prevent the war which would also engulf Jim and Spock," she finished.

His eyes went bleak.

She smiled. "We always knew there was no way out but forward, James. Nothing has changed. Nor does either of us run, as Jim would doubtless say, 'worth a damn.'"

He met her eyes and finally nodded. "I have to assume that you know your territory—and there is at least a chance."

She lifted her head. "If there were not, I *would* run. I am not alone now."

"No," he said very softly.

He started to come to her, but she held up a hand. "There is one thing."

He inquired with a look.

"There is now no choice," she said. "If we continue to make Warp Eight, I can stop at Thorva briefly on the way. With that mission accomplished and the Thorvan tribute-liege in my hand, my case will be strengthened. I will return not so much as the *bruchón* of the Omne affair, but as the victor of Thorva."

James grinned. "I might have known you would have something up your sleeve."

She nodded. "I have. The high card. The Prince of Thorva."

His eyes widened as he saw it coming. "You're not talking about choosing a 'script'?"

She shook her head. "It was been chosen for us, James. There is now only one cover story I can provide for you and only one chance for your survival. When we leave Thorva you will be my tribute-hostage, and you will act the part. My princeling—protected by ancient custom—even from yourself."

She straightened. "My kinsmen will, therefore, protect you, even if I fall. And no man will fight you. That is your 'script.'"

He started to protest, but he saw her eyes and knew that there was no argument.

# CHAPTER III

THE COMMANDER eased the scoutship down toward the appointed place. There lay before them the crown jewel of a glittering diadem of planets which wove a complex filigree of orbits around a triple-sun. It was the royal planet of a hereditary league of worlds which stretched beyond the planets of the triple-sun to a small globular cluster. Who ruled it ruled a power which could challenge the Empire.

S'Tal would have had the Commander land on Thorva with an armed party. That, of course, was the last thing she could do.

But there was precedent for coming alone. The planet was hostage for her, under the guns of her starships.

Nevertheless, the precedent for lone acceptance of tribute was rare. The odds on returning alive and with tribute in hand were not exceptionally encouraging.

The Commander had never understood that better.

She was to require a woman who commanded a planet and an alliance to surrender a male who could be hostage for that woman and for the fate of that planet and league.

The difficulty with that theory, of course, had always been that a male who could be hostage to fortune for such a woman might well not be surrendered, at any price.

The Commander understood that very well.

She watched James slip out of the miniature cabin of the scout and ease in beside her, fastening the chin strap of the Romulan helmet.

She looked at him with both approval and annoyance. The helmet covered a multitude of invitations to sin. But the mouth, the eyes, were still visible. "The idea," she said, "is for you to fade into the background. That is the uniform of an *arvan*—call it an aide-de-camp—in whose presence I am alone."

He sighed. "I'll try to keep that in mind."

"You will do more than try. Eyes down. Mouth shut. Speak not unless with my express permission, or on direct order of the Doyen."

"Sounds like I already *am* the princeling," he complained.

The Commander laughed in her throat. "Not at all. You have not yet begun. But you will maintain the *arvan* persona at all costs. It will, therefore, be reported that I came alone, as my ships believe. In no case are you to move to defend me."

He started to protest, but she held up a hand for silence.

"We are here. Make no mistake, James. Both of our lives, and your freedom, depend on that."

"My freedom?" he said.

"I cannot leave you on my flagship. The chance of discovery is too great. I can't leave you here on the scoutship for the same reason. I must take you with me. But if I should lose, I'm afraid you would be considered spoils of war. You would, however, be alive."

"While *you*—would not?" She could see the stubborn set reach his jaw.

"I will not lose," she said, feeling the same set in her own.

She put the ship down beside the arena.

A sullen honor guard met them carrying lethal edge-weapons and dressed in the chain mail of ancient ceremony—and very little else.

She saw James having some difficulty with the eyes-front, eyes-down routine. Not his fault if the Doyen's planet was hot as the Origin World and costume of choice for ancient challenge was chain mail and silk or skin loin cloth for male and female.

The honor guard contained both. The women were tall, statuesque, long-legged, and of an easy power. James seemed to find that somewhat remarkable. The Commander had pointed out to him once that her research into his species indicated that in the rare Human culture where males and females were fed and exercised alike—ancient Sparta for example—anthropologists found it very hard to distinguish male from female skeletons.

The Commander accepted a sedan chair carried by two women and motioned James to full in at her side.

He got used to the idea that she would ride in the sedan chair and look as if she belonged there.

It had not occurred to her to think that he would find that unusual.

What else of Romulan culture, or of this offshoot of it, would he find unexpected?

For this *was* Romulan culture—merely a slightly earlier version and variation.

There was a strong streak of female-rule in the parent culture which had spawned both Romulans and Vulcans. And the fact that it competed with an equally stubborn and even more pervasive streak of male dominance made for spectacular variations and combinations.

Nonetheless, this planet and the hereditary Thorvan League of Planets which its ruler commanded were part of the Empire and had shared its culture—until the League had recently seceded from the Empire and its policies.

The Commander wondered now if Omne's fine hand could be seen even in that. It was the same sentiment of secession he had cultivated on worlds throughout the Federation.

The difference was that the Federation would probably ultimately be hoist by its own Prime Directive and its tendency to respect revolution, and would have to let defecting worlds go.

A warrior people was under no such obligation against an upstart league of colonies, and indeed, could not afford to be. There was nothing worse than a warrior empire which became fragmented. That was the formula for an instant war of all against all.

Therefore the Empire sent its best troubleshooters against any threat of disaffection.

The Commander had shot this trouble once by disabling the Thorvan fleet in space. The planet and League Council had formally surrendered under terms of royal tribute hostage.

If the Commander could have collected the hostage then, it might well have been all over.

But she was called on unanswerable immediate priority to the Omne crisis.

It remained to be seen whether the Doyen of the League fully considered herself bound by that Council surrender—or whether she ever had.

The Commander saw the Doyen being carried in on a sedan chair. The Doyen was tall and lithe, wide-shouldered, strong, poised, and of that rare golden coloring known as the mark of a Romulan royalty which extended back to the time before the beginning, across many worlds.

The Doyen's face had that beauty which is only carved by millennia of breeding—an arrogant perfection of line, expression, a lift of dark-gold eyebrows and upswept ears, a startling fire in the glowing amber eyes.

The Commander was subliminally aware of James' perception of that face's beauty, of a similar arrogance of perfection in a body both strong and lavishly female.

The Commander did not look at James.

Her eyes did shift to the man who walked beside the Doyen's litter—a pace behind.

He wore a cloak and mask.

It was the Doyen's ancient right. The countenance of the Prince belonged only to the one to whom he belonged.

It would be the Commander's prerogative, of course, to unveil it when he was hers. She could even unveil it permanently by stages, if she chose.

But the salient point was that even this world, apart from the Doyen, would not know if the Commander unveiled another "princeling" entirely.

She saw James flash her a startled look—beginning to understand better what this was all about and how she could hope to make it work.

But he was appalled.

A man in a mask?

A man in a silken cloak, drawn about him under the hot sun . . . ?

The mask was carved with features which virtually looked alive and might or might not resemble the living face they masked.

If they did, the man might well be worth a Prince's ransom.

The masked Prince bent his head, reached up and handed the Doyen out to face the Commander.

James, taken aback, bowed slightly, gracefully, and handed the Commander out with some look of expertise.

It was, by all ordinary standards, close enough to the behavior of an *arvan*.

The Commander saw immediately that the Doyen did not judge by any ordinary standard, and that James had caught her eye.

She looked him over, and a trace of puzzlement formed between her eyebrows. There was a touch of appreciation in the Doyen's eyes. Yet she could be concerned with only one thing.

She raised the open-handed salute which their culture shared with the related Vulcan one—paired fingers divided to a "V."

The Commander returned this signal greeting, but she perceived that it did not signify peace and long life.

"I acknowledge your presence," the Doyen said. "I concede your defeat of the Thorvan fleet. I recognize the Thorvan Council's decision, during my incapacity from that defeat, to sue for peace. However, I am no longer incapacitated. The Council is advisory only. Its decisions are not binding on me. I do not surrender what is mine. I believe you have recognized that in me by coming alone. It will be settled between us."

The Doyen drew herself to her full height. "*Kalifee,*" she said.

The ancient ramshorn curl of a great horn sounded its low, shuddery demand for attention. Bell-banners sang. The Headsman stepped forward with his longaxe.

The Commander shook her head. "The question is settled, the debt of honor incurred and concluded. Whoever spoke for you and in the name of the planet under my guns bought time only by pledge of a value which must now be surrendered. I grant no dispensation and answer no challenge. I will leave with the Prince momentarily. First I will speak with you—alone."

The Doyen's golden eyes glittered. "You will leave with him over my body."

The Commander nodded. "Quite possibly."

For a moment there was an expression of amusement in the Doyen's eyes. She gestured to the ranks of her guards. "One can only admire your idea of a suitable opposition," she said.

The Commander looked at the Doyen more directly, also with a certain appreciation. "It is said one is known by the quality of one's opposition—and of one's hostages." The Commander nodded toward the Prince.

"Then let us challenge and have done with it," the Doyen said. "Unless the *bruchón* of the Black Hole fears honest challenge."

It was meant to goad, but the Commander answered levelly:

"I did not come to leave my bones, or yours, to bleach on this planet. If they do, they will have company. My ships hold the power. I *will* speak with you alone."

The Doyen's eyes narrowed in respect. After a moment she said, "Very well," and turned beside the Commander to walk toward the colonnade of the arena.

Unobtrusively James fell in just behind the Commander's shoulder, on the theory that she was still alone in his presence.

In an instant the Prince had also moved to fall in behind his Doyen. The two exchanged some look, but James chiefly kept his eyes to himself.

"The Prince is mine," the Commander said. "Make no mistake, I will take him if one or both of us has to die here, or if *he* does—or if your world must pay the price you would not pay." Then as they passed out of earshot, she turned to the Doyen more directly. "On the other hand, under certain circumstances, I am prepared to make an agreement of honor, whereby I will provide for the Prince's safety and you may work toward having him back within a reasonable time."

The Doyen looked at her incredulously. "Why would you do that?"

"For a purpose of my own."

"What is a 'reasonable time'?"

The Commander shrugged. "When key aspects of my own plan have succeeded sufficiently or when I have come to trust you implicitly."

"Or when Hal Voh Ra freezes solid?" the Doyen said in a savage tone. She had been baited on ground where baiting was not to be endured.

The Commander smiled to herself. The Doyen had answered the question she had not asked. She asked it anyway as they turned in the door of the arena's audience room. "Is your resistance to letting him go a matter of pride, or a matter of *him?*"

The Doyen turned. "How does that concern you?" she said.

"It will concern *you.*"

The Prince moved to stand beside the Doyen. Absently her hand found him and guided him to sit down beside her. Her hand came to rest on the silken mask-cowl where it swirled into the enveloping cape. The gesture was also an answer, and eloquent.

The Doyen's severe features belied the gesture and looked stonily at the Commander. "The Prince is of the ancient royal line. The males of the line are given to dreaming, as you know. Sometimes the dreams are dangerous. Sometimes they are the pride of a world. His are." She looked at him and then at the Commander. "Neither the world's pride nor mine matters a singular Voh Rah to me. I want him back."

The Prince looked up at the Doyen with an odd kind of astonishment which registered even through the mask.

The Commander nodded. "I had hoped so. If we agree, it will be necessary for me to place more than my life in your hands. I do not do so on a basis of trust. Your Prince's life will be my guarantee. I see that it will suffice."

The Doyen did not remove her hand from the Prince's neck. "It will," she admitted. "What do you wish? It is said you are a traitor. I have seen no evidence. However, do you wish me to compound your treason? Done. I am a secessionist, myself, but even if I were not, I would do what I must."

The Commander nodded. "For now I require only silence. Later you might consider the possibility of an Empire where secession would be a right, but not an advantage."

The Doyen chuckled. "I *have.*"

"You control many planets," the Commander said, "and influence many more. You have expressed a wish to be able to trade freely outside the Empire, even with the Federation worlds. You do not wish to fight the Hundred-Years War with the Federation for a second hundred years. Nor do I. As a command officer I will carry out direct, lawful, proper orders. As an officer with discretionary powers, I will exercise them on my best judgment. As myself, I will seek to reach the position where the discretion is mine."

The Doyen looked at her soberly. "In that event," she said, "you will not require a hostage against me."

The Commander nodded gravely. "Thank you. I accept. However, I do require the hostage."

Anger began to come back to the Doyen's eyes. "I offered you friendship, support. You can't have it both ways."

"I am prepared to try," the Commander said. "The Prince I must have. The support, I would welcome. The friendship I value even now."

The Doyen's eyes dropped to the man at her side. "What do you need him *for?*" she asked bitterly.

"I am not prepared to say. It will become apparent to you in due time," the Commander said.

"I will know now, or there will be no deal."

"No deal, no Prince," the Commander said simply, ruthlessly.

She saw that her eyes caught and held the Doyen's. And the Commander knew well enough that it was really unanswerable.

"You do not want him yourself," the Doyen said in the flat tone of insight. "You have not asked to see his face. Yet you want him with you for some reason beyond a guarantee of my behavior."

Her eyes turned slowly to James. "I have not heard it said that you have consort—or even an *arvan*. You are called the lone skyeagle. Now you bring an *arvan* on this mission. And he is very quiet, and if he did not hide his eyes, he would be very beautiful."

"*Arvan!*" the Doyen ordered suddenly. "Look at me!"

Almost instinctively James looked up, and for a moment his stance was the confident poise of a starship captain. Then he lowered his eyes to a veiled look through his lashes again.

"Take off your helmet," the Doyen ordered. He looked to the Commander for approval, denial. She said nothing but shrugged fractionally and waved negligent permission. She would not have made a fuss over an *arvan*.

The Doyen was much too far along the right track. But—possibly she could be diverted.

James took off the helmet.

The coloring which McCoy had given him on the Commander's instructions was almost exactly that of the Doyen and his eyes were the same dark gold as those of the Doyen and of the Prince, who was probably the Doyen's first cousin.

The Doyen's eyes widened. "He cannot be of the blood-royal. That face would be known halfway across the galaxy."

It *is*, the Commander thought. But she shook her head. "The genes are recessive," she said. "Rare, but they can crop up anywhere. He is my *arvan*."

"Or—the greatest secret in the galaxy," the Doyen said. She turned to James, "Are you *her* Prince?"

James contrived not even to look surprised. "If I were, would she need one?" he said.

It was a good answer, and it drove the Doyen back for a moment. Then she nodded. "Possibly in that case—most of all."

She turned to the Commander. "You don't want *mine*. You want a place for *yours*."

The Commander faced her gravely. "Even if it were true, I would need yours, as a guarantee of the safety of mine."

"You would need a guarantee," the Doyen said. "But not the living body." She drew a breath, made a decision. "This planet is set to kill you before letting you leave with him, whether I live or die. I will see that you both live, and give you my word."

The Commander stood quite still. It was always possible, even likely, that the Doyen had done exactly that—set the planet to kill them—and that they would be killed as they left, whatever the fate of the Doyen or of the world, or even of the Prince. If the Doyen could not have her Prince, it was quite possible that she would see to it that no one else could.

Finally the Commander shook her head. "Would you take my word—on the matter of his life?" she said, indicating the Prince.

"No," the Doyen said reluctantly, acknowledging truth.

"Neither will I take yours for a life which is mine," the Commander said in the same tone of truth. "You will have to call off the death trap, for I *am* taking your Prince as guarantee, and at need I will see that the trap closes first on him."

It was the Doyen's turn to stand very still.

"I cannot call off the trap," she said. "I set a last line of defense which even I could not recall."

# CHAPTER IV

THE COMMANDER traded looks with James, and it was their shared belief that the Doyen was not bluffing.

"There is a way," the Doyen said.

"Name it."

"There is a man who regards my honor at his own, above his own. If I sent a message now, he would regard it as under duress, and disregard it. He would kill you as you go. You will stay here until tomorrow. That will place you under the honor of my house as guest-friend. Then—we will meet in the Trial of the Three Challenges. Honor protects the challenge. While we meet in trial you will be safe. Win or lose, that man will be obliged, in honor, to let you go."

"And you?" the Commander said.

"We will not do the challenge trial for nothing," the Doyen said. "The three trials are of mind, body, and inner power. If you win, I will follow you gladly. But if I win, you will leave the Prince here and take my word for my honor. If I lose, you will take him—and give me your word to return him in original condition within a time we will name."

"We might quibble over original condition," the Commander said. "Apart from that: done."

The Doyen touched the Prince's arm. "Go and tell the Chief of Chambers that we have guests."

He dropped on his knees in front of her. "Yes, my

liege." And after an instant, softly, "Thank you, my lady."

The Doyen touched his shoulder. He rose gracefully.

James was looking at him with utter astonishment.

And it was only as the Prince moved away and out the door that it was possible to see a pantherish stride which was as male and as powerful as James' own.

The Commander read James' thoughts.

How could that power be leashed?

What manner of culture—or woman—would leash it? And what kind of man permit it?

And how was *he*, born unleashed and with no such concept, ever to play the Prince, or allow anyone to believe that he could be tamed?

If James had been given to panic, she would have seen it then.

The Commander signalled S'Tal with the proper code-within-code to indicate that she remained a free agent.

Within reason.

She walked carefully and kept her eyes open—including the eyes in the back of her head.

It was not clear to her how far she could or should trust the Doyen. On any other matter the Commander would, in fact, have been disposed to trust her. Even now she suspected that she had found an ally who might ultimately prove both a staunch friend and a crucial force in her plans for the Empire.

But she also suspected that the Doyen's trustworthiness ran very thin where the Prince began.

Dinner was laid in a hall of barbaric splendor.

It was in the old Romulan mode of unsparing simplicity, a cleanness of line which was a statement of the ancient warrior virtues.

But some particular personality had given the ancient simplicity a richness here in gleaming, deep-polished woods, rich fabrics, ancient weapons and shields on the walls. And in the great hall alcoves: sculpture.

James walked in with the Commander down the aisle of sculpture. The alabaster statues had the warmth and sensuousness of flesh, the texture of skin, the look of celebration of life.

Several were by the great master sculptors of the Origin World and the Twin Planets.

And several were by a hand as fine, an imagination perhaps more subtle, but the works were unfamiliar to the Commander, and the material looked contemporary.

She stopped at one and James drew close to her shoulder and whispered. "You had your Sparta and Athens—together."

She laughed silently. "Of course. It is a source of astonishment to me that you could have had yours apart."

An alcove opened in front of them, evidently one not ordinarily opened. Lights came on in it and they were looking at the sculpture of a man.

The Commander found her breath taken.

She recognized the hand of the contemporary master sculptor. And she was certain that she recognized the model.

It was a masterwork on the level of a handful in the galaxy. Earth's *David*, Vulcan's *Young Surak*, her own homeworld's *Atavar*.

But this was no statue of untouched youth. This was the image of a mature man who projected still that sense of essential innocence in the face of knowledge.

It reminded her, almost painfully, of James. The body might almost have been his. The face was—almost—as beautiful, although it bore no real resemblance. The features were fine, sensual, with a curious purity containing almost a sultry look of inner fire.

The Commander had never seen body or face, and she was certain she had been in the presence of both.

She caught James' eye, and he was whispering, "Is it—?"

"Good evenwatch."

They turned to find the Doyen with the Prince at her shoulder.

The Commander bowed her head. "Watch in Life," she responded. "Thank you for the private showing." She nodded toward the sculpture. "One could raise an argument in some quarters whether artist, model, or artwork would be worth more of a Prince's ransom."

The Doyen nodded silently. "In some quarters," she said. "In others there would be no argument if the living work of art could be ransomed with the stone."

The Commander nodded. "Almost I could be tempted. But my appreciation has always run rather more to the lively arts—and artworks."

The Doyen looked at James. "I rather thought so."

The Commander did not attempt to deny the direction of the glance, or its meaning.

Whether she could trust the Doyen or not, the woman had been too astute not to see how it was. Curiously, the Commander found a certain pleasure in that. This was perhaps the only person in the Empire who could be permitted to know the Commander's choice, and who was capable of appreciating it. There was a danger in that. Letting the Doyen know the truth might well be fatal. Yet the Commander saw now that against a woman of this caliber it could only have been avoided by leaving James on the ship. That would certainly have been fatal if he had been discovered, or the Commander had not returned, or if he had been taken by Omne.

Therefore the Commander had no regrets. She merely knew that she had to win the challenge and leave with both living works of art, or the life of hers would be in the Doyen's hands.

"I would like to get to know very well the sculptor of the unsigned works," the Commander said.

The Doyen shrugged. "It might be arranged." For a moment she met the Commander's eyes, and her own lambent eyes did not conceal a certain laughter. "Possibly you could allow that sculptor the use of a model."

The golden eyes lingered on James with a certain appreciation.

James colored faintly—a slightly Romulan bronze. But the Commander suspected that the Jim Kirk in him would have liked to make some remark which would get them both in trouble.

"I think not," the Commander said firmly—and was a little surprised to hear how firmly.

The Doyen did not look surprised.

"The evening is prepared," she said coolly, bringing the moment to an end. "Come."

She turned and they followed her to a dais where a dining table and couches were laid out.

The Commander noted that the manner of ancient days was indicated.

And she noted that a vein pounded in her temple.

To refuse would be mortal offense.

She found herself considering how long it would take S'Tal to beam them up . . .

The Doyen indicated a couch to the Commander, settled herself in regal splendor on the other one, and turned to James.

"You may serve me, *arvan*," the Doyen said, indicating a place for him on her couch.

The Commander had seen Jim or James in many states. She doubted now that she had ever seen either completely nonplussed. James looked at her. She nodded fractionally. He looked demoralized. The Prince moved to the end of the Commander's couch, and she saw James' jaw begin to set.

"I was not aware that you followed the ancient custom of evenwatch exchange," the Commander said.

"I do not," the Doyen said flatly. "I make an exception."

It was a statement that death was the alternative.

"Exception noted," the Commander said. She caught James' eye. "Proceed, James."

She saw the dangerous glint in his eye and the stubborn set of his jaw saying silently, dangerously: '*Proceed? All right, I'll show you "proceed."* '

Clearly he did not take well to being exchanged. Certainly not for a Prince who would take his place.

And perhaps he did not like the look she had given the stone sculpture, or the artwork now sitting in living flesh on her couch.

The Prince sat on the Commander's couch, the silken evening cape flowing back from his shoulders now, baring them.

Except for the mask he was dressed only in the silken loin wrap, cloak, and sandals which were the standard evening wear of his station, and which they had found laid out for James as well in the quarters assigned to them.

James had worn them under considerable protest and over nothing else but objections.

The Prince bowed to the Commander. "Allow me to serve your pleasure, my lady."

She made a place for him beside her. "The pleasure is mine."

James set his jaw, gathered himself, and marched to the Doyen's couch. He sat on it as if leading a charge into the breach of a wall. "Allow me to serve your pleasure, my lady."

The Doyen chuckled appreciatively in her throat. "The pleasure is mine."

"That remains to be seen," he murmured. "Perhaps it will be mine."

The Doyen nodded and let her eyes drift down his body. "The evenwatch is yet young."

He colored, but the captain in him was undaunted. "Then let us not waste youth—or beauty," he said. From the corner of his eye he watched for the Commander's reaction, but saw chiefly that the Prince was pouring a drink from a carafe.

He turned back and did the same, pouring *kavit* into a viridian goblet, and the Doyen in turn tipped the goblet to pour the spiced mead from her viridian cup into a silver cup for him. The Commander tipped her cup to pour a drink for the Prince and she and the Doyen toasted each other silently, and then nodded permission to the men to drink.

The Prince murmured thanks and toasted the Commander with his eyes. After a moment James followed suit.

Presently the Prince served food from the exquisite cold and hot delicacies and the Commander served from her plate to his.

James was a quick study. It could not have been apparent to the Doyen that he didn't know the custom from a Klingon *kvatch*.

But when the Doyen drew him to sit in the curve of her arm, he almost blew it.

He caught himself, however, in good time, the Commander noted rather sourly. And he settled in without noticeable reluctance. The Commander had caught one look at her from under his lashes, rather accusingly seeming to say that she might at least have warned him. On her own head be it . . .

She felt her own irritation rising and she gathered in the Prince as he would expect, and as it would have been an insult, both to him and to his liege, not to do.

James' eyes flickered with a sudden dark light and he turned and murmured something to the Doyen which was pitched to be inaudible even to Romulan ears across the table.

"Now you will tell me your name," the Commander murmured to the Prince, pitching it just audibly for Human ears.

She could almost see James' ears move to pick it up.

The Prince looked into her eyes. His own were a match for James' eyes, behind the mask. "I am called Trevanian," he said. It was the first time she had heard his voice above a murmur. It had a low melodic quality not unlike James', but without the years of being the starship captain.

The Commander suddenly felt herself curiously touched. This one would have been here all of these years, almost a prisoner of his beauty, his royalty, his Doyen.

And yet it was his place and, the Commander suspected, his love.

Covertly, when he had not thought she was watching, he had looked from under his lashes across the table, and the Commander thought that his eyes burned.

He was a little stiff in her arm—not enough to give offense, but perhaps a reminder that he had never before been given in this manner.

Or perhaps it was a reflection of the question which neither he nor the Commander could ask:

Evenwatch was one thing. Nightwatch was something else.

With dinner came entertainment, a series of dancers beyond a force field curtain, building to a climax with a dancer who looked made of gold. It was the meaning of Trevanian's name: golden; it meant, in fact, "poured of sunlight."

The golden dancer was joined by another dancer—and suddenly the dance became a drama: a capture-dance, and the great figure which came out to dance in a black light, the face unseen, the body massive—made the Commander's hackles rise.

She sensed more than saw that the impression caught James, too. And she could feel his tension.

In truth the dancing figure might have been a trifle smaller than the giant he made them think of, and doubtless did not radiate quite the power, but the illusion was compelling.

"Doyen," the Commander said carefully, "when you planned your secession, were you in contact with anyone outside the Empire?"

The Doyen's tone was harsh irony. "I should have thought you would have asked me before, Commander. You have just come from burying him."

The Commander felt the chill congeal her spine. She should have known. Omne had been here before her. Selling some version of his alleged passion for freedom to someone in whom the passion was real.

And the Commander had proposed to trust that person with James' life. *Had* trusted her with it. James was in the Doyen's hands even now. And the usual formal knife was at the woman's belt. If she counted herself Omne's friend, and the Commander as cooperating in Omne's death . . .

"I should have asked," the Commander said very quietly. Her arm locked around the Prince. "How do you stand?" she asked the Doyen flatly.

"On my word," the Doyen said. "I will meet you in challenge."

The Commander eased the arm lock fractionally. "What was Omne to you?"

"A man I could not control," the Doyen said in an odd tone. "Perhaps—a friend. Almost certainly an enemy, at some point, if he had lived. Possibly, however, in truth an advocate of freedom. Certainly a giant. The galaxy is safer without him, and poorer. If you had killed him, I would have required you to answer for his blood."

The Commander sighed. "I did not," she said, "but it was not for want of trying."

"I thought so. If you had not said so, I would have required a blood answer, in any case. Why did you try to kill him?"

"For the safety of the galaxy, and of what is mine."

There was a long moment of silence. "I accept that," the Doyen said. "If necessary I would do the same thing, for the same reason."

She turned to watch the dance come to its conclusion, a lift and carry, as if darkness carried away light.

"It is difficult to believe that he is dead," the Doyen said. "I ask you on your honor, did you see his dead body, beyond possibility of error?"

There was only one answer which the Commander could give and she gave it, truthfully, and lying in her teeth: "Yes."

There was a moment of silence. "Very well. I had to know."

The Doyen hit the switch to bring the lights up.

The Commander unlocked her arm from around Trevanian, suppressing the impulse to do it hastily.

The Doyen didn't move hers from around James. He looked a little flushed and flustered and slightly disarranged.

The Commander felt the pounding of the vein in her temple again, but she kept her face impassive. He would answer to her, but not here.

And she rather thought that he had learned his lesson in those moments in the dark. Romulan women were not to be counted in the same category as the women with whom a certain starship captain had earned a reputation which extended even into the Empire.

Here a man might run into a clash of cold steel in the dark, or find himself in strong hands.

James kept his eyes down, but he looked up into the Commander's eyes.

And for just a moment she saw the simple, heartfelt plea: *Get me out of here.*

She did not permit herself to smile.

Instead, she devoted a certain attention to the Prince, absently, as if she took it, and him, for granted.

She had a feeling that he was flashing a similar message to his Doyen.

But the Commander spoke as if politics were on her mind. "Omne's advocacy of freedom I regard as sham or worse," she said. "Freedom itself I honor. He believed that empires and alliances destroy freedom. I believe they must be made to preserve it. If they cannot, or will not, they must be taken apart until they can. Omne believed conflict and even war could preserve pockets of freedom. I believe peace must preserve more than pockets. But my true enmity for Omne is personal. If he were to rise from the dead and walk through the door, I would kill him. There can be no friendship between us unless that is understood."

The Doyen nodded. "There is no friendship between us, yet. When I give friendship, it is forever—barring confirmed betrayal. Nor do I give friendship to one who holds hostage a value which belongs to me. But when all questions are settled, if we both live . . ."

The Doyen did not finish and looked at the location of the Commander's hands. For a moment the look was lethal.

Then she nodded. "It was I who made the exception. What would you do if I made it also for nightwatch?"

"Challenge you now," the Commander said evenly, flatly.

The Doyen laughed. "I thought so."

She released James with a strategic pat, and let him up.

"Strictly speaking," the Doyen said, "I should do it, for if you win tomorrow, I will have no option, and I shall regret it, perhaps fatally. However, I will not pay the price tonight." She extended a hand toward the Prince.

The Commander nodded and let Trevanian go. "I quite understand," she said, reaching her own hand to James.

He came and sat on the end of her couch. And his eyes thanked her, but did not quite forgive her.

That was just as well. She did not forgive him.

The Prince crossed over and slipped into the Doyen's arm, as if claiming his rightful place.

James bowed his head to the Commander. "Allow me to serve your pleasure, my lady."

She looked at him and nodded. "The pleasure is mine, James—as you are."

In some curious way, he almost accepted it.

But then she could see the starship captain looking out of his eyes, stiff-necked and incredulous.

"Mine," he said under his breath, "as *you* are."

But Romulan ears heard him and she saw the Doyen swivel toward them with the startled look of not believing her ears. Trevanian looked at James oddly. It was unheard-of behavior for a male in James' position. And it was dangerous. The Commander knew that he saw the fire in her eyes. "Attend me," she said, and left with him.

# CHAPTER V

THE COMMANDER woke to a strange sense of unease.

She had slept only on the first level, which was tanta-
mount to waking—the light sleep-watch, in a chair.

She had kept the nightwatch over James and knew
that he was safe.

What, then, did she sense?

Treachery from the Doyen?

Always possible, when the matter of Trevanian came
down to the wire—but doubtful before.

Someone ready to violate the honor of the Doyen's
house by attacking a guest?

The Doyen's own political enemies?

Possible.

But the Commander had a chilling sense that it was
none of those.

Omne?

It seemed too soon for him to be here. And yet there
was that uncanny way in which he seemed to be everywhere . . .

She got up and checked the locks, the weapons, everything which she *could* check.

It was pointless and worse than futile to go roaming
through the corridors of a strange palace, let alone a
hostile one, at night, trying to check a vague premonition.

She considered waking the Doyen.

But how could she warn the Doyen against a man who was dead, much less a dead man who had been some kind of friend . . . ?

The Commander tried to shake it off, but it would not shake.

In the end, she sat up, watching James, watching him sleep with that terrible innocence . . .

*"Why did you let her do it?"*

*"You do not regard custom as a sufficient answer?"*

*"No."*

*"Nor do I. What answer occurs to you?"*

*"None."*

*"Don't be sullen."*

*"Why not? You—handed me over."*

*"You moved with some alacrity."*

*"You command here."*

*"Yes."*

*"You wanted me to see what it would be like—as a princeling, really—no exceptions, no exemptions, no accommodation to my Human frailities or my stiff neck or my private customs . . . "*

*"Close."*

*"And you wanted to see if I would take you up on it, make the most of it."*

*"Closer."*

*"We have a saying: 'What's sauce for the goose is sauce for the gander.' "*

*"I trust it does not refer to cooking one's own gander."*

*"You speak English too well."*

*"You do not think in Romulan. It can be fatal."*

*"I did what you wanted."*

*"No."*

*"What you ordered."*

*"Yes."*

*"If you had challenged tonight, it would have been to the death?"*

*"Yes."*

"Don't scare me like that again. I suppose—it wouldn't kill me."

"Don't bet on it."

"Oh. That's why you would have challenged? To save my delicate neck?"

"Do you think so?"

"No."

"You liked it that I would challenge."

"I—loved it. Don't ever do it again."

"Don't make me."

"Don't let me see you look at him."

"The artwork?"

"The masked marvel. Leave him to her. Let her hide him in the hills."

"For their sakes?"

"No. For mine."

"It is for your sake that I cannot. She could betray you at any time. He is your life."

"He is not. You are. The challenge tomorrow is not to the death?"

"No."

"What if she uses it to kill you? Or even—an accident?"

"Then you will be hers. Live and prosper. Spock will find you, eventually."

"I would not prosper nor live long. And it would be more likely that Omne would find me first."

"She would keep you, even from him."

"It would not matter. You are not to die. If she kills you, I will kill her, or die trying. You are to know that in any moment when you might weaken."

"I forbid it."

"If you die, you will be in a poor position to command."

"Be still."

"Is that an order . . . ?"

In the dark of dawn Trevanian brought breakfast.

The Commander slipped out without waking James to take it.

"Thank you, Trevanian. That was not necessary."

"It was. I have come to ask you not to meet the Doyen in challenge. I will go with you now. I know a secret way. Your James will be safe."

"Why do you come?"

"It is a death matter—for you and for her. You may kill her even if you do not intend it. If you do not, but are winning, she may kill you, or try."

"She has no word?" the Commander said.

"Her word is bond. I have not known her to break it. If she would break it, she would do it over this. But if she would not, there are others not so scrupulous. She could be caught in it. Come with me now. She will not attempt to destroy you while I am with you."

The Commander shook her head. "If I were her, I would do nothing else until I had you back. It is one thing for her to yield you for a time to an honorable opponent who guarantees to give you back reasonably intact. It would be another to come after a word-breaker who accepted guest-friendship in her house and used it to steal you."

The Prince sighed. "I will tell you that I grow tired of honor."

She chuckled, remembering a similar sentiment.

She reached out and lifted his chin. "I will not kill her unless I must, and I will not betray her. Who is it who is not so scrupulous?"

"The War Minister burns for her. But also—there is—the other one."

"Who?"

"The dark one. The giant." Trevanian swallowed and set his jaw. "The—dead one."

The Commander stood very still. "You mean—there *was*."

"I mean—*is*." He looked solidly into her eyes.

"You believe you have seen him? Omne?"

He shook his head, but the solidity did not waver. "I have not seen him. But—there was always an aura about him, a power. I have experienced such an awareness with no one else, but with him it was certain. I always knew when he was here. As if I could sense his presence. I sense it now. Since the middle of the night. I offer no explanation. I accept your word that you saw his body. Nevertheless, I know that he lives."

"Trevanian," the Commander said, "if you wish any of us to live through this day, say nothing of this to anyone—especially not to the Doyen. Can you do that?"

He smiled slightly, and somehow she liked the smile very much. "Seldom," he said. "However, I will."

The Commander looked at him speculatively.

"So you would protect her by silence—and even by leaving with me?"

He lifted his eyes from the proper lowering and for a moment looked directly at her. She saw the primordial male, untouched by training or culture, and not to be denied his ancient right to protect and defend. "With my life," he said simply. Then he lowered the eyes again. "My lady."

"You will find that I will take a very dim view of deception—of your lady—when I *am*."

"I don't doubt it." She thought that she caught just a trace of irony in the fine, strong, sculptured mouth below the mask.

"You had better leave before you are missed," she said. "It is more than likely that what you are sensing is merely the tension of impending events, or the presence of someone who would like to alter them. However, we will take precautions."

The eyes did not quite rise to directness again, but they met hers. "If that is what you must tell me, so be it. I know what I know."

"Trevanian," she said, "to whom are you bound?"

He looked down, and finally up from lowered eyes. "To you, my lady."

"Name the right."

"You named it. I have been awarded to you by lawful right by the Council during the incapacity of the

Doyen. By ancient law even she cannot revoke that obligation. Nor can I. However, you must understand that she has—no choice. I believe you do understand."

He looked toward the room where James slept.

"Because I understand and because the Doyen does, I accept the challenge," the Commander said. "Else I would have taken you at once. Go now and be bound by silence."

"My lady," he said and bowed his head and left.

The Commander picked up the tray and found James awake in bed. She saw that he could have seen through the doors by the wall mirrors.

Had he awakened in time to hear the main point?

She saw that his mouth was set.

"Omne," he said.

She slid the table tray over his lap. "Unconfirmed. Merely a premonition. Little more than we have had ourselves. It may merely be Trevanian's overwrought imagination."

James shook his head. "I'll tell you a secret. If I were psychic, I'd be having the same hunch."

She raised an eyebrow. "But—you *are*, you know."

"Psychic?" He chuckled.

"You call it seventeen other names. Intuition. Hunch. What are the symptoms this time?"

He grinned sourly and set the tray aside onto the table. "No appetite. Maybe I sense the presence, too. Unease." He reached out suddenly and touched her face. "Fear. I'm afraid for you. And—I'm afraid for me. I don't want you hurt, killed. I don't want you to leave me—alone. The challenge may be rigged against you. By her. By her friends or enemies. By Omne. All she wants is Trevanian. Let her have him."

"I cannot."

"But—you don't *want* him. Do you?"

"Irrelevant. Even if he were not your life. But he is."

She leaned forward and kissed him, to find that his mouth was stiff under hers, almost sulky. But she did not release him and she felt the slow melting rise to become a kind of molten fury.

"Don't do it," he said against her mouth.

"Be still . . ."

He didn't ask whether it was an order . . .

# CHAPTER VI

THE COMMANDER rode her *varal* to fling the white lance down to quiver in the sand, denoting the challenge-not-to-death.

Flames burned in the arena fire pit. The challenge gong sounded. The great-horn played its distant note, speaking of forgotten gods.

The Doyen rode her great *varal* at a gallop, its single-horned head dancing like an echo of her lance, and cast her own lance to sing its quiver-note not an inch from the Commander's.

The lances were scarcely less white than the faces of the two men who stood under guard by the Headsman: James—and what could be seen of the face of Trevanian.

The Commander did not blame either of them. If it had been James whose life was now in his own hands . . .

She much preferred to have her own life in hers.

She wheeled her white *varal* to face the Doyen.

They wore the leather briefs, leg greaves, vests of the light chain-mail armor, and the shaped, slim-shields on their left arms. They picked up the trial-lances now—long, slender, flexible, with slightly blunted points.

The lances were not intended to be lethal—a fact which would not prevent them from killing unless both parties exercised great skill, daring, and possessed more than reasonable luck.

Without preamble the two challengers rode at each other.

It was a simple contest.

No rules.

One objective: one's opponent unable to proceed, or under control.

The standard procedure would be the lance-charge, which might be deflected, with luck, by the slim-shields. Or it might end the contest abruptly with one or both dead.

The Doyen leveled her lance. She was taller, heavier—in a brute crush she would have the advantage.

The Commander kept her long-lance leveled until the last instant,

Then she dipped it to the ground and vaulted on its long, flexible length, swinging to take her opponent out of the stirrups with her legs.

But whether it was an instant response or a similar plan to get outside the phalanx, the Doyen was with her, swinging in a shorter vault, meeting her in the air.

They struck with the shields, but blocked each other, then dropped to the ground, breath knocked out by the impact.

But they turned and squared off with the long-lances like quarterstaves.

The Doyen attacked and the Commander caught it on her lance, and for a moment they looked at each other warily and with some approval.

"You will do," the Doyen said through her teeth.

Then they dissolved into action and for some moments were only concerned with blocking, parrying, attempting to find a moment for the disconcerting battle-vault.

Then the Commander did get in a half-vault and took the other's lance out with her feet, and bore her down to the sand.

The Doyen was out of it in a moment, and then they were meeting in the Second Challenge, hand-to-hand.

The Commander knew at once that she had never fought a more formidable opponent of either sex or any species. Omne would have been more formidable, Spock would. Short of that she would have taken her chances with any male opponent, as compared to this.

The Doyen was better trained and less vulnerable. She would be top-rated in the Romulan unarmed combat skills, ancient and modern. And she was very strong. The Commander was feeling the height-weight advantage; and it took every scrap of her strength and training to stay in the fight.

She knew at once that the Doyen had that indomitable quality of will which would not lose, and which had always been the Commander's own chief advantage.

Now she found it matched.

And the Doyen was fighting for Trevanian.

Without effort the Commander could have been undermined by sympathy. But she hardened her mind with the more abstract knowledge that this was for James' life.

She could have ended the fight, perhaps, with a lethal blow, as could the Doyen. And the Commander knew that both of them were tempted. No action would be taken—probably not even against the Commander. Accidents happen. Challenge is frequently lethal, even when not so intended.

One blow, and Trevanian would remain free—or James' life would be guaranteed.

And does honor stand against that?

Briefly at intervals the Commander caught the faces of Trevanian and James, strained, wondering, barely held from somehow intervening.

But the fatal blow did not fall, and the Commander did not raise her hand to give it.

Then she managed to cut the Doyen's feet from under her and had her down in an arm lock which would snap the arm if she moved.

Now it was a question of whether the Commander could hold it, and for how long—and of whether she could use it to force the Third Challenge.

She pressed her fingers into the nerve centers of the Doyen's face and reached out . . .

Then their minds were locked.

They met as a sheet of fire, and the Commander knew the Doyen's searing, utter determination to keep Trevanian.

It was matched only by the cold flame of her own determination that James should live.

In the mind lock both absolute resolves had a lethal intensity, and the Commander knew suddenly that the two challengers could both leave their bones on this sand, minds burned out by the deadly inner clash.

She felt the Doyen realize it too.

And yet the only alternative was surrender.

The Doyen had never surrendered.

In the link the Commander got a sudden vision of what this woman was, how she had forged an effective political unit out of a loose hereditary league of planets, moving worlds. The power was hers not merely by right of birth, but by right of what she was. And she had moved always by honor, intelligence, passion, until she found her own passion in Trevanian.

The Commander allowed some vision also of what she herself was, but she blocked recent events, and James.

She caught a hint of Omne from the other's mind, but knew that the Doyen was blocking that, too. What danger might be in that secret? Would the Doyen stand with the dark giant, finally, and plunge the Empire into civil war again?

Would she betray James to the dungeons of the Empire?

The Commander found power in the fear, and suddenly she was bearing down with her mind and with a power which did not seem to be her own, which rose from some depth she had never touched or needed.

The power was beyond resistance and yet the Doyen was resisting, from her own depths.

They were locked into it now, and the end was death.

And yet the Commander could not yield. She would have lost, publicly, and she would have no cover for

James. He would die, while Trevanian, if *she* won, would live.

She tried to project that to the Doyen. Yield. We will all live . . .

Suddenly someone was with them, kneeling beside them, his hands touching the Doyen's face.

'Let me go. Don't die. Do it for me—' Trevanian projected in the link.

The Doyen was distracted, undermined.

She did not surrender. But suddenly the balance had shifted. The Commander's fixed will was unanswerable with the Doyen's attention divided.

Suddenly they both knew that it was over.

'For you—' the Doyen projected to him bitterly.

'I will take care of him,' the Commander sent.

'If you fail, it is war to the knife . . . '

'While I succeed—peace and alliance.'

'Yes. You have won.'

The Commander slowly released the mind lock—and barely found the strength to release the Doyen from the arm lock.

They were helping each other up.

Then Trevanian seemed to be lifting them both.

And from somewhere there was James, drawing the Commander away.

His strength was sufficient unto that.

And *he* had not broken her concentration.

The four of them walked out of the arena together, past the baleful look of the War Minister, and the—perhaps—relieved looks of the Council.

The Council's judgment had been upheld.

Peace had been ransomed with royalty.

It was a Romulan tradition millennia old.

And each time it must have been new.

# CHAPTER VII

THE COMMANDER had allowed the Doyen and Trevanian their fair walls while she dressed and attended to the not-negligible results of the physical fight.

James swore over her injuries in English and attended to some of the results.

She set a light healing trance and kissed him on his consternation. "Come, I have had worse in a hundred fights."

"*That* is what worries me."

"I am pleased that you did not try to intervene. Perhaps you are learning something."

He laughed. "Are you kidding? I had pretty much the same idea—only I was held by a ten-ton truck. Trevanian landed *his* truck on the sand. He's tough as a boot if he has to be. And *I*—" He looked at her bitterly. "I had to stop, or the guard would have known I was Human, and you would have died just as surely. *Bruchón*, with your Human treason."

She sobered. "You see, you have learned something. You did stop."

"Yes. And that could have cost you your life. It was some kind of fatal mind lock, wasn't it?"

"Yes. You must learn to trust me for that last reserve of will, James. If it had been Spock, would you have tried to intervene?"

He looked startled. "Maybe—not."

"You would have expected him to win."

70

His eyes agreed, but finally he shook his head. "Yes. But if I thought that he was dying, I would have moved. You cannot ask me to trust you to be immortal—or to stand and see you die."

"That is what you must do if it will break your cover. And you must now be the Prince."

He stood back. "I don't know how."

"I will teach you."

They met in the great hall by the statue in the secret alcove.

The Doyen had opened the alcove.

The Commander bowed to her fractionally. "You are the sculptor, of course."

The Doyen nodded acknowledgment. "You have known that I would permit no one else the model."

She did not say that she now would have no option and that the original model would belong to the Commander.

She didn't have to.

The Doyen would have cold stone, and the Commander would take the living reality.

Even now the Commander considered it an open question whether the Doyen would not kill to prevent that—or whether someone might not on her behalf.

And where was Omne?

Was he merely keeping to the background for some purpose of his own?

Or had he approached the Doyen with some offer? The power of the Phoenix on the side of her quest for freedom?

What if he had offered another Trevanian? One for the Commander to take, while the original stayed safe with the Doyen?

The thought chilled the Commander—and yet she did not think that Omne would have surfaced so completely, if he were here at all. If he, in truth, lived. He would be saving his big guns for some moment when he could act crushingly against her, Spock, Jim, James.

It might be through the Doyen, but not just yet.

The Commander turned to her. "We have pledged alliance. I shall hold you to that."

"While he lives and prospers," the Doyen said. "If not, I do not care what the cause or cost. There will be no ransom and no excuses I will accept. I will lead not merely my planets but the new alliances I have forged—into a war. We will now be strong enough to win."

"Until I fail," the Commander said, "you will back *me*. You will forge still more alliances, as will I. By family and personal obligation I already can call on substantial power. Yours will strengthen my hand, as mine will ultimately strengthen yours. However, neither will be sufficient. We must reach others. The faster we do it, the sooner I will return him."

The Doyen shook her head. "I will have a time-name, now. I will not wait for you to achieve power. At some point you must trust me—or you must kill me."

The Commander nodded. In truth she was debating whether the time should not be now.

She looked at Trevanian, at the Doyen, and she knew the agony, and that nothing could concern the Doyen until she got him back. Desperation might force her hand to treachery. Or—Omne might.

On the other hand, generosity now would forge a bond which the Commander would bet would be unbreakable.

She would bet . . . anything but James' life.

And against anyone but Omne.

She set her jaw and named a time.

The Doyen must have read that it had been close. She turned and confronted the Commander. "Your impulse was to give him to me. Do it. I will see that you do not regret it."

"I believe that," the Commander said. "There is only one thing I would not risk on it. But that is what is at stake." She shook her head with finality, "No."

The Doyen's face was not to be read.

Nor was it to be read as she escorted the Commander and James to the Commander's scoutship.

The Commander turned to the Doyen. "By custom a royal tribute hostage may be accompanied by a kinsman who will attend him. I have asked you for no kinsman. I assume that your Prince's private calling-name would be known to no one to whom you had not given him in evenwatch exchange."

"To no one," the Doyen said.

"Then my hostage, James, will be attended by his kinsman, Trevanian," the Commander said.

The Doyen nodded and extended her hand. It held a simple eyemask. "I had thought so. You will want the mask of a kinsman of noble station."

"I have one," the Commander said, but she took the offered mask. "Very well, you may change now, Trevanian."

She saw the Doyen's eyes darken, but it was almost a look of gratitude. The Commander had correctly understood that this would spare the Doyen the imagining of the moment of unveiling.

Trevanian almost looked to the Doyen for permission, then caught himself and did not. He reached up and took mask and cowl off.

For a moment the Commander merely looked at him. The face had a startling purity of beauty that even the master sculptor had not fully captured. And it had a look of the mature man which even the statue did not promise—a curious look of innocence and maturity together. It was a face which, as in an old Earth legend, could have launched a thousand ships. And it was very probable that it would.

The Commander looked at the Doyen for a moment in acknowledgment of what she had chosen.

The beauty was startling on a sheer physical level, too. The coloring of the skin was fair and golden, to match the golden eyes. But the hair and the winged eyebrows were dark—they were the color of hair of that other strain of Romulan royalty which went back to the Origin World—that living, iridescent black which was almost blue-black, silky—the color, in fact, of Spock's hair.

The Commander nodded. She saw that even James was startled by the sheer physical presence of the man. The Prince had the look both of a sheltered nobility of breeding, and of a strength which had never been tried. There was something in his eyes, the set of his jaw, which was a throwback to his most savage ancestor. But there was something in the mouth which was sultry, exotic, sensuous, and—almost sullen.

This was the last man in the galaxy to take well to being the princeling and the property of the victor. Well, almost the last. The Commander looked at James.

James was looking, for once, completely nonplussed that the man he saw here could have been made to behave with the deference and decorum which James had done.

The Commander got a sudden flash that James was going to know the reason why—or else—and that the process of finding out was going to be quite an education for a Romulan Prince, and for a displaced starship captain.

The Commander turned and put the cowl mask on James. He did not protest—in front of the Doyen—but the Commander could feel the rebellion in his whole body.

Yet he was held by the knowledge of the necessity.

"You are the Prince, now, James," the Commander said.

Then he said, "Yes," very quietly, and he moved . . .

She had not intended it, but she realized only as he did it that she had wanted it, almost commanded it in silence.

James went to his knees and knelt in front of her. "My lady."

Perhaps it was an acknowledgment to Trevanian, in front of *his* lady, that what Trevanian could do—even while possessing that streak of fierce and elemental maleness—James could do, and would. Perhaps it was silent eloquence to the Doyen—arguing that the plan would work.

But it was doubtless also some tribute to the Commander. She knew that James would have done it for no one else, taken that role for no one else.

She saw a look of respect on the Doyen's face.

"It is even possible that your 'Prince' will carry it off," the Doyen said.

"He will," the Commander said. "Rise, James."

Her focus was on James, but she saw beyond him that the look on Trevanian's face amounted almost to worship. Trevanian stepped forward to stand at James' shoulder. "I will be his hand," he said.

In another moment the Commander ordered them aboard the scoutship and they were gone.

# CHAPTER VIII

KIRK got the report in the gym. They were already in the dark nebula which wrapped the stars of the Hegemony systems as if diamonds were caught in spider webs of midnight. The view from the bridge was spectacular, but Kirk had left it. They were barely an hour out of the capital and conference planet of Voran, and he needed to clear the cobwebs out of his own mind and body.

It was almost the first time he had had to try to work the odd stresses and strains out of his body, or his soul.

He needed it, and he could barely force himself to it.

The report which Uhura's runner brought from the bridge was almost a welcome interruption, until Kirk saw it.

And then he looked up to see the Vulcan watching him as he hadn't stopped doing since the morning after the night of the Phoenix.

Sometimes the watch was unobtrusive—watching from his bridge station, in the dining room, over chess, off in a corner doing his own exercises. And sometimes the Vulcan was sitting on Kirk's neck.

Kirk threw in the towel and draped one around his neck and went over to the Vulcan.

"Mr. Spock, have you had your eyes examined lately?"

The Vulcan raised the necessary eyebrow. "I have experienced no symptoms, Captain."

"That large spot before your eyes is a rare bird, known as an overwatched starship captain."

"Now that you mention it, sir," Spock said, "I believe that the specimen is just about your size." Kirk started to grin, but the Vulcan was going on—and then was caught by his own words. "They are vanishingly rare, you know."

Kirk saw the Vulcan's face go tight with that look he had been wearing lately. Kirk sighed. "Come on, Mr. Spock. Business as usual. Try this for size."

He handed the Vulcan the report and watched the quick dark eyes scan it.

He doubted that the Vulcan had had any real sleep since before that day which seemed to date a new era in their lives. They tended to think of things as before Phoenix and after Phoenix. Perhaps there would come a time when the galaxy would date everything from that event. Meanwhile, Spock had closed his eyes only on order.

Moreover, they had been so busy that there had hardly been time to talk. One crisis after another—and the Vulcan was still locked behind his wall.

In truth, Kirk also felt some need to recover. The psychic burnout still screamed in his skull, and he was locked in there with it—he and the Vulcan locked in separate cages.

But Kirk kept trying to get through.

And at night there were the nightmares.

Also—by day. Spock looked at the report—another catalog of disasters, with a final note: Intelligence probes and analysis predicted that the Voran Hegemony would stampede the conference delegates into secession from the Federation.

"As Ambassador Plenipotentiary," Spock said, "you are ordered to prevent secession, if possible, but at all costs to prevent war."

Kirk nodded. "It amounts to being elected to preside over the dismantling of the Federation, Mr. Spock. Which will *lead* to war."

Spock nodded. "It would appear so."

Kirk sighed. "We beam down in one hour, Mr. Spock. Collect the final intelligence reports and meet me in the transporter room."

Kirk went to the showers, feeling somehow very alone.

He dressed in white civilian formal wear and met Spock in the transporter room. Scott himself stood by to work the controls and McCoy simply stood by.

"Intelligence final update, Mr. Spock?" Kirk said, nodding to them.

"The Hegemony heartworld, Voran, is prepared to receive the Ambassador Plenipotentiary of the Federation," Spock said. "The delegates assembled represent the largest dissident interstellar convention ever assembled. The old Hegarch has announced that the new Regent is responsible, and in recognition of that and other achievements, not specified, the Hegemony will honor the Regent with its Dynastic Liberation Prize. It has been presented only five times in history—once to Zephrem Cochrane for the warp drive."

"And a conference of dissidents is supposed to be in *that* class?" McCoy muttered. "Cochrane opened the stars."

Kirk nodded. "What else?"

"Romulans will be in attendance," Spock said. "The Hegarch has declared the Hegemony heartworld a free-port for the purpose, and since the conference planet, Voran, lies very near the Romulan Neutral Zone, any Romulan violation of Federation space to come here would merely be violation of that part of Federation space controlled by the Hegemony. If we attempted to prevent the Romulans from passing, it would certainly be taken as violation of the Hegemony's right, and of the Prime Directive, to say nothing of an act of war."

"Let 'em come," Kirk said. "Although we have defended the Hegemony from the Romulans along that Zone for a century, with our ships and our blood. However—if there were an alliance between a secessionist group led by the Hegemony's new Regent and the Romulans—"

"The Federation could not stand against it," Spock said in that tone of dispassion with which he often pronounced doom.

Kirk grinned sourly. "Come on, Mr. Spock, we have not yet begun to fight. Any word on the nature of the Romulan Delegation?"

Spock shook his head. "The favors you called in to spread the 'rumor' into the Romulan Empire were performed, but the result is unknown. Two Romulan fleets—one of three starships, one of five including a dreadnought, are approaching from the dark side of the nebula."

"That sounds more like a war party than a diplomatic delegation," Scott said.

"Yes," Kirk agreed.

But McCoy turned on him with a suspicious eye. "*What* 'rumor' did you spread into the Romulan Empire?" he said accusingly.

Kirk shrugged with his best look of innocence. "I believe it would translate as 'Please don't throw her into the briar patch!' "

McCoy did a double take. "You don't mean—"

But Kirk had already steered Spock up onto the transporter platform.

"I believe," Kirk said judiciously, "that some person or persons unknown started a rumor to the effect that only one thing terrifies the new Ambassador Plenipotentiary of the Federation: that the Romulan Empire might send as a delegate the Romulan Commander who won the trust of the dissident delegates before—the only Romulan who might unite them now against the Federation—a Commander who may have pretended a certain cooperation with a starship captain, while perhaps actually being in league with Omne."

"You don't believe *that*—" McCoy began. Then the implications caught up with him. "You intend to get her off the hook on the charge of consorting with the enemy!"

Kirk chuckled. "Can I help it if there are rumors?"

McCoy swallowed. "Say—hello," he said softly.

Kirk nodded. "If it works. And if she brings him. Take the con, Mr. Scott. Energize."

# CHAPTER IX

KIRK and Spock beamed down to conference co-ordinates which were on—and under—the sea of Voran. The conference center was set in a transparent force field the shape of a globe as if a brandy snifter floated half-under the waters but open to sky and stars. Great sea creatures peered in through transparent crystal walls, into what was, perhaps, the most elaborate formal reception which Kirk had seen in a lifetime of diplomatic fetes.

This particular fete looked as if it had been staged in a tradition so old and so honorable that it could adapt even to starships and alien life forms.

Kirk saw most of the Class M-compatible life forms of the Federation, and a few that were new even to him. In pressurized compartments around the walls of a vast floating amphitheater were the noncompatible life forms—swimmers, oozers, mass-mind multiunit forms, breathers of methane or other Class M-lethal atmospheres. Around lower tiers were special areas for marginally compatible forms. Seating, lying, and perching arrangements were available. On the vast open black-onyx field floor, under a force-field roof open to the night sky, were the glittering life forms of a galaxy, some in mobile life-support units or force-field belts, some with power-assisted units to aid them against gravity or protect their vulnerabilities. A delegate who stood a foot high might not wish to mingle on an even footing with one who stood ten feet tall. Someone had arranged for both of them with thought and care.

The reception was more elaborately staged and arranged for the convenience of disparate life forms than even the Babel conference or Omne's last Hole-in-the-Wall conference.

Many more delegates were in attendance—by the looks of things almost every Federation world, and many which for one reason or another had not joined the Federation.

Kirk traded a quick look with Spock. A decision against the Federation here would be an unmitigated disaster.

A kind of hush had fallen over the delegates as the Federation Ambassador and his First Officer materialized, as if everyone had been waiting for the drama which they represented.

Some of these delegates had been present on Omne's Black Hole planet at the last conference to see Kirk dash into a fire, and the Vulcan return to the *Enterprise* with Kirk's body. Many had seen Kirk's and the Commander's subsequent speech to the effect that the reports of Kirk's death were exaggerated, and that their host, Omne, had been beaten in a fight by the Vulcan, and had killed himself.

Now a man whom some of them had seen dead—was *here*. Kirk and Spock's names were announced and they were greeted by a winged biped with gleaming bronze feathers from one of the Hegemony's member worlds.

Kirk made the ritual sign of greeting-of-unspecified-ranking which Spock had unearthed from the computer files on Hegemony customs.

The feathered glide-wing spoke: a music sequence which the implant translators rendered as speech, but which still reached the ear as music.

"I am V'Rlee, D'Vor of Protocol, Ambassador Plenipotentiary Kirk, Mr. Spock. I am in charge of arrangements. Ambassador Kirk, as senior diplomatic representative of the Federation you are to accept the Dynastic Medallion of Liberation from the old Hegarch for presentation to the new Lord Regent. You will place the medallion around the Lord Regent's neck."

Kirk looked at V'Rlee skeptically, trying not to betray discomfiture. "I am honored. But surely the honor of presenting the award would be better reserved for one who knows the purpose of the award and the nature of the achievements of its recipient."

V'Rlee nodded, but the gesture was apparently a negative. "It is the custom. So long as the Dynasty owes allegiance to the Federation. Unless, of course, you as Federation representative wish to question the judgment of the Dynasty in choosing its Regent or making its award, or to deny its right to that custom under the Prime Directive . . . "

The music was silken, but the warning was plain.

Kirk had the sudden sense of a trap closing around him—and yet there was still nothing but silken protocol and what might be an innocent honor, and even a welcome sign that the Hegemony's relationship with the Federation was still honored.

Kirk looked at Spock. The Vulcan's impassive face was unreadable, but less than encouraging.

But there could be no deep-laid trap in this—no more than the obvious dangers. Omne, even if he lived, could not have been everywhere at once, starting all the fires which had brought delegates here. More likely, many of the fires, perhaps all, were merely the natural course of events from the last conference. Perhaps, even, Kirk *had* killed Omne, permanently. But even if not, Omne could not show himself. He was a dead man to the galaxy. And if he was not, he would have to explain immortality.

"May I ask the name of the Regent?" Kirk said pleasantly.

"You have asked," V'Rlee said just as pleasantly, as if it were an answer, and turned, offering a winged arm to Kirk in a polite gesture, as if to escort him in.

Kirk restrained himself from an impolite answer. He found himself wondering whether the D'Vor was male or female. Possibly another feathered biped could tell.

He could not. Possibly it should not matter. It did. His reflexes were not attuned to it. It was not as if the life forms were so different that the question didn't seem to arise. He was accustomed even to that, but he never quite got used to it, or liked it.

Nevertheless, he took the offered arm in what he hoped was the proper manner. "So I have," he said. "Who is the Regent?"

The D'Vor nodded negation. "The identity is to be known only in the moment of presentation of the award and ascension to the Regency. It is the custom of ancient days, that none may envy beforehand, nor oppose before the fact. Thus we affirm the judgment of the Hegarch. However if you wish to withdraw participation of the Federation in Hegemony affairs from this time forward, your participation in the ceremony will not be required."

Kirk smiled, and if the D'Vor had been Human of either sex he/she would have recognized the smile as dangerous. "One can only admire the iron fist in the feathered glove, D'Vor V'Rlee. You have made your point admirably. The Federation of course recognizes the right of the Hegemony to choose its ruler and to present its award. If you wish me to act as representative of the Federation in presenting the medal, I will regard it as an honor to the Federation."

The D'Vor shook his/her head in satisfaction. "Thank you, Ambassador Kirk. That will be satisfactory. It will not be necessary for you to kneel to the Hegarch."

Kirk tried not to sigh visibly. He had done it before for diplomatic reasons, and had never liked it. He looked at the Vulcan with a microscopic flicker of relief. The Vulcan looked skeptical. He had warned of the strictness of the custom of kneeling.

"However," the D'Vor continued smoothly, "the exemption applies because the Hegarch is unable to sit or stand. You will kneel to the Regent."

The feathered person detached an arm to put it around Kirk's shoulders and steered him toward a low platform backed by shimmering force-field curtains. "You may wait here, Commander Spock," V'Rlee said at the edge of the platform.

The Vulcan stopped. For a moment his eyes debated it with Kirk, or with himself. This was a strange crowd, some of it almost certainly hostile . . . The Vulcan was not easily dislodged from Kirk's shoulder at the best of times.

But there was little choice. The Vulcan stood where indicated, and Kirk remained under the D'Vor's wing.

They stepped up onto the platform and approached an incredibly old man lying propped up on a couch. He looked older than God, and not much less determined. A boy—almost a grown man—sat beside him.

"The Hegarch is addressed simply as First Born, or Sir," V'Rlee trilled. "You will address the Lord Regent as 'my lord.' "

He handed Kirk on ahead and fell back.

The lights fell to leave Kirk alone in a spotlight and he saw that he was almost on top of the old ruler. The Hegarch beckoned Kirk down close to him, and Kirk dropped to one knee beside the couch. It could do no harm to pay respect to a dying monarch. The Hegarch looked into Kirk's face as if trying to read some riddle there.

"Your health, sir," Kirk said. "The Federation's best wishes, and mine, to the First Born of the Hegemony."

"It is far too late to wish me health, Ambassador. Best wishes are accepted and returned. I suspect we will both need them." He pressed a heavy medallion into Kirk's hand with a bony, translucent hand which had once been powerful. "You may wish health to my great-grandson, last survivor of the royal Dynasty. He is a sweet child, but a prisoner in his own skull. He will be the new First Born."

Kirk understood suddenly that this was a dead man, breathing only by virtue of some last assignment he had given himself. Kirk turned to the handsome teen-age boy and smiled, and was answered by a smile like morning, but the smile of a child. The boy held the old man's hand lovingly.

"The award for—liberation—has never been more truly earned, Ambassador," the Hegarch said, as if Kirk should understand him.

"May I ask for *what* liberation?" Kirk began.

But at that moment the feathered glide-wing was alerted by a signal at its belt. "The Romulan Delegation," V'Rlee intoned and moved off to offer greeting.

Kirk looked to the transporter platform.

Two figures shimmered. Then they solidified to become the Commander in civilian dress, with a man in a mask. Kirk restrained himself from the appearance of doing a double take, but did one anyway. He could barely believe the cowl mask, and even the stance was fractionally different, but he recognized the masked man well enough. Too well.

The loud-translator announced, "Commander Charvón, Ambassador Empowered, of the Romulan Empire, attended by royal hostage of the Thorvan League of Dissidents."

Kirk watched the Vulcan digesting that package.

Then the transporter shimmered again.

This time it was a dark Romulan male of massive stature and obvious authority, reminding Kirk a little of the enemy Commander of a Romulan ship he had faced once.

"The Commander-in-Chief of the Romulan Forces, Rovan, in observer capacity," the speaker said.

The Commander stood very straight in her white civilian gown, as if untouched by the fact that she had been sent to do a job, while being watched by her ultimate superior—on suspicion of treachery.

She greeted V'Rlee and was shown to a position beside Spock, with James standing masked at her shoulder. The Commander-in-Chief followed at a slight distance. The Commander bowed fractionally, formally. "Mr. Spock."

"Commander Charvón," Spock said, his tone giving no hint that he knew also her private calling-name.

Spock did not look at James, except with the brief glance which one might give a stranger. The impassive Vulcan face served Spock well. But it remained tight. Kirk suspected that his own face looked much the same. His eyes met the Commander's only for a moment, and James' eyes still less. So it was the "princeling" script. At least they lived. And they were not—yet—in the dungeons of the Empire.

Kirk suspected from the look on Commander-in-Chief Rovan's face that Kirk's "rumor" might have reached the Empire about one-half jump ahead of the Commander's arrest for treason.

"That completes the cast, Ambassador Kirk," the old Hegarch said. "You will present the award now, for a liberation which I will not name, but which you are uniquely qualified to honor." His hand made a slight signal to V'Rlee.

"Beings assembled," the glide-wing announced, "the Lord Regent of the Dynastic Hegemony steps forward to be honored with the Dynastic Liberation Prize presented by Federation Ambassador Plenipotentiary James T. Kirk."

Kirk rose to see the Vulcan's face—the skin looking stretched to breaking over the bones now. The Commander's face was also dead-calm and drawn tight with the same premonition which was gathering suddenly in the pit of Kirk's stomach.

"The Lord Regent," V'Rlee said in deep bell tones.

The hall went dark under the stars. Force-field curtains parted and for a moment only massive darkness could be seen. Then a pinpoint spotlight flared on the unmistakeable face.

There was a low, odd murmur as some delegates recognized a dead man.

Omne.

Kirk stood very still, feeling himself caught in a spotlight, too, trying not to let the shock be visible in his body. He lifted his chin to meet the giant's black eyes, seeing the man's silent enjoyment of his shock, and the silent, deep anger.

Kirk had killed him.

And this man had seen him beaten.

Kirk's own flesh went cold and then hot with the knowledge that this man had beaten him—with a terrible ease which had reduced him almost to surrender. This man had seen him cry, and had tended his injuries with the giant hands.

The slow look of amused appraisal was on the giant's face as the hard eyes looked at Kirk. And what did the look reveal of that contest between them which Kirk had lost?

From the corner of his eye Kirk saw Spock start to move very deliberately up the low stairs. But Kirk saw that the movement had nothing to do with the civilized company in which they stood. This was the elemental Vulcan, bone-white and lethal, standing out in frozen flickers of motion as strobe-lights caught him, moving toward the menace who had done what he had done to Jim, to James, to all of them on that day and since— and who would do what he wanted to them now.

Without hesitation Kirk stepped between the Vulcan and Omne.

And still without hesitation Kirk took another step and sank down to kneel before Omne.

"My Lord Regent," he said.

And he said it easily. He had knelt to a shrewish Elaan of Troyius, to the insane Garth of Izar. He could do it to stop Spock—with that same ease with which he had once begged Omne on his knees for Spock's life. And he could do it in front of the galaxy.

He sensed that the Vulcan had stopped, frozen.

Omne looked down at Kirk. "I am honored," he said in the heavy voice.

Kirk rose. "I honor the choice and the custom of the Hegemony," he said flatly.

Omne's black eyes glittered dangerously, "Merely that, Ambassador?" he said. "How scrupulous you have become of custom. What became of the true son of moral certainty? Where is the man who set his own judgment against his sworn Prime Directive—and against the customs of the galaxy?"

"The man who set his judgment against a dead man is here, my lord," Kirk said carefully. "The dead man, of course, cannot be."

"Of course," Omne said. "One is so easily afflicted with imposters and doubles these days, as you know best of all." The wolf smile appeared on his face.

"Because I do honor choice," Kirk said, "I will present this award on behalf of the Hegemony for a liberation which I will not name."

He stepped forward a half-step, trying to separate the catch of the short, heavy link-chain which was to bear the prize medallion. It would hang above another gold shape-medallion, almost the shape of a face, which was the sole ornament of Omne's black formal dress.

"Shall I name what you will not name?" Omne said voicelessly—a sound which would not have carried three feet—except to Spock's Vulcanoid ears, and to the Commander's.

"Name what you must," Kirk said, as quietly. "But take great care."

"Do you threaten me, my original?"

"Yes, *my lord*," Kirk said savagely, softly.

Omne looked down at him. "That will be most interesting."

"Once before," Kirk said, "you believed that I had no power to threaten you. Do not make the same mistake twice."

"I never do," Omne said.

Then Kirk stepped forward quite deliberately and reached up to put the chain around the man's neck. There was no help for it. He could not end this without doing it, nor betray the effort of doing it.

"On behalf of the Dynasty," he said aloud, stretching up to encircle Omne's neck with the chain, trying to lock its clasp.

The physical presence of the giant was overpowering. Kirk had known the bone-bruising impact of that corded steel strength. The man could have broken him in half as easily as he had broken something inside him.

He looked into the carved, amused, deadly face, met the obsidian eyes from a distance of inches.

Omne had forgotten nothing.

Then Omne leaned his head forward and whispered in Kirk's ear, "*I will do the one thing I cannot do . . .*"

Kirk froze and the ends of the chain almost dropped from his nerveless hands. Those were Spock's words, the last words the Vulcan had spoken only in Kirk's mind when he had tried the impossible deep-link on the night of the Phoenix, and found that he could not do that either, could only send Kirk down into darkness and oblivion . . .

But Omne could not have known those words—not even by tapping an intercom. Only by tapping a mind . . .

*Could not have known—*

Kirk felt the ground leaving from under him—

Unless it *was* Omne . . . that night . . . and since—

Kirk felt the knotting in his whole body—that Spock whom he had trusted as always, and more than ever, that Spock who had not let him out of sight . . . If *that* Spock had been *Omne* . . .

Kirk suddenly pulled the curtain down on that thought. He could not think about it now.

And perhaps there was another explanation.

Omne *was* Spock—had his memories, might have divined what Spock *would* have done and said, even the impossible.

With savage precision Kirk found the clasp ends and locked them home.

He started to step back, but Omne whispered, "Kneel."

"Once," Kirk said in his throat. "Not more."

Omne looked down into his eyes without touching him. "I do not threaten."

With the effort of his life Kirk lifted his head and straightened his back. "Go to hell, my lord," he said between his teeth.

He stepped back and inclined his head briefly. "My Lord Regent, there are many here who will wish to congratulate you on your new—life. I shall leave you to them."

He started to turn.

Omne's hand settled on his arm—a social gesture now, but with the bite of steel. "On the contrary, Ambassador, you must meet the delegates."

He turned Kirk and stepped to face the Vulcan.

Spock stood as if carved in stone.

"You have forgotten something, Vulcan."

"Nothing," Spock said.

Omne chuckled. "More than you know. But at the moment—you stand in the presence of the Lord Regent of the Hegemony. The custom is to kneel." He did not quite move to stress his hold on Kirk's arm.

Spock's face fought to maintain the Vulcan mask of impassiveness, but the lines of his face stood out in ridges. "Do you wish me to kneel?" he asked flatly.

"No," Omne said. "It is another form of tribute which I have wanted from you. Such as a Vulcan's wish to kill me."

Spock nodded. "That tribute I have paid," he said without pleasure.

Omne smiled. "Indeed."

He bowed fractionally to Spock and stepped past him to the edge of the stage. He gestured with his hand and the stage sank to floor level.

"Good evening, my dear," Omne said to the Commander, moving to face her.

She stood without moving and inclined her head minutely. "Regent."

Omne laughed. "Such formality, my dear, and such a stiff neck. No matter. We meet upon the level. Custom is satisfied." He turned to raise his voice slightly to include the delegates standing nearby. "Formality is dismissed on the level, for the evening. The Regency begins. Let us celebrate the next thousand years."

"Do you expect your Regency to last that long, Regent?" the Romulan Commander-in-Chief said.

Omne bowed to the Commander-in-Chief slightly. "I make no predictions. Those who have boasted of a thousand-year plan have uniformly come to bad ends on a much shorter time-scale. However, there must come a time when life forms here do begin to plan on the scale of a thousand years. Some life forms *have*. Organians. Metrons. Melkotians, others. Have you a thousand-year plan for the Romulan Empire?"

Commander-in-Chief Rovan inclined his head slightly. "Not for my personal stewardship of the Empire," he said, "although I am beginning to get the impression that some people *have*." He looked at the Commander. "It was extremely foresighted of you, Commander Charvón, to forge an alliance by hostage with the Doyen of the Thorvan League. But if you hoped to stay my hand—"

"I hoped only to complete what I had started before you sent me to deal with the matter for which you now wish to accuse me," the Commander said.

"To deal with *me*," Omne said. "Which you did most admirably, my dear Dí'on." His voice fell to pitch the last word low.

Silence fell in their immediate circle. Commander-in-Chief Rovan's eyebrow rose. Omne had used the Commander's private name. That he knew it implied a degree of knowledge which the Romulan Commander-in-Chief would not have expected. Romulans exchanged private names only under special circumstances. Kirk had never known the Commander's first calling-name-of-choice until it had become proper for Spock to tell him after her life-path was bound to theirs on the day of the Phoenix.

How well *had* Omne known her?

She had said that she was not Omne's ally, but she was privileged to do as she pleased on his Black Hole planet. What had she been to him?

"My choice-name is not for strangers," the Commander said.

"There are no strangers here," Omne said.

A man stepped forward from the background and

Kirk recognized the Varal of Voran, largest planet group of the Hegemony.

"I note," the Varal said, "that it does appear there are no strangers here. Regent, you have been pronounced dead by this man, Kirk. Are we to assume that you have known the Federation Ambassador before?"

"Yes," Omne said. "I have known him."

Kirk remained silent.

Then Kirk met the Varal's eyes. "What I said in my speech to the previous conference, with Commander Charvón, was the simple truth."

"Then you lie now, Ambassador Kirk," the Voral said, "or else you have knelt to a man you pronounced dead, a man your First Officer fought to the death, a man you accused of kidnapping you."

Kirk turned to the Varal and shrugged slightly. "Then I have knelt to that man," Kirk said. "It has been said by some here that neither I nor the Federation I represent have respect for others' customs. Perhaps I wished to illustrate the contrary."

The Varal was not easily diverted. "Perhaps you wished to stampede the conference with that impression. What you did on stage was a most dramatic performance. Most gracious. Most astute. Do I get the impression that it also saved your First Officer's life?"

"My First Officer, Mr. Spock," Kirk said steadily, "was quite logically concerned to see what he could only regard as either a dead man or an imposter for a dead man. In either case, quite possibly an enemy possessing hostile intent—and with easy access to the Hegarch and the representatives of a galaxy."

"Come," the Varal cut in, speaking to Kirk. "Your peaceful, logical Vulcan fought Omne to the death, or he did not. Which is it?"

"You must find your own explanation, Varal," Kirk said. "As must the galaxy."

The Varal's coppery eyes narrowed, looking Kirk over—a look bordering on contempt.

"You called Black Omne 'my lord,' " the Varal said.

"Yes," Kirk said tightly.

"A courtesy which *you* have omitted, Varal," Omne said smoothly, dangerously.

Kirk looked up in astonishment.

The giant's face was impassive, but his black eyes locked with the Varal's.

In a moment, as if there had been no contest, the Varal said, "My Lord Regent, my congratulations upon your new life, and your old—friend. Or perhaps the Federation's Ambassador comes under the heading of 'Know thine enemy.' "

"There are times," Omne said silkenly, "when one may prefer one's enemies to one's allies." He bowed slightly to the Varal and turned Kirk away from him. "Ambassador, a word with you." He steered Kirk as if to move with him through the force-field curtains nearby.

But the Commander moved and stood in front of Omne.

"A word with you," she said. "We will ignore the matter of my choice-name, for the moment. That is the personal. The political is that your behavior once required me to act in concert with *my* honorable enemy, Captain Kirk—a matter which has caused me some difficulty."

Omne chuckled. "One is known by the enemies one keeps, my dear." He did not, quite, look at James.

"However," the Commander continued, "the matter may be turned to advantage. I am empowered by the Empire to offer Romulan alliance to worlds seceding from the Federation."

Kirk turned on her. "You are quick enough to turn from an honorable enemy to make alliance with a 'friend' who knows your private name, and tells it to the galaxy. Maybe you were always with Omne."

The Commander laughed. "You did not suppose that I was with *you*, Captain?"

"You had your own plan, all this time," Kirk said savagely.

"Of course," she said coolly.

Kirk saw that the Romulan Commander-in-Chief was

taking in that exchange, and beginning to revise an estimation. As intended . . .

Omne looked at the Commander with appreciation. "Up to your usual form, my dear. We must have a private summit conference on that subject. Among others. How is the princeling business these days?"

"Adequate," she said. "Let us have that conference now."

It was as gallant an offer as she had ever made, and Kirk knew that it was made to get him off the hook and away from Omne.

Omne smiled the wolf smile. "Delighted, my dear. Anytime. However, I do have a prior engagement for a summit conference with the only man whom I have allowed to tell me to go to hell, twice—and once to pay for my ticket to ride. I will take a raincheck, Commander."

Omne's eyes were suddenly chips of black basalt and he turned Kirk to walk along the edge of the force field, shutting the Commander and Spock and James out with his back.

"You ought not to tempt me to illustrate, my original," Omne said. "Do not play poker with me. Nor galactic confrontation. I never bluff. There is the political, and the personal."

"Yes," Kirk said. "The elemental. Answer me now," he said through his teeth. "Name 'the one thing I cannot do'—or admit that you play a game with that, too."

"Of course I do," Omne said. "Your problem is merely to determine *what* game. And—what player. I am Spock, too, you know. Even in *this* body. Of course Spock would have had to try to mark you with the tracing link. But did *he* do that to you—or did *I?*"

Kirk could not keep the shudder down. The searing terror of the Vulcan's last drive to establish the link was with Kirk still, and the shock which had knocked him into nightmare oblivion still seemed to permeate his body, his whole being.

And now—if it had not even been *Spock* . . .

Somehow the shudder reached some snapping point.

Kirk wrenched against Omne's arm, trying to break the giant's hold, careless of the galactic audience. Some things were beyond endurance. But even Kirk's body could not remember the totality of the dark strength of the giant. It was like being held by more than flesh. Kirk's wrench barely moved the corded arm. Then the steely hand crushed his arm with a power which he had forgotten. And Omne was bundling him into an alcove in the force curtains, so smoothly that Kirk doubted that most of the guests even knew that he had made any effort.

Omne touched a control on his belt and a light force curtain opened and closed behind them. Kirk could see out. But the field closed in the Vulcan's face and blocked his effort to come through.

Kirk could see the Vulcan's face through the curtain.

Then a heavier field closed to black, and Kirk could no longer see the Vulcan nor hear sounds from the reception.

Kirk was alone with Omne.

"It was *not* you, that night," Kirk said. "If it had been, I would have killed you."

"You *did*," Omne said. "Once."

"It was—too soon."

"No."

"You would have had to die, again."

"No. But if necessary, do you doubt it?"

"He is still Spock."

"Is he?"

It was the question which had been hammering in Kirk's brain. *Was* he? Had he been? How long? When? *Now?*

"You would have had to—put him back—when you left."

"No," Omne said. "It could as easily still be me."

"You wouldn't do that. You wouldn't—share—the memory."

"Are you certain? Now that I have the Vulcan's power to merge memories again through the mind meld? No, Captain, you and your Vulcan have taken away the last limits on the Phoenix process. Nothing can stand against it, or me, now. Least of all you. Don't you suppose that I would want to test that power against your legend? Against that friendship which has become famous throughout a galaxy? If I could be Spock to Kirk, so completely that *you* never knew it, who could I not be? Who could detect imposture if the legendary friendship is not safe against it?"

"Not possible," Kirk said obdurately. "I would have known. Spock would. You would still have had to put my Spock back at some point. I do not believe that you would let another Omne run loose."

For a moment he caught an odd look on Omne's face, and he thought that it was the look of being understood.

"In the long run, that is possibly even true," Omne said. "It guarantees nothing about the short run. But if I *did* wish to put your Spock back, or if I *have*, it is still no problem. I have Spock's Vulcan powers now, but with an added power factor of my own. Or has it escaped you that the Vulcan has, even, the power to alter your memories—to make you forget? He *has* used that power on you, and so can I. I could stun Spock, keep him in suspended storage, take his place in his own form, and, when I wanted to, meld with him, erase unwanted memories, even plant false memories—some version of the fact, perhaps, to match with the memories which I would allow you to keep. Neither you nor he would ever know that he had been gone. I could do the same for your memories—block them, make you forget the moments when I might have shown something of myself."

Kirk had a sudden numbing sense that it could be true—perhaps even that it *had* been true.

If he could not trust Spock . . .

In some very quiet way Kirk felt something at the bottom of the structure of his world crumble. If he behaved sanely now, it would be by rote, by some brute knowledge of what he had to do.

Omne had done the one thing which was not possible, and the one thing which Kirk could not bear. He had taken Kirk's certainty of the Vulcan away.

Spock could be with Kirk now, and Kirk would never know. It could just as easily be Omne.

Kirk launched himself against Omne with a knee smash and a body block. He didn't care if he were flattened in the next instant.

Omne blocked him with a muscled thigh and twisted him in an armlock to hold him helpless. It was not even the beginning of a fight.

"I gave you warning," Omne said.

And after a long moment, "Kneel."

The giant forgot nothing, never bluffed. It was the price Kirk had known he would have to pay at some point when he defied Omne on stage by refusing to kneel. He had bought defiance, and now he would have to pay for it, have to take whatever he had to take, one more time . . .

Kirk felt the helplessness which would finally bring him to his knees. Omne could put him there in an instant. But that was not what Omne wanted.

It took a time which was counted in eternities.

But Kirk knew the end result.

And he knew that he was utterly alone. Vulnerable. Undefended.

He could not stand against that. This man had him beaten. In body. Perhaps even in soul. Omne could demonstrate that at any time.

Finally Kirk went down, by inches, by millimeters, but went.

"Say it," Omne said.

Kirk found himself immersed in the nightmare of the day of the Phoenix, and in the nightmares since, in which Spock was Omne . . . Nightmares in the dark— or in the daylight.

Omne had mastered him in both. And nightmare was here.

"My lord," Kirk said.

Omne looked down at him. "How shall I punish you for killing me?"

Kirk looked up at him bitterly, knowing that it was more than this man which had broken some will in him to resist. "You have punished me enough," he said. "You have taken the Vulcan away from me, the certainty, the trust—even the memory. Even the future. I will find him by my side, and doubt him. *That* is what you have done."

"Yes," Omne said. "I have."

# CHAPTER X

THE COMMANDER said under her breath, "Mr. Spock!"

The Vulcan turned back to her with that look which she had not seen since the day of the Phoenix.

They both knew that the force fields were of Omne's impenetrable kind. Behind them Omne could exact whatever vengeance he wished against Jim Kirk, or against both of them by keeping Kirk there as hostage for their behavior.

The look on Spock's face was betraying to the assembly exactly how grave the matter was.

"Mr. Spock, a word with you," she said and turned him so that the Vulcan's face was less visible. She could not be seen in this manner with the Vulcan. But she could not leave him alone in this moment. James also moved to stand beside Spock on the other side.

"You cannot reach him," James said. "You must depend on Jim to survive. He has before, even against Omne."

"He had not killed Omne before," Spock said.

"If Jim could kill Omne, he is not helpless," the Commander said. "Do you have the directional tracing link with Jim?"

"No," Spock said with effort. "I attempted it. A burn-out."

The Commander looked at him with appalled comprehension. "You are not merely shielding, then?" But she knew. The sense of psychic presence which the Vulcan had always projected was cut off, as if by a wall. And there had been something—not right—with Jim, either.

"No," Spock said. "Condition unknown. Unprecedented. I will beam to the *Enterprise*. Omne's force fields cannot be as complete here as on the Black Hole planet. I will try to penetrate them."

"Complete enough, I suspect," she said. "Nevertheless, I will try too."

They had been moving along the edge of the force field toward the transporter. Now Spock stopped her and looked into her eyes, and she saw that deep strength in him which could rise even in the worst crisis.

"I have caused you to betray yourself," he said. "Your Commander-in-Chief will have read your concern and will no longer believe any appearance of enmity. He is coming, and I suspect that he will now arrest you for treason. You must beam to your ship and get James to a place of safety. Will you consider outside the Empire?"

"No," she said and stepped onto the transporter with Spock, and with James at her side. "But I will get James to safety."

She saw Commander-in-Chief Rovan making his way through the crowd as they gave the separate coordinates.

"There was not, after all, much time for us, Mr. Spock," she said.

He turned to her. "Certain moments are—all the time there is," he said.

"And worth the price," she answered.

Then the transporter took them.

# CHAPTER XI

KIRK looked for the Vulcan.

Omne was walking Kirk back into the reception through another force-field curtain. He had given Kirk some time to deal with the series of shocks and to regain some semblance of a normal appearance suitable for a captain, an Ambassador.

Kirk doubted if it had helped, much. But he attempted to keep his face set to stone, and his thoughts the same.

Nevertheless, they caught speculative looks, heard a kind of low murmuring sweep through the crowd. Kirk walked beside Omne without restraint now. Could the crowd see that there was something gone from Kirk's stiff-necked resistance? What could they see?

Oddly enough, Omne had talked to him quietly and sanely toward the end.

It was the first time they had not been under the gun of immediate and fatal crisis—unless you counted those other few minutes in Omne's safe-house, when Omne had tended Kirk's injuries while his tears dried, and told Kirk that Kirk had not broken, had not surrendered.

This time he *had*.

"My lord . . . "

Kirk did not know how to deal with that. He could tell himself that it had been a tactic—to save his life, his mission, his freedom to act without a broken body. It had been that but he knew it had also been more, and he did not know how to deal with surrender.

At the moment he only knew how to keep putting one foot in front of the other. And—how to look for Spock.

Spock was not there.

"Where is he?" Kirk said under his breath in the tone of murder. "If you've done something to *him*— Where are the Commander and James?"

Omne shrugged. "If I told you that I do not know, you would have no cause to believe me."

"No," Kirk said. But after a moment he set his teeth. "I have not known you to lie, unless by implication or in the form of a question. I am asking."

Omne turned to him, acknowledging that effort. "I don't know," he said with grave courtesy. "I will inquire, if you like."

"Yes," Kirk said. Finally he added, "Thank you."

Omne summoned someone to him and murmured an order.

Someone else took the moment to buttonhole Kirk, "—caused quite a stir, you know," the being said. "Your Vulcan looked as if he would take the place apart. And the Romulan Commander with him."

Kirk could not quite focus on the being's flowered face. Then he made himself do it. "Where did he go? And—she?"

The person spread its tentacles. "My impression, he beamed to ship, and she to hers, with her hostage. Her chief was not pleased."

"That is my report, also," Omne said. He steered Kirk away from the flower person and walked him back toward the force curtains.

Kirk stopped as they got close.

Omne permitted it.

"I do not have planetary shielding here yet. Merely limited force fields. I trust your Vulcan would not do anything rash?"

"I thought he was *your* Vulcan."

"We still have not established when or for how long," Omne said.

Suddenly there was a transporter hum and the Vulcan materialized directly in front of them.

Kirk looked at the prehistoric face and was certain that it must be the real Spock. And yet he had been equally certain all along . . .

By some terrible instinct faster than thought, Kirk recoiled away from Spock. He saw the knowledge of that reach the Vulcan's eyes, together with the sight of Kirk.

Spock came toward them.

Hell broke loose.

Afterward Kirk could isolate certain moments and visions as if in slow motion. Now it happened beyond the speed of thought.

Kirk saw some effect sweeping toward them through the crowd—felling everyone in its path. A slow stun-wave, death? He didn't know.

He saw the Vulcan start for him. And he started to move toward the Vulcan.

Suddenly Omne caught Kirk up and turned, shielding him with his body and plowing with the giant's terrible strength toward the force field, his hand opening the belt switch.

Kirk twisted and tried to get to the Vulcan, but Omne's strength held him.

Kirk saw Spock fall as if axed.

The effect hit Omne and the fractional spillover caught Kirk's legs and convulsed him in agony. He could feel the giant cut down as if pole-axed.

But the great bull strength and will of the giant held out. The massive legs gave under him but carried them another step through the force field.

Omne fell then like a broken colossus but he somehow broke the fall with his body and shielded Kirk from most of the impact.

Kirk felt his breath leave and blackness claimed him. But he knew that he lived.

And if the effect was death, he owed his life to Black

Omne. Omne had taken the full effect with his body.
Kirk doubted that Omne had immortality here yet, either. And perhaps for the giant this blackness was final.

But Kirk's final blackness was the picture of the Vulcan falling . . .

Kirk woke still in darkness.

But the giant was crawling, dragging him along.

"What—" Kirk murmured, trying to move and finding his legs a dead weight.

"Unknown," Omne rasped.

"*Spock*," Kirk said.

Omne heaved Kirk through a force-field curtain and
they emerged into light. A laboratory.

Kirk saw the body of the old Hegarch emerge in a
transporter shimmer—automatic machinery . . . And
another shimmer brought the stunned, living body of
the Hegarch's young great-grandson. And Kirk understood.

He knew then that he had underestimated Omne, and
that he was looking at the Phoenix equipment, and at
Omne's secret inner stronghold.

But there was only one thought on Kirk's mind.
"*Spock*," he said urgently again.

Omne looked at him with some unreadable expression—perhaps mere astonishment.

"Because I ask," Kirk said desperately. "Because you
can afford the luxury."

Omne smiled the enigmatic wolf smile.

Then he dragged himself to a control console, set a
dial, and Spock's body emerged in a transporter shimmer on the floor in front of Kirk.

The Vulcan was not breathing.

And there would have been no automatic Phoenix
equipment set to record the Vulcan's mental emanations
at the moment of death. If it was too late—

Then Omne had crawled back and was working over
the body.

McCoy had said that Omne was a doctor. And he

knew Vulcan physiology. He was using external heart massage on the lower abdomen, compressing the chest to start breathing.

Time merged into eternity.

Then the Vulcan coughed. And breathed.

Kirk felt shock catch up with him again and collapsed into blackness. But this time there was no nightmare.

Except at some deepest level the thought—Now what mad evil was running loose in the galaxy?

Kirk woke to find Omne standing over him, shaking him as if to waken him from a bad dream.

"Enough," Omne said.

"God, yes," Kirk said before he was awake.

Then he remembered.

"Spock?"

"All right."

"How many dead?"

"One."

"From *that?* It was a catastrophe."

"It was an extraordinarily powerful stun effect of an unknown type. But it was apparently more a warning than an attempt to annihilate. There are some serious or critical conditions among the less fit delegates and certain vulnerable life forms. Including Vulcans. But it is likely that they will recover. The old Hegarch died. However, as you may have noted, he was prepared."

"Yes," Kirk said. "It worked for him? You could play his mind-recording into his grandson's body?"

Omne nodded. "Two who are one."

"The boy still lives, too?" Kirk asked, seeing an image of the sweet, imprisoned face. "Is he—free now?"

"Of course. They both are. Together."

"The attack was not your doing?"

"No."

"Then whose?"

"Possibly Spock's."

"He was caught in it."

"Perhaps inadvertently. He could have hoped to beam out with you."

"He would not attack an interstellar conference, a mass of innocent beings."

"He thought I had taken you."

"You had."

"Yes."

Kirk was silent. "Not Spock," he said finally. And then with effort, "If it *is* Spock."

For a moment Omne had a look as if he would relent about something. Then he shook his head. "I will not answer the question which you do not ask."

Kirk set his jaw and asked, "Did you save Spock—or *yourself?*"

"I will not answer."

"In any case, I thank you."

Omne nodded. "My pleasure."

"Also for *my* life," Kirk said.

"You would not have died. Unless of shock."

"You could not know that."

"No."

"You shielded me with your body."

"Yes."

"I am the enemy."

"I have not finished with you."

# CHAPTER XII

KIRK walked out into the conference hall with Omne.

There was a murmur from the hall—some peculiar, undefinable response. Kirk faced the eyes. It was a rump session—hastily organized by delegates able to move again after an hour, or by their backup commanders from a number of starships. The mood was volatile, dangerous, edgy; faced with an unknown threat.

And faced with the unknown of the two men before them . . .

These were the two antagonists around whom the poles of opposition should have organized. Yet it was clear enough that by some obscure cross-circuit, they now stood together. And Kirk sensed that someone had seen, and all knew, that Omne had carried him off the field of battle.

The Varal stood up. "Lord Regent, what explanation do you offer?"

"None," Omne said.

"The protection of the conference is your responsibility," the Varal said. "Yet you left the reception unattended and, apparently, unprotected—with the Federation Ambassador. It was clear that you had incurred the wrath of his Vulcan First Officer, who left in a state which can only be described as dangerous. The Romulan Commander also transported to her ship, followed by her Commander-in-Chief. Commander Spock appeared to attempt to retrieve his Captain by the transporter under cover of the confusion of the attack. He did not succeed—because you left with the Captain. Some say Spock was caught by the effect—it appears to lower blood pressure beyond a critical point for Vulcans. The Vulcan delegate was found in critical condition on the edge of the effect. Spock was at its heart. Now he is nowhere in evidence. You have spent some time being scarce yourself, together with the Federation Ambassador. Yet he is your enemy. You seek to disassemble the Federation. He must preserve it. He has called you a kidnapper—and a corpse. Yet you saved him from death or severe injury at the focal point of the effect. Lord Regent, you will pardon a certain confusion. Have you and the Federation Ambassador arrived at—a separate peace?"

"No," Omne said.

"Is that your only answer?" the Varal said dangerously.

"That was your only question," Omne said.

"What evidence can you offer that the Federation and/or its representatives here did not stage this attack for the purpose of breaking up the conference before the conference broke up the Federation?"

This time Omne paused to give weight to the answer. He looked out over the delegations as if measuring the consequences of the answer.

"None," he said. He turned to look accusingly at Kirk, and the black eyes were opaque now. "I withdraw the Dynastic Hegemony from the Federation and move an immediate resolution of secession."

There was a stunned silence, a threatening murmur—and then cheers.

Kirk felt the slow burn rising.

And with it the temper and the incorrigible brute stubbornness which had deserted him for one crucial moment that night.

Broken? Hell. He had not yet begun to bend.

So Omne would turn this against them, knowing

damn well they were innocent, and try to stampede the conference?

Well, look the hell out, my Lord Regent.

Kirk shook himself imperceptibly, as if coming out of some state of deep shock.

And that was about what it amounted to, he told himself firmly. Only that and nothing more. Probably he had not really been out of a state of shock since the day of the Phoenix, but he had never truly allowed it to hit him, to run its full course and wear itself out. So it had hit him tonight, with the impact of Omne alive in the flesh, in control, with the galaxy about to fall into his hand.

Kirk stood straight now.

He stepped to the microphone beside Omne.

The cheers and the quick consultations were beginning to die down, and as he stepped up, silence fell.

"I do not defend the Federation," Kirk said.

The silence became a hush.

"The Federation needs no defense," he said. "Some of you have complaints against the Federation on the matter of the Prime Directive. Some of the complaints are even legitimate—or at least arguable. I am here to tell you that they can be argued only because the Federation defends the ground on which you argue, and the starways on which you travel to come here. They can be argued only because the Federation, alone in the galaxy, has had the temerity to commit itself to a moral policy of that stature. Right or wrong, honored in the breach or the observance, that is a moral aspiration of the highest order. To equate a freely formed Federation which holds that aspiration, and which even recognizes the right to secede, with the great empires of force is— ludicrous. To declare a plague on all their houses is both injustice to the Federation and—suicide. Declare an impartial neutrality which condemns the just and unjust alike, and you will be swallowed by the empires of force. Your defender will fight crippled, blinded, hands tied. You will deserve your fate, but the Federation will not. Nevertheless, it will not impose its will on you now."

He paused for a moment and looked out over the audience, picking out the Varal, locking eyes for a moment. "Every Federation starship captain—and every command officer—swears an oath to die before violating the spirit of the Prime Directive. That is all I will say on the matter of whether I or my First Officer would break up a freely assembled conference by force. Except that the attempt would represent a new low of stupidity, since it would lead to the very backlash which you are seeing now. My First Officer has never been accused of stupidity. If this were his work, his timing was superlatively bad."

Kirk looked out over the audience coldly. "Commander Spock died tonight."

There was a sudden murmur of surprise.

Kirk put up a hand. "His heart and breathing stopped. Quick medical action revived him. For that I have the Lord Regent to thank, and always will."

Murmurs of astonishment.

Kirk turned to Omne. "However, purposes do cross. The Lord Regent Omne has allowed you to infer that he cannot rule out Federation guilt, in fact, suspects it—and calls for punishment on suspicion, speculation. I suggest that you might well look for who would benefit by such an action. This conference in its sober mind would not be stampeded into secession. In the middle of some night after catastrophe, it might."

He looked at Omne. "Who would benefit from that, my lord?"

For a moment Kirk thought that Omne would smash him to the ground, there on the stage.

But he did not. "The man who could turn the stampede," Omne said with a certain appreciation. But his eyes were cold. "That is a pretty speech, my Captain. Someone should have made it on behalf of the one or two benevolent, reasonably free powers of history, who were always judged guilty only by the standards which they alone set. Nevertheless, Captain Kirk, the Federation has set those standards, and it has violated them, as *you* have—in the judgment of many here. They do not regard you or your First Officer as above suspicion. Nor do I. In what they regard as a good cause, or under personal stress, men will do remarkable things. It is against creeping benevolence that I warned you. It is perhaps more dangerous than naked force, for almost any being will fight undisguised force to be free. It is when they will fight *you*—the most attractive example of moral meddlesomeness—that beings will have learned to be free."

He turned to the audience. "I have made no accusation and my motion does not depend on one. I move the question."

Under the old Robert's rules of order, there was no debate of a call for the question. The delegates were enraged, chiefly against the Federation, and would go to an immediate vote against it. However, under Hegemony rules—

"I call for formal Challenge Debate of Champions," Kirk said, "by the ancient custom of the Dynastic Hegemony."

There was a startled murmur from the audience—of the kind which could not have been heard since David had pulled the same stunt against Goliath.

The Dynastic Debate of Champions was not merely argument. It was war: continued as an extension of policy, but confined to two persons—and binding upon both their sides.

It had not been used for decades, but it was the bedrock reason for requiring an ambassador with full powers.

The two champions might be required to meet in any kind of confrontation, from argument to demonstration, to unarmed combat—or, armed.

Omne looked down at Kirk, startled, even impressed. Then he chuckled. "You do not quit, do you, Ambassador? At least, not for long. I approve. But surely you must concede by now that *I* am alpha here. You cannot challenge me."

"I concede nothing," Kirk said. "I did challenge you." He stood straight and faced Omne. "I did defeat you," he said.

Only Kirk could have seen the low jolt of that reach Omne. "The alpha wins," Kirk said. "That is the definition of alpha. I won."

Omne looked at him grimly. And then the features set in a certain acknowledgment. "Yes. You did."

Kirk's eyes widened fractionally. He had not expected the giant to admit it here. He inclined his head in acceptance.

"The alpha dies hard," Omne said, "and lives to fight another day."

Kirk nodded acknowledgment of his own. "The alpha knows what he is willing to give up before losing."

"On that count," Omne said, "I showed myself willing to give up more than any man."

Kirk nodded. "Yes. But the winner is he who gives up *least*."

He found a slow smile on his face and knew that Omne wanted to break him where he stood.

"I did defeat you," Kirk said. "And—I will again."

"Over my body," Omne said softly.

Kirk nodded. "Quite probably."

"The delegation is polled," the Varal said from the audience. "Challenge is entered and will be binding on the conference. It will begin with Debate of Words in the matter of the Prime Directive. The topic is stated: 'Resolved: The Noninterference directive is a policy of mass murder.' The Ambassador from the Federation will take the affirmative."

Kirk looked down at the Varal, surprised. "That is not the Federation's position, nor mine. The question is undebatable in that form."

"That is the form," the Varal said, "and it is the contention of some here that that *is* either the Federation's position, or your own, or both. However, even if it is not, the custom here is to argue first the opposite position. Begin."

Kirk shook his head. "Let us not debate straw positions. I do not believe that it is even my opponent's position," he said. "Or—*is* it, Lord Regent?"

"No," Omne said, "although there is some truth in it. But it would be my contention that it *is* your position, whether you know it or not. And it is becoming the Federation's position—as witness the fact that your own world-changing has been condoned. You have not been cashiered or court-martialed for violation of your oath. And it is *you*, the son of moral certainty, who are sent with full plenipotentiary powers to answer in this matter. Very well, answer. But defend your true position. It is Death which is your old enemy when you change a world. Make your argument from life. I will state it for you. On every less advanced world which the Federation refuses to change or to help because of the Prime Directive, billions die of diseases for which we already have cures. They suffer from insanity, crime, war, sickness, and ignorance—for which we have cures or help. They suffer and die in silence, and alone—and we deny them the stars. By what right? Are they so fragile that we must make that choice *for* them? And what contempt for them do we display by protecting them from greatness and shielding them from the light?"

There was a low, stunned murmur from the audience. They had expected Omne to be the outraged defender of the Prime Directive.

"You play Devil's Advocate very well, Lord Regent," Kirk said. "That is doubtless why you have been able to champion the Prime Directive with one hand while the other hand changes the fates of empires and arranges wars and rumors of wars. No Federation representative would so arrange things that he became Lord Regent of a member confederation. None would try to change a viable culture by force. None would encourage formation of an alliance to foment war. And none would defend that argument, except in earnest. You are right: Death is my enemy. When I see battle, murder, and sudden death, or worse: slow death in silence and alone—yes, I am tempted. That is the genuine dilemma on which a starship captain stakes his honor and perhaps his soul."

Omne smiled. "I was never merely the Devil's Advocate, Captain. Some have suggested that I am Devil enough. If your soul is for sale . . . " He bowed with a slight shrug.

"Merely on the line," Kirk said. He turned to look at the audience. "That is always the stake. On any new world millions, even billions, may die if it is left to its own devices. Yet if an advanced alien civilization interferes, even to save it, there is the risk that it will never develop along its own path, or even that it may be destroyed. But what we fear most is the destruction of the path not taken. That loss is incalculable—and perhaps fatal, in the long run, to a galaxy. We might become one wall-to-wall empire: homogenized, safe, and— sterile."

The Varal spoke from the audience. "Surely *that* is your opponent's argument?"

Kirk glanced at Omne. "Yes. We share a certain taste for the path not yet taken."

Omne inclined his head. "And a distaste for the homogenized, the safe?"

"At least—for the sterile," Kirk said. "But it is my job to keep both the untaken road and the high starways open. Sometimes it is my job to decide whether a world suffers alone or struggles in full knowledge. Sometimes, if I do *nothing* I condemn millions to early death. If I do *something* I may condemn the seeds of greatness. Except—who is to say that the untaken path would have had as much to offer as paths already taken? Should all beings not have that choice? Who denies it to them? By what right?"

Kirk lifted his head and looked out over the audience. "*We* make that decision, he said, "all of us who have reached the stars—by the right of the fact that it is ours to make. We have the knowledge. At least we are beginning to know how much we do not know. There may come a time when we need to think through the Prime Directive again. The time may even be now. We have already made certain qualifications in the langauge: The 'normal' development of a 'viable' culture. It leaves room for judgment. Judgment must be used. Judgment can be wrong."

Kirk shook his head. "Even when judgment is wrong," he said, "it is better than using no judgment. It is better than making no attempt to follow a moral policy. This I believe: the Prime Directive is the highest moral policy ever attempted by a galactic power. It is also, as an Earth statesman once said of democracy, the worst policy—except for all those others which have been tried from time to time. In practice, both democracy and Prime Directive have become the defense of choice, of the right even to be wrong, as long as you impose your choice on no one by force. That right I do defend with my life, my ship, my honor."

There was some low murmur in the audience. Assent? Appreciation?

"How does your honor stand, Ambassador Kirk," Omne said, "on imposing your own choice on the galaxy—even on the question of immortality?"

Kirk turned to Omne slowly. Was this the form in which Omne was going to expose the real question to the galaxy?

"It is a pretty problem in logic," Omne said. "To withhold immortality: is it murder? Mass murder of millions, billions, trillions in a galaxy? There are those in this room who came close to death tonight, who will die in a week, a month, a year, a decade. One did die tonight, and what would he have given for another life at the head of his Dynasty—or even merely for another life? What would any being in this room not give—especially in that last fatal moment when oblivion comes, for you, or for the one you cannot let go?"

There was a murmur from the delegates, a sense of unease, as if they knew at some level that Omne spoke of more than the topic of debate.

Kirk stepped in. "By your own argument from the Prime Directive," he said, "even immortality could not be introduced. It would be the most radical alteration in a culture, any culture, every culture, which is possible."

Omne nodded. "You notice that?"

Kirk said, "There was once an argument on my world: Should the advanced nations move into less advanced countries with their customs and their medicine, their sanitation and their swamp-clearing, and bring down the death rate—then hear complaints of overpopulation and accusations that they were meddling and homogenizing the world? Creating Tasmanias. Obliterating customs. Saving lives which might die of the problems of civilization, but not until later. One suspects that the question was not often asked of those who were about to die."

"Nor of the Tasmanians?" Omne said.

Kirk shook his head. "The details of that case have been obliterated in the name. They do not support the principle or the poetry for which it stands. The Tasmanians were killed, murdered, not shocked out of existence by mere cultural contact.

"There *was* the cruelty from which we learned the Prime Directive," Kirk continued, "but also, we did not stop the medicine and the swamp-clearing. Millions who would have died lived, mingled, struggled, quarreled—and finally made it to the stars."

"Where you have not stopped the meddling yet," Omne said. "There is Capella, where you object to Klingon interference, but keep a medical mission because the Federation needs their dilithium crystals, and where you yourself saved a life in direct violation of custom—and touched off a civil war—"

"Where I saved a woman and an unborn child from a treacherous coup and restored the legitimate succession," Kirk said.

"The coup was within custom," Omne said. "You were not. True or false?"

"True."

"And when you cut the Federation in for a piece of the action and sent missionaries to gangland on Iotia?"

Kirk shook his head. "I am not here to answer a catechism of questions on my actions or the Federation's. In that particular case, we dropped a stitch some time ago, and I knitted it up again with the best yarn I could think of at the time. Could be I dropped a bigger one, which we will regret in another hundred years. And some starship captain will have to try to knit one, purl two—while keeping his neck out of a noose and his anatomy out of a sling—and his eye on the Prime Directive. Now try to work in that position—"

Kirk grinned a little sourly, then sobered and turned to the delegates. "I will say to you now that those are not even the most difficult of the decisions that any starship captain faces. I have seen one captain destroyed by the promise of an immortality which he could not bring home. I have seen another—Garth of Izar—the man who wrote the book, and *was* the book, for starship captains—finally driven insane, and I have knelt to him, not in the homage which he deserved as that hero, but to save my life and that of my First Officer. I have seen men destroyed, both in honoring the Prime Directive, and in its breach. I have gambled, if you like, my own soul or sanity or peace on a hundred worlds. I have pulled the plug on computer war as a civilized custom, with sanitized casualties, in favor of brute war—or peace. Peace prevailed. I could have lost—and lost two worlds. In any case, I decided. As the Lord Regent would doubtless like to point out, I have even decided against immortality."

Omne raised an eyebrow and there was a questioning murmur from the audience.

Kirk turned to face Omne. "The question is: immortality, at what price? I decided against it on Vaal's planet when the innocent immortals came to murder me. If I introduced the apple to Eden, the serpent was already there—as in most Edens I have seen. In the legends of many worlds, the forbidden fruit is from the tree of knowledge. To eat it is the end of immortality, and the beginning of life. One day, knowledge will become the key to immortality. When it does, that decision, too, will be in the hands of some one man, one person, one being."

Kirk looked out over the audience. "You are always in the hands of that being—the one who will make the decision on life and death and immortality. No directive and no secession will save you. One day one being will face the decision of immortality. Perhaps someone already does. On that day, all that will save the galaxy is that being's commitment to a decency of the caliber aspired to by the Federation. You can undermine that being. You can reject that aspiration. You can secede and reject the system against which the worst real accusation is excessive benevolence. But then do not be surprised if the jackals come out to feed. The Federation will be cut in two—and the jackals of war will snap up your bleeding half, too. You will wonder how you were safe when the skin was whole."

There was some sound of approval, but there was a larger mutter which was ominous. Kirk knew the sound of a house divided, and one still chiefly against him. It could not be settled in words.

He turned to Omne. "You have said that when giants clash, there is room for pockets of diversity. I see room only for blood. But if there must be a clash, let it be between you and me."

Omne bowed fractionally. "My dear David. I do admire your notion of odds."

"If you care to refer to that legend," Kirk said, "Goliath lost."

Omne laughed. "An unpardonable contribution to the history of legend. But that is the risk which the stronger always faces in accepting challenge. If he wins, it is no virtue. If he loses, it is a cosmic joke for three thousand years. Why should I accept challenge from you, beyond debate? And with what weapons? Slingshots at forty paces?"

"Starships," Kirk said. "Our single swords. Why? Because you would enjoy it."

Omne laughed. "High noon on the starways? Captain, we have *played* that game."

Omne's eyes were suddenly dangerous with the memory of the ending of it, and Kirk locked with the black eyes, not letting him forget. He nodded. "An unpardonable contribution to the history of legend."

For a moment he thought Omne would come for him, there on the stage.

Then the giant bowed urbanely. "I will meet you. Choose your ground." The black eyes were cold as nighted space.

"Here, before the conference, after the hunt."

"Hunt?" Omne said.

"Let the duel be over the real essence," Kirk said. "Something struck here tonight which you and I know came from neither of us, nor from my First Officer. Therefore, there is some other force loose, and it is deadly. It was fatally intended, at least for Vulcans, and fatal to the Hegarch. The turn of a dial could have made it fatal to us all. The source was not detected by my ship nor by your defenses. It can strike at will. This minute."

Kirk looked out over the delegates, who sat very quiet; then he looked back at Omne. "I propose that the challenge be a hunt—to find that menace. One or the other or both of us will return to report to the delegates. If only one of us returns, that solves our problem. If both, the delegates will decide."

This time there was a sound of assent from the delegates. They liked that idea. Omne heard it and knew that he had lost the momentum for secession at this time.

He bowed, "I accept the challenge on condition we hunt together. Our two ships, and swords, joined. Nothing less will serve."

Kirk drew a breath and it felt like the first one he had drawn for a long time.

He would sooner join ship and sword with the Devil. But it was what he had angled for from the moment they stepped throught the force field.

"I accept," he said. "I shall, of course, require my First Officer."

For a moment Omne's eyes clashed with his, seeing the progression Kirk had led him through, and knowing why.

"Of course," Omne said, as if it were not a problem.

But they both knew that what Kirk had won was the guarantee that Omne would let the Vulcan leave the impenetrable force field alive.

Kirk did not draw another whole breath until Omne brought out the bone-white Vulcan, barely on his feet, and they left directly from the conference chamber to transport to the *Enterprise*.

Minutes later in Sickbay Omne had given McCoy a crisp medical report on the treatment he had given the Vulcan, and suggestions for a follow-up treatment.

McCoy's eyes narrowed in professional respect. It was all he could do to accept Omne's presence in this room where they had all fought him, and Kirk had killed him.

Once Omne's eyes flickered to the wall where he had stood, dying, staining the wall with his blue-green blood. Then he met Kirk's eyes.

Kirk's eyes didn't waver. He had made his stand here and he had won.

Omne inclined his head to Kirk in acknowledgment.

"A victory for the lamb," he said. "I recommend we get to work, Captain. I have unleashed rather more of a wolf even than I intended."

Kirk turned to Omne. "You do know who unleashed the stun effect on the conference, don't you?"

Omne nodded. "Yes, Captain, *I* did."

McCoy looked up. "I thought you two had joined forces to hunt somebody."

Omne nodded. "Myself."

McCoy turned to Kirk, the question written on his face.

Kirk sighed. "It is the one effect of the Phoenix which we did not anticipate, Bones. We knew he could come in the body of Spock." He looked at Omne. "But what if that other Omne went into business for himself?"

"My God," McCoy breathed.

Omne nodded. "If you pray, Doctor, begin. The Captain is quite right. The wolf is loose. My—Other."

# CHAPTER XIII

KIRK saw the Vulcan's eyes open to reveal the depths of a strain which was still very near death.

"Then that is why you pulled away from me," Spock said to Kirk with effort.

Kirk put a hand on the Vulcan's shoulder. "I did not know—who you were, " he said very quietly.

"Omne has been here," Spock said, "on the ship. In my place. With you." It was not a question.

"Yes," Kirk said firmly. The thought still gnawed at him, but it was his time to be strong for both of them. "Omne claims that his 'wolf' could link with you, take your memories, and give you false memories of having been here with me. Neither of us would know the difference. Then Omne could link again with the 'wolf.' Omne has one memory which only you and I would know—from the link on the night of the Phoenix."

"I did link with my 'wolf' once," Omne said. "I have all of his memories, including those which you believe are yours, Spock. Call it payment for that memory of mine which you wanted to take. It is for you to wonder at what point I came in your body, and when my 'Other' left to pursue his own course. I will not help you. I do not forgive."

Spock's face went still more white. He started to sit up, but Kirk restrained him with a touch. "It's all right, Spock. One day we will sort it all out. But for now you will rest. That is an order." Kirk tried a smile. "It is all right. If he was here, he was constrained to play your part so well that he served me well, too."

"I find that thought singularly unhelpful, Captain," Spock said.

Kirk nodded. "I know."

Spock's eyes narrowed. "Then murder is loose, wearing my face, possessing my memories. You must be prepared to kill a man whom you cannot distinguish from me."

"At least," Kirk said, "we must find him."

Spock shook his head. "Whatever we have known Omne to do, it has not been murder—"

Omne laughed. "You noticed that?"

" but this other Omne, other Spock, *is* prepared to murder," Spock said. "You must hunt him down like a mad wolf."

Kirk set his jaw and looked at Omne. "He is right, you know. This—other Omne—murdered Spock. You, the original Omne, would, perhaps, have made Spock pay a price at some point. But not then nor in that way. Is—the Other—really *not* you in some way? More desperate—?"

Omne chuckled. "How astute, my original. My 'Other' has a time bomb ticking inside him—a self-destruct circuit. It was my guarantee that he would return to merge his memories with mine. It worked, once. But not totally. He was able to conceal from me that he had, as you said, gone into business for himself. Now he must fight me—and on a very short fuse. He must draw me to him, with my key to the destruct circuit, before it kills him."

Omne touched the golden shape-medallion on his chest.

"My 'Other' may not feel that he can fight both me and his second other self at the same time," Omne added. "He is Spock, too—even more than I am. And he has experienced taking Spock's place, as if it were his own. Mr. Spock is in grave danger."

For a moment they stood in silence.

"He is—if he does not rest," Kirk said. "Bones,

watch him like a hawk. Spock, rest." He flipped the intercom, "Security to Sickbay, Kirk out."

Then he turned to the giant.

"Omne, come with me."

The giant nodded slightly and followed Kirk out.

On the bridge of the *Enterprise* the crew stared at Omne as if he had materialized out of some mythical tale. Only Scott could know even the fraction of what Omne was, but they all knew that he had announced Kirk's death at the Black Hole planet, and in turn been pronounced dead by Kirk.

They had followed the broadcast of the conference and seen Kirk kneel to him.

"My ship will keep station," Omne said and touched a control at his belt. On the viewscreen a ship rose like some great copper-gold bird and settled off their left nacelle. "The Phoenix ship," Omne said simply.

Kirk looked at it very carefully. "There isn't another ship like that in the galaxy," he said.

"There is one," Omne said. "I wish to stop at Razar, Captain. It is on our way toward the Romulan Zone."

# CHAPTER XIV

KIRK dragged himself off the bridge, to the transporter room, then stopped by Sickbay, but Spock was sleeping—in a healing trance—and McCoy was practically sunk in a gloomy trance of his own.

"You had to bring him *here?*" he grumbled.

"That's right," Kirk said irritably—then softened it. "The only game in town, Bones. He and I just plowed through all the records of strange things happening since the day of the Phoenix. Omne confirmed his responsibility for a stack of them—and added some we didn't know. That leaves a stack of 'unknowns'—and they're worse than the 'knowns.' Tougher. More ruthless. The dark side of the Phoenix. Some of those things we talked about—and some we never thought of. The tests against greed, power-lust, evil. Duplication. Switches. One mind in another body. New bodies for old."

Kirk felt his shoulders slump. "I'm going to bed, Bones. We raise Razar in the morning."

"Where is—*he?*" McCoy said uneasily.

"Beamed to his ship. He'll check his own monitors. 'Night, Bones." Kirk stood looking at the sleeping Vulcan for a moment.

At least this one was real.

Then he realized that he didn't even know that. McCoy, supposedly, had not left Spock. But now Kirk had to reckon with the thought that even memories could be altered.

And for that matter, even McCoy could be a ringer. If someone could deceive Kirk as Spock, then nothing was safe or certain. Anywhere.

McCoy glommed Kirk and gave him a spray-hypo shot—and Kirk turned irritably and then suddenly felt more cheerful.

"Same old Bones," he grumbled happily, and made it to a Sickbay bed before the shot hit.

Dimly he knew that McCoy sat up over the two of them.

CAPTAIN'S LOG PERSONAL, STARDATE, 9789.2 In orbit of Razar. We have ascertained that Razar is in a state of civil war. There is, apparently, an imposter claiming the Residency. Some reports say that the two claimants are identical. The Resident has no twin. Is this the work of Omne's Other—taking the risk of what true doubles might reveal about the Phoenix process? Omne has exercised some caution. But he believes the Other would risk it—as part of a plot to create dissension. Razar is a pivotal planet along the Romulan Neutral Zone.

We are beaming down. Omne and I and a security team. I am leaving McCoy with Spock, and Scott taking the con.

But I do not know what Omne wants to check on the planet: the political situation—or something else?

They beamed down, but abruptly Kirk knew as the transporter effect took them that it was not the *Enterprise* transporter. It was Omne's own silent version from his ship.

Kirk emerged drawing his phaser, knowing that the security guards were not with them.

He leveled it on Omne.

Omne laughed. "It is not treachery, Captain. Merely irritation with excess baggage. Also, your security guards are quite likely to get killed in the city, and I shall have enough trouble looking after you."

He turned on his heel and strode off, leaving Kirk, after a moment, to follow.

They were not in the city. The coordinates also had been changed. Omne walked up to a cliff. He touched a stud on his control belt and half the cliff moved away.

It opened on the most elaborate underground hangar installation Kirk had ever seen. There was space for a small starship. And it was conspicuously empty.

"My Other has the second Phoenix ship," Omne said very quietly. "The Phoenix process—and the galaxy—are him."

"I suppose—you couldn't lock the ship against *him,*" Kirk said.

Omne frowned oddly. "I locked this memory away from him with a Vulcan technique before I gave him my memories. He must have found some way to break that lock, too."

Kirk found himself smiling for some reason he could not quite name. "Perhaps you should have reckoned with his Spock half more thoroughly. He may have learned things from it which you have not."

Omne looked at Kirk with a certain respect. "One does not assimilate a Spock with ease," he conceded.

"If it were anyone but *you,*" Kirk said, "I would bet on Spock to assimilate *him.*" He frowned thoughtfully. "Could that be *happening* to the Other—especially in the body of Spock?"

Omne shook his head. "No. The ego strength is sufficient. But it could be a source of stress, making him act with increasing desperation. Perhaps one reason why he wished to be rid of Spock first."

"Is it a source of stress for *you?*" Kirk asked.

Omne merely looked at him. "Yes," he said.

"Of desperation?"

Omne laughed. "I am Omne."

Kirk indicated the phaser still hanging loosely in his

hand. "You will have caused consternation on my ship. Why did you bring me here?"

Omne shrugged. "These coordinates are not to be known. But also I made no pact to lie down like a lamb. A joint hunt, yes. But the old wolf does not change."

Omne touched a stud on his belt and they were caught by the silent transporter again.

This time it set them down on the planned coordinates in the Resident's palace.

Without pause Kirk flipped his communicator. "Kirk here. I am in no difficulty. Take no action. Rook to King's pawn one."

"You have changed the codes," Omne said. "Even since my Other was with you."

"The old lamb does not change, either," Kirk said.

"And is that the code for 'Hands off' or for 'Come and get me'?"

Kirk shrugged.

Then they heard flamer fire from within the Residency.

Omne cut in front of Kirk and looked around the corner, then pressed Kirk back against the wall as Omne drew his own weapon.

The drama unfolded in front of them.

Suddenly they saw the two identical men meeting at flamer-point.

They were doubtless not bad men—perhaps even good ones. The Resident of Razar had a decent record.

Yet here were the two Residents locked in mortal combat.

Kirk stepped forward suddenly with drawn phaser. "Drop it, gentlemen. I understand your problem."

They looked up and saw that he had them covered from half-behind a column—and some giant covered his back.

"Impossible, on both counts," Resident One said, not firing, but not ceasing to cover his double.

"Agreed," Resident Two concurred, also not dropping his gun.

"You are both dead men," Kirk said, "and you are both absolutely genuine."

This time they swiveled to look at him in astonishment. "How would *you* know?" One said.

But Two shook his head. "Still impossible. *I* am genuine."

"Did you die?" Kirk said.

Two grimaced. "Yes."

"Then what remains impossible?" Kirk asked. They were silent. "There is one place, and two men. You must share it. Or one or both must leave it. Or one or both of you must kill the other, as you were about to do. That exhausts the alternatives. I cannot help you with the moral dilemma or the shock. I will undertake to see to it that one of you is resettled somewhere with a reasonable new identity."

"As Resident of a planet, Captain?" Two said with harsh irony. "Is the Federation dispensing rulerships these days?"

"Or new wives and children?" One added.

"Or is Star Fleet running in android ringers or surgical doubles?" Two said. "Is this your latest breach of the Prime Directive? I guarantee, *I* am the legitimate Resident. Who or what *he* is I don't know. What is your game, Captain? You—who were reported dead—and the dead man who is with you?"

"It is Black Omne, is it not?" Resident One asked.

Omne inclined his head. "Whatever exists is possible. There is even in the galaxy the spirit which can deal honorably with your dilemma. I have seen it done. I do not believe that spirit exists here, but for his sake I will add to the Captain's generous offer a comfortable fortune for one or both of you—off Razar." He jerked his head toward the sound of flamer fire outside. "There are people out there dying for you. Make up your mind. If honor is important to you, and not merely position or power—both of you abdicate and leave. If both go, you would not leave your planet to civil war or to a possible imposter, but to a legitimate successor. You could make private arrangements out of the public eye for your family—even for both of you to remain close. You might become close friends. It has been done." Omne looked at Kirk and back at them. Flamer fire was coming closer from outside. "Decide—or get on with killing each other," Omne snapped.

For answer Resident Two whirled and fired at Kirk, who narrowly ducked and was pulled back behind the column by Omne.

Lethal flamer fire split around the column and crackled around them, and Omne pinned Kirk to the column. Kirk saw fire shimmer across the giant's shoulders, crisping the black silk, and the skin. One tendril of fire caught Kirk's wrist and he gasped, almost cried out.

Omne's jaw clenched and veins stood out in his forehead. Then it was over and he was alive.

They heard the almost simultaneous whine of two flamers and Omne looked around the column, then allowed Kirk to look.

Resident Two was gone, a flamer disintegrator burn marking his spot. Resident One was dying of a partial hit.

An armed party burst in from the garden and a man in a cloak hurried to kneel by the Resident, his back to Kirk.

"The Federation is doing this," Resident One gasped. "Captain Kirk. The dead giant . . . Dead men walk—and I am one of them."

The Resident slumped into the arms of the man in the cloak. "You are, *now*," the man said.

The man turned slightly and Kirk could see his profile, then most of his face—a strong, responsible face.

Omne pulled Kirk back behind the column. "Do you want to confirm the accusation?" he said. "That is the legitimate successor. Will you stop him?"

"No," Kirk whispered. "Let's get you to the doctor."

Omne touched the belt stud.

His transporter took them silently.

But when they emerged, it was not on the *Enterprise*.
Kirk saw the look of engineered luxury and knew
that they were on Omne's Phoenix ship.

"Dr. McCoy has to take care of your back," Kirk
snapped. He went to look at Omne's shoulders and saw a
charred expanse of skin which would have felled an ox
with shock and pain. It might well have killed a Human. The small sear on Kirk's own wrist was white fire.

He reached for his communicator. "It's much worse
than I thought. That's the second time you have covered
me—"

Omne's hand closed over the communicator and took
it out of Kirk's hand. "Merely the logic of the situation," Omne said, "in both cases." He crossed to a cabi-
net, but Kirk noted that the giant's walk was not quite
steady and his face was white. But Omne smiled. "*I am*
the doctor here." He tossed Kirk a silver spray can of
the healing foam he had once used on Kirk. Then he
tossed the communicator. "Take the foam for your
wrist," he said. "I have adequate supplies and automatic
handling machinery. It is my custom to take care of myself."

Kirk hung the communicator on his belt. "New custom," he said. "I meddle."

In the end he meddled successfully, and Omne allowed him to remove the fragments of shirt and apply
the molecular growth-forcer foam Omne had invented.

Kirk understood that it was perhaps the first time in
decades that Omne had accepted help from anyone.
Kirk was careful to maintain the gossamer thread of
matter-of-factness which would allow Omne to accept.

Finally the healing foam was clearing away the
deeply charred tissue over most of the upper back and
shoulders and covering it with a healing layer.

"There is the Vulcan healing trance," Kirk said finally. "It is within you now. Use it."

The black eyes were thoughtful for a long moment.
Then Omne said, "No."

"Is it because—you would not put yourself into my
hands to wake you?" Kirk said. "I will call Dr.

M'Benga. You would be simply a patient to him—protected by his oath and his honor."

Omne shook his head. "God help you, I would be protected by *yours*, if you let me do it. I will not put you in that position, nor accept that from you."

A very ancient oath gathered on Kirk's lips, and was cut off by a signal from his communicator. He raised an inquiring look at Omne as he reached for it. Omne nodded.

"Kirk here."

"Scott here. Where *are* you, Captain? We lost your readings during a pitched battle at the Residency. We thought you took a direct hit. Now we have a message demanding your return to answer charges of interference with the Prime Directive, staging an imposture, inciting to civil war, and—perhaps—murder. Rook to King's Level One, sir."

"Castle Queenside, Mr. Scott."

"Aye, sir!" Scott said, relieved.

"We are on Omne's ship. What is your position?"

"Tenuous, sir. I had a bit of an argument with the man in charge there—maybe more than a bit. Told him more or less what to do with his charges. He was not pleased. I do na' know if he would fire on a Federation ship. But I do na' like to trust a planet in civil war. Recommend we move to a higher orbit and put up all shields—or move out. But Omne's ship isn't keeping station without Omne on the *Enterprise*."

"Move out, Warp Factor Three, Mr. Scott. I'll take care of it. Kirk out."

A moment later he was at the controls of the Phoenix ship, moving it out under Omne's direction.

Kirk suspected that it could have been done automatically, but Omne wanted the pleasure of watching him discover the sweetness and power of the ship. And Kirk wanted to get his hands on it.

It was the most beautiful bird he had ever flown. There was his own silver bird, but the gallant lady was a stately starship—not a fiery, high-spirited ship which you seemed to lift with your hands and fly with your body.

He took the Phoenix up out of orbit, hot and clean, and practiced its handling.

He found himself looking back at Omne in simple tribute.

Omne looked back at him with another kind of tribute. "What you have seen on Razar, Captain, is the test of the Phoenix against less than the best of a galaxy. Not the worst. Merely less than the best."

Kirk cut the power. The ship's viewscreen signalled and filled with the face of Spock, still—or again—pale as death.

"Captain," Spock said without preamble. "We are receiving a coded burst signal from the Commander. The Commander-in-Chief is closing in on her and James."

Kirk felt the chill settle on the back of his neck. If she was in trouble in the Empire, he could not take the *Enterprise* there . . .

# CHAPTER XV

THE COMMANDER punched a printout of the statgram.

After a long moment's thought she handed it to James. It was very simple:

MY FLEET PROCEEDING TO ACCEPT YOUR SURRENDER TO STAND TRIAL FOR TREASON. YOU WILL SURRENDER YOUR TRIBUTE HOSTAGE AND ATTENDANT KINSMAN.

It was signed by the Commander-in-Chief.

James looked up at the Commander. "Can he require you to put your own neck in the noose?"

"Or fire on my ships," the Commander said. "But it is not merely my neck—or my head—which the Commander-in-Chief is hunting. The demand to surrender personal tribute-hostage is within law and within his discretion, but custom and honor would normally forbid it until after conviction. He is declaring that my guilt is self-evident, and that you are a prize for which he will stake his honor. He knows you are a key to war or peace. I have only one recourse now: to leave you with a kinsman who will protect you even if I lose."

"You know I don't want—"

The Commander felt her eyes go hard. "What you want has become immaterial," she said flatly. "This makes it impossible for me to keep you with me. Even if I stand any chance of beating the charge, I will not surrender you. If I *would*—the moment I handed you over, you would be unmasked, literally and figuratively. As a Human. Perhaps even as a Kirk. The Commander-in-Chief has been with Jim too recently."

James' eyes went hard, too. "I can't let you go alone—to your death. If you do not surrender me, they will certainly take that as evidence of treason. You can't go. It *is* death. Run for the border again. There are other ways to fight."

The Commander stood straight. "Not for me, James. This is my world. And my fight. I have enemies, but I have also support. You would not run from a charge against you by your service or your government. Nor will I." She tore the fax printout in two. "However, I have not seen this just yet. I told Spock I would bring you to a place of safety. We are orbiting Themas. The Proconsul here is my kinsman and influences several worlds. I will confirm him in my cause. He will keep you for me by kinsman's right if a fleet comes after you. Which it will."

"No—" James began.

"Prepare to beam down," she said and turned to leave.

At the door she turned back. "If it will help you to know it—you must stay not only to keep yourself safe but to keep Trevanian for me. As long as he is safe in my kinsman's trust, the Doyen will rally her support to me. If he is lost, she will destroy me, and go to war. Come."

"Di'on—" he said. But he followed her.

# CHAPTER XVI

TREVANIAN moved down the stone-carved corridor, wearing the mask which had been his, and which was now supposed to conceal the face of James. Somewhere ahead of him was that indefinable aura which he associated with the presence of one man out of a galaxy—and that man was dead.

Nevertheless, that man was here.

And that was a personal matter to Trevanian. He had lowered his eyes at too many conferences between the giant and the Doyen. But the giant had always raised the hackles at the back of Trevanian's neck.

And neither the Doyen nor the Commander was here to require him to lower his eyes, or his hackles, now.

Nor was the Commander here to protect James.

Trevanian also sensed that the threat was to James. When the attendant came too early to escort James to meet with the Commander and the Proconsul, Trevanian had left James in the water-fresher, where the Commander had ordered him to accept the water-offering and guest-gift clothing.

The attendant had come long before the time the Commander had named.

It was Trevanian who had answered the door in the mask.

Trevanian permitted himself a smile within the mask.

It was not yet clear to James that all his ingenuity

and daring had not been able to conceal from Trevanian the fact that he was no Romulan.

James was very good in the dual role of Romulan and Prince. But for the Romulan role there was an occasional matter of simple, everyday strength, as if a three-year-old attempted to open an aircar door. Trevanian had been with James too much to miss it. There were the subtle ways in which James contrived to have Trevanian deal with certain everyday objects—to open a pressure-top on a container, to loosen a water-fresher valve which had been turned off too tightly.

But James had perhaps not noticed how thoroughly Trevanian had learned to leave tops and valves closed loosely, to open heavy doors before the question arose, to see that the highest temperature of a fresher did not rise to what he suspected was building for James.

Trevanian had sworn to be his hand. No man had ever needed one more.

James was an alien. Doubtless an enemy alien. Trevanian had heard the Commander accused of treason with the Federation. Possibly James was even a Federation agent. She had taken him to some event in Federation territory which Trevanian had not been permitted to attend, and they had returned looking grave.

What kind of game the Commander played in concealing James from the forces of Empire, Trevanian did not know.

But if she lost, someone would claim Trevanian permanently—ultimately over the Doyen's body.

It was reason enough.

And yet Trevanian wondered whether that was the real reason he went to meet a dead man now. There was something in the simple, natural way James treated him as friend which Trevanian had not known from a man before.

And perhaps the truth was merely that Trevanian had known that James could not stand for a moment against the dead man: Omne.

Trevanian's escort-guard turned a corner. A long-fingered hand reached out and closed on the guard's shoulder. The guard dropped in his tracks.

And Trevanian froze in his.

The aura told him unmistakeably that this was Omne. But the man who turned to face him was certainly not the giant. He was powerful in a tall, lean mold, and his appearance was Romulan—or at least a similar species.

"James, come with me—" The translator rendered the words.

Even as the man said it, his eyes narrowed.

He did not speak and his manner did not change, but Trevanian was suddenly certain that the man had known in the first instant that this was not James.

Therefore the man knew James very well.

Trevanian knew from experience that there was nothing in his appearance in the cloak and mask to betray him at first glance. It must be something almost telepathic, empathic.

How close had this man been to James?

Was there some treason deeper than Trevanian could know?

For this was Omne. Impossible or not.

"Come," the man said, and took Trevanian's arm as if there were no question, and turned him back toward the way he came.

So the man would accept Trevanian as a substitute. Should Trevanian play along? Find out the game?

Or did Omne want them both? James would be charging down this corridor at any moment . . .

Trevanian belted the man under the ribs with an elbow and reached for a throw-hold.

But the man slammed him against a wall and smiled Omne's smile with the unfamiliar features.

"That's quite all right, Trevanian. You will do nicely. Better, in fact. Hostage for the Doyen as well. Now we will just collect James, too."

"You are Omne," Trevanian said flatly.

"Very good," the stranger said approvingly.

Trevanian went at him.

They locked again and suddenly Trevanian knew that this also was a galactic-class fighter.

The training which the Doyen had allowed Trevanian was beyond anything which was expected or permitted by Romulan custom for a Prince.

But this stranger had a depth of experience which Trevanian could not match.

The man did not want Trevanian dead, or he would have died. He was driven back against the wall. He sagged and covered his face.

Between his fingers he saw the man's surprise and the stranger's hold eased slightly. Trevanian brought his knee up, and it was only by a last-instant fighting reflex that the man partly blocked it.

Then the world seemed to explode.

Something hit Trevanian. The report from his nerves, blocked by shock, did not come for an instant, and in that instant he turned and saw that the Proconsul's guard had regained consciousness and fired his projectile gun from the floor—doubtless at the intruder.

But it went low past the intruder's side, and into Trevanian's body.

Omne turned, drawing the sidearm he had not used against Trevanian and fired at the guard. The guard slumped down, stunned or dead.

Omne turned back to Trevanian, his eyes inspecting the wound. Trevanian read the verdict in his eyes.

Then he saw James turning a corner and breaking into a run, seeing the stranger.

"Spock!" James called. Then James saw the wound. "My God, Spock. Trevanian—"

"Help me get him to the ship," Omne ordered.

James came trustingly, astonished, but reaching to support Trevanian from the other side.

Trevanian felt the blackness rising, but he lifted a leaden arm to smash at Omne's weapon. "James, it's —Omne."

The weapon fell and James recoiled back. "Omne?" James said, his eyes narrowing.

"Either way," Omne said, "Trevanian is dying. He has one chance. With me. Help me get him to the ship."

"Omne," James said, and Trevanian saw him torn. It might well be the only chance for Trevanian's life. But if he put himself in Omne's reach, there would be no lifeline for Trevanian or for himself.

James dived for the phaser.

Omne was already freeing a hand from Trevanian to touch a switch at his belt. He laughed and kicked the phaser aside. "All right. You will come after us, James."

A transporter started to take them—and Trevanian felt his consciousness fading.

But he saw James reach his ship's communicator and say, "Beam me up."

# CHAPTER XVII

JAMES stepped off the transporter platform and started to walk past the startled Romulan technician who was not quite sure *who* he was without the proper mask.

But no one could question his right to beam up. *Down* was something else.

"Good evenwatch, Ral," he said casually, and the man accepted the familiar voice.

"Evenwatch," the Romulan technician said, a little confused.

James stepped past him and chopped him on the shoulder. It was like chopping iron, but the nerve center was there and the man dropped.

James pulled the guard's Romulan uniform on over the negligible formal guest-wear of the Prince.

Then he strode through the corridors of the Commander's flagship, hardly drawing a look, answering with the proper salute and passwords.

He reached the landing craft bay, set the automatic controls, punched in the Commander's personal code, and took the fast long-range scout.

Its controls were stiff to his hands, like everything here, but he had practiced what he could, and desperation gave him strength enough for the rest.

The scout's sensors barely picked up the reading of a strange ship from what seemed an incredible distance. He shoved the scout to Warp Factor Ten, where it started to shake apart.

Omne's ship was still pulling away—but leaving a slight, fading sensor trail which James might follow.

He boosted the ship up another notch and tried to keep the trail in range. And somewhere he wrestled with the problem of how he would deal with Omne in the body of Spock.

# CHAPTER XVIII

KIRK listened while Spock translated the Commander's full message. Security cameras in her kinsman's house showed that Trevanian had worn James' mask against an intruder: Spock, or his double. Trevanian had fought the intruder, who wore a Federation Star Fleet uniform. Trevanian was mortally wounded, and James had gone after him. The Commander had gone after both of them, with the Commander-in-Chief in hot pursuit. Her kinsman had been required to surrender the damning security films to the Commander-in-Chief.

And the Doyen's fleet was converging from another direction, having heard the report that the Prince and his kinsman were missing.

Spock looked at Kirk grimly. "Permission to take a fast scoutship, Captain."

"Denied," Kirk said.

And in fact there was no way even by fast scout to reach the scene of the action in time to be of any use. And yet—Kirk would have to try.

Kirk looked at Omne carefully. "A joint expedition. The two of us?"

"We have an engraved invitation," Omne said. "I know where my Other will go. The Anomaly."

"The Anomaly is a death trap," Kirk said. "Even the Romulans haven't claimed it."

"Precisely. It is the one break in the Neutral Zone border, claimed and patrolled by neither side, since too

144

many ships were lost there. Therefore potentially quite valuable. I tested it with probes long ago and found the one way into the star system and planet at its center. The planet is a killer, with a vortex of the Anomaly at its heart. Its gravity exceeds Vulcan's and its geophysical conditions are extremely variable and dangerous, but parts of it are marginally habitable. I have a base there."

"But wouldn't the Other know that you would expect him to go there—and therefore avoid it?"

"That is why it is an engraved invitation. He wants us there, where he hopes to settle with all of us. It is why he would go to take James. Trevanian is a bonus. Or perhaps he always intended to take both. Trevanian in his hands will split the Empire wide open."

"Then shouldn't he get clear—run for the border?" Kirk said.

"No choice about that," Omne said. "Captain, have you not wondered how my Other could have done his work at the reception without detection, and then reached into the Empire so quickly? I know you have wondered how I have managed what you have called the 'Flying Dutchman' effect, to be everywhere at once."

The figures, times, distances suddenly clicked in Kirk's head. "You've done it," he said. "What every expert has said was impossible. A transporter ship . . . "

"Two," Omne said. "The capacity to transport the whole of a Phoenix ship is limited by extreme power requirements. But it is useful. My Other will have used that capacity up going in, as we will. He will be on ordinary warp drive now, and will have to refuel at my base. He will make a virtue of necessity and meet us there. The two of us, Captain."

"Three," Spock said from the screen. "Under no circumstances will you go into the Anomaly or against the Other as a two-man expedition. Clearly the invitation was to all of us."

Kirk felt his own jaw harden. "To you most of all, Mr. Spock. It was you he tried to kill. You are a target.

Perhaps *the* target. And you are not recovered from the last target practice. I won't risk it. I need you to bring the *Enterprise* around the edge of the Neutral Zone and meet us at the Anomaly. I can't leave her under anyone else in these circumstances."

"Captain," Spock said with the sound of barely leashed patience. "Mr. Scott is quite capable of bringing the ship. If I am a target, I am a target here as well. The Other can have counterfeited a dozen assassins to stalk me. I am functional. More than Omne is at the moment. And, to name only one factor, if Omne is killed or injured in the Anomaly, I am the only one who would stand some likelihood of keeping you alive on that planet, or of calculating a path out of the vortex fluids."

"That may be, Mr. Spock, but—"

"*But*," Spock said, "that is only one factor. I name the fact which none of us can forget. Not only the Other is the enemy. The Original is still Omne—and a joint hunt does not change that. The wolf does not lie down with the lamb. Omne has given us no cause to trust him."

Kirk sighed. The last thing he wanted to do was to test that premise. But he heard himself saying, "He has the only transport ship in town, Spock." And to Omne: "I'll go, thank you."

Omne inclined his head. "You're welcome. However, I quite agree with Mr. Spock."

"You *do?*" Kirk said involuntarily.

Omne laughed, then sobered. "My Other wants a confrontation with all of us. If he does not get it, he will come after us separately. Me he must certainly kill, if he can, and there can be no guarantee that he cannot, since he *is* me. That would leave you in an unenviable position. Under hostile conditions, I cannot have my hands tied by the need to slow to your pace. You will require someone of Vulcan strength, at least, merely to stay alive on the planet. I cannot make a lifework out of pulling you out of the fire." His look indicated his charred shoulders. "There is a certain amount of wear and tear." The curve of Omne's mouth was irony, but Kirk could see that the giant was suddenly ready to drop.

Kirk stood up and moved quickly, but Omne warned him off with a hand.

Kirk ignored it and took the giant's arm, steered him to sit down, and for once Omne allowed it.

"All right," Kirk said very quietly. "Spock will come." And still more quietly: "Thank you."

Omne grinned rather sourly. "Never thank the wolf. Benevolence is not my nature. I promise nothing. I merely do not care to have someone else determine the fate of my chosen enemies."

"Merely the logic of the situation?" Kirk said. "I still thank you." He turned back to the screen. "Mr. Spock, brief Mr. Scott to meet us at the Anomaly, and prepare to beam aboard."

"Immediately, Captain," Spock said, and for the first time his face did not look quite so white.

Minutes later they had made the first transport jump. There was a limitation on range and a slight waiting interval before a full charge could be built up again, but the transporter ship was still faster than anything the known galaxy had developed.

Finally Spock turned to Omne. "You will now go and enter the Vulcan healing trance. It is now in my logical interest to attend you, for the assistance you can offer in finding your Other and in keeping those who are valuable to me alive. Therefore no imposition or question of trust is involved. Merely logic. You know me. Go."

To Kirk's surprise, Omne merely looked at Spock and said, "Very well."

He went and stretched out face down on the medical table. "There will not be sufficient time, but you will rouse me before the last jump to the area."

"Proceed," Spock said.

Omne closed his eyes and Kirk saw him will himself down into the healing trance, as easily and deeply as the Vulcan would have.

It wrenched at him again, suddenly and deeply, that Omne *was* the Vulcan.

Kirk sat down rather suddenly himself, and he let the Vulcan fly the Phoenix ship while some of his own weariness and cumulative shocks caught up with him.

# CHAPTER XIX

KIRK found that he had dozed off and Spock must have stretched the auxiliary control chair back to a reclining position for him.

Kirk sat up a little sheepishly.

Spock was the one who should be resting.

But he could see the Vulcan sitting steadily at the controls, scanning and tracking. There never seemed to be an end to the Vulcan's stamina when he was needed.

Kirk saw Omne still stretched out in a trance which was close to coma—almost unbreathing, very close to death. Kirk looked at Omne's back in astonishment.

The healing foam had cleared away the debris from the deeply charred muscles and its molecular growth-forcer had helped the trance draw a thin film of new skin over the breach.

It was somehow shocking to see the translucent newborn skin on the giant.

It was the first time Kirk had felt that there was a breach in the giant's invulnerable strength.

Omne was in their hands now, deep in the trance, and would need one of them to wake him from a sleep which would otherwise be death—even for an immortal.

They were the last two men in the galaxy to whom Omne should have trusted his life.

And Kirk knew very well that they were the only two men to whom he would have.

He stood over Omne for a long moment and then padded forward to Spock.

"We have cut the trail, Captain," Spock said quietly, as if he had followed Kirk's progress, and even his thoughts. "Too late to intercept James. Very shortly ahead of the Commander—who is barely one jump ahead of the Commander-in-Chief. We are on warp drive for the Anomaly. I cannot raise James and have not risked a directional beam to the Commander."

Kirk nodded. "Do you want me to wake Omne?"

Spock turned and stood up to face him. "With the ship's equipment and computer databank I have calculated and programmed the path in, and out, of the Anomaly. The information on Omne's refueling base and what is, perhaps, his ultimate refuge at the top-of-the-world vortex of the Anomaly, are here in a sealed code. I have been able to break the language by eidetic recall of certain memories from my link with Omne before he killed himself. By deep reconstruction of those memories I am able to deduce much of what Omne would know or predict about his other self."

"You are saying that we do not, in fact, need Omne," Kirk said carefully.

"There is his strength," Spock said as carefully, tonelessly. "He is an army. But he is the enemy army. And we must assume that he is a prime target. The Other must force him to yield the key to the self-destruct process."

"And if he never came," Kirk said, "the Other would die." Kirk looked at Spock steadily. "Are you saying that we should not wake Omne?"

Spock met his eyes as steadily. He spoke after a pause. "This Omne may save your life a dozen times over, and yet betray you at the end. The Other—we cannot live with." Spock lifted his head. "Jim, if the decision were to be made, it would be mine, not yours. He is beyond the point where a Human could revive him. He knew that he would be."

Kirk stood straight, not offering argument. "And against all that?" he prompted very quietly.

Spock looked at him bleakly. "He counted on my honor."

Kirk nodded.

"Is there a point," Spock said, "where honor ends?"

His face wore that look of the prehistoric Vulcan who had never known the thousand years' peace.

Kirk understood entirely. It was Spock who had suffered most—down to the uncertainty now of his own memories since the day of the Phoenix, and the knowledge that even Kirk could not know when he had been with the real Spock—and would never know while any Omne lived. Spock's own memories, his life, everything he was or wanted, belonged to Omne now. Nothing was private. Nothing was safe.

Kirk looked at Spock. "If there is a point at which honor ends, the question is whether for you this is it. If it is, I will know why. For myself I will say only that it would be my honor, too. I let you make the commitment, knowing what it would mean for you." Kirk hesitated a moment. "But I thought that *I* could revive him."

Spock took a step toward the medical area and looked down at Omne's back. "How was he wounded?"

"Covering me."

"You do not remind me that he covered you before, or that he saved my life?"

Kirk shook his head. "No. You need no reminder."

Spock stood still for a very long moment.

"No," he said, "I do not." He looked at Kirk. "Unfortunately. And unfortunately Omne knows me too well, and you better. It is the second decision which we may live to regret for a thousand years—if we survive the day."

He reached down and put his hands on Omne's temples. "If honor ends—it is . . . not yet." His eyes began to cloud. "I . . . am . . . sorry, Jim. I gave him . . . my word."

Spock's whole body stiffened in agony, and Kirk recognized the Vulcan's look of being caught in a link, drawn down into it, down into the trance-meld which would become unbreakable.

Kirk seized Spock's shoulders, as he had done to bring him back from too-strong links with Nomad, with the Horta—so many times . . .

But this time he shook Spock and Omne, too—realizing suddenly that there might be a special danger in linking these too-similar minds. If the link became indissoluble—

Perhaps the Vulcan had known of that danger, too.

"Spock!" Nothing. Kirk turned to shake the giant.

"Omne!" Still nothing.

"Omnedon!" Kirk thundered it, and tore the Vulcan's hands away from Omne's head, flung him back, and as the giant's hand suddenly came up, blank-eyed, Kirk slapped him in the standard way of breaking the healing trance.

The giant's hand caught Kirk's wrist and nearly snapped it. Spock slumped bonelessly toward the floor and Kirk managed to topple him into the chair.

Then he looked into Omne's face.

"Who calls Omnedon?" the giant said.

Kirk stared into the unclouded, suddenly young-looking face, and knew that Black Omne was not back from wherever he had gone.

This was the man Omne had been, the man Spock had called "the Alexander of his world, but not by conquest."

"My lord," Kirk said carefully, mindful of his wrist strained to the snapping point and of the starship hurtling on autopilot toward the Anomaly. He chanced the title. Omne's implant translator would render it. "*I* called, my lord. You have been ill. Allow me to bring you—" He tried subtly to disengage the wrist, as if it were a foregone conclusion.

It was not. The giant's hand remained locked. "You touched me," the young face said in simple astonishment. "Without permission. In fact—you struck me."

Kirk inclined his head in assent and stopped trying to

free the wrist. "Indeed, my lord. It is a specific remedy. You have been gravely ill."

"Not in my right mind?" the man said quickly, facing it gravely. "I do not recall . . . However, if true, I thank you. But I do not know you. Call my customary attendants."

It was the casual order of royalty—an embattled royalty to whom a stranger might be enemy, assassin, the other half of that civil war which had killed Omnedon's life mate, his sons, his world. A stranger must be checked out.

Kirk sensed that he had tapped a level which was before Omnedon's final tragedy. Kirk must keep it that way—until he could recall the giant fully to the present.

The Phoenix ship could not contain the black grief and rage which had turned Omnedon into Black Omne.

But now Omnedon's eyes were focusing beyond Kirk, on the ship.

"My lord, you required medical care far beyond the available facilities. You were brought here."

"It is not the Federation starship," Omnedon said alertly, decisively.

"And it is moving. Are you a rival political entity?" He twisted to look over his shoulder and saw Spock. "Romulans?"

Kirk shook his head. "We are of the Federation. He is a Vulcan. We are a second ship, recently arrived at your world. A more advanced ship. You needed much care. Perhaps more than we can offer. However our base—"

"Your story might also offer plausible justification for a kidnapping." Omnedon said. "Tell me the name of your first Federation ship, its Commander and First Officer, and the name of my eldest son."

"My lord, I cannot," Kirk said immediately. "I spoke only to give you time to gain complete possession of your faculties. The truth is that I *am* a Federation starship Captain, and my friend here is my First Officer, but we are not from the time which you remember now. You are remembering only a portion of your memories,

from your early life. We know you from your later life,
and of the time of Omnedon we know little more than
your name and stature, which we honor. You must now
release me, and I must revive my First Officer or re-
store your later memories—or at a minimum, change
course, or we will be destroyed by a hazard which is
ahead."

Omnedon's eyes widened and finally he chuckled. "At
a minimum that is the most ingenious lie I have heard
in some time. Show me the hazard."

He stood up, a trifle unsteady, but with the bearing
of a world-king, and moved forward.

For a long moment Omnedon merely looked at the
splendor of the stars, the speed of their movement, the
ominous roiling haze of the Anomaly just ahead.

Then with that calm which was able to assimilate any
truth—however rare, unwelcome, or bitter—and to decide the fate of a world, Omnedon released Kirk's wrist.
"Go wake your Vulcan," he said quietly. "I see that
these are not my stars."

"I think—they *are*," Kirk said, inclining his head for
a moment in tribute. "I once wished that I could have
known Omnedon, sir. I am glad that for a moment, at
least, I have." He reached and slowed the ship, swinging it slightly off course to buy time.

"My later self does not bear my name?" Omnedon
said.

"No. A shorter form of it."

"Is my later self—your friend?"

Kirk turned to look at Omnedon gravely. "No. He is
my enemy."

Omnedon looked startled. "I find that—remarkable.
It would be my estimate that you are a man of honor,
and that the stars are also *yours*. Are they not *his*?"

Kirk smiled ruefully. "The galaxy is his. He has defeated death."

Omnedon's eyes narrowed sharply. "It is an old
dream."

Kirk nodded, not sure how far he could or should
pursue this. He was not certain that Spock could be

roused. Perhaps Spock would only come back if Omnedon came back to being Omne. But to try to rouse Omne could be fatal. What if Kirk tapped into Omnedon's deadly grief?

Perhaps it would work the other way around. Start with Spock—

Kirk bent and felt the Vulcan's heartbeat. Slow for him, and faint. "Spock!"

The name made Omnedon blink.

Kirk slapped Spock. The Vulcan did not stir.

"The Vulcan is your enemy, too?" Omnedon said.

"No. My closest friend."

Omnedon sighed. "Your remedies are impartial, if somewhat heroic. Why are you here with your closest friend and your enemy who defeated death?"

Kirk looked up at him. "To hunt the man who is both."

"You speak in riddles, Captain."

"Yes."

"How was my later self hurt?"

"Saving my life."

"And the Vulcan?"

"Saving yours."

"And now?"

"Spock will die, I think, unless you come back to your later self. You are mentally linked—your later self and my friend, and you already have my friend's memories, from your process which defeated death. I cannot explain the riddles further now. For your life and his—and mine, and others you would not know now, you must come back. *Now.*"

He stepped to face Omnedon.

"I am going to say your later name now, Omnedon, and mine. You must return into your memory and let the self who is my enemy come back."

Omnedon looked down at Kirk.

"I am reluctant to do so," Omnedon said. "If what you say is true—and I believe you—I suppose that I no longer exist. I am—the child of whom your enemy is the man. And he has arrived at the enmity by some path which I cannot change, since it did happen. But it is impossible to *feel* that. For me, the future is still untaken. We meet across that gulf and I would not have you for an enemy."

"Nor I you," Kirk said. On impulse he extended his hand, the offer of a handshake.

Omnedon took his forearm in a locked-arm shake reminiscent of Rome.

"I will remember Omnedon," Kirk said. "That part of my enemy will be my friend. Now you must be— *OMNE.*"

He put every force of will he had into it. "Omne! Spock! Both of you! I am Jim Kirk. Disengage and come back to me *now*. Omne! My enemy—"

The giant's eyes clouded and his hand bit into Kirk's arm.

Kirk shook the giant's shoulder—and the Vulcan moved as if shaken.

"OMNE!"

Suddenly he could see the giant's face begin to transform itself, going through the terrible grief, the rage, the loss of innocence—a terrible and awesome transformation, compressing decades into a moment.

The giant's eyes blinked and suddenly they opened and Kirk knew somehow that they were the fathomless black eyes of Omne.

Omne looked down at Kirk.

Spock shuddered.

Omne put a hand to his temple and his eyes dissolved into the look of Vulcan concentration.

Spock's head lashed from side to side. Then suddenly his eyes opened and were his own, alive, and sane.

Then Spock slumped in the chair in simple unconsciousness.

Omne swayed, then put Kirk aside, strode forward to the controls, punched up a review of Spock's calculations, made a correction for Kirk's course change, set an undiscovered control for some kind of hazard evasion, and kicked the autopilot to take them into the Anomaly.

The he turned to Kirk in black fury.

"Never attemp to recall Omnedon again," he said in his throat. For a moment he looked as if he would smash something—perhaps that earlier self.

Then he turned and went to examine Spock.

"He will live," Omne said after a moment, and turned back. "No thanks to his honor, or yours. Foolhardy nobility, Captain. You should have let me die."

"Don't tempt me," Kirk snapped and went to Spock. "I owed you his life," he said. "We are even on that count now."

Omne chuckled. "Oh, no, Captain. I do not release you from that obligation. I will call it even with the Vulcan for one of the times I saved yours."

"Go to hell," Kirk said without raising his voice. He found the Vulcan breathing adequately and went to the communicator to try to raise the Commander.

# CHAPTER XX

JAMES sat on the trail of the impossible ship, and he knew that he was being led down the garden path.

The great golden bird ahead of him had mass-energy readings which could not exist, and it could have flown circles around James' fast scout.

But it had kept just enough ahead of him to leave a plain trail and, as it pulled into the Anomaly, had slowed enough that he could easily follow it by sensor and once or twice by sight.

It was leading him on.

All right. So be it.

Omne/Spock wanted him.

And that was nothing to the way James wanted Omne/Spock.

Sensors showed ripping fields of force on all sides and strange gaps into nothingness. It was impossible to tell whether the Anomaly was in space, time—or both. It was a shifting morass, a quicksilver quicksand of unknown force fields where hapless ships could sink through to destruction, or perhaps to some unknown otherwhere or elsewhen.

Federation attempts to chart it had proved essentially fruitless—and costly in lives.

It was perhaps a natural feature in space, but not an eternal one. It was believed to have appeared something over a hundred years ago at about the time when the first Federation ship had disappeared in the sector. And the Anomaly had engulfed a small cluster of star systems which had been charted in the area.

The Federation had thought during the Romulan war that it was a Romulan trap. But the Romulan ships had been observed to avoid it religiously.

Now if Omne had made it his private preserve, he was truly invulnerable.

Federation, Romulans, Klingons—no one could reach him here.

Only Omne—or his equivalent—could get in, or out . . .

James looked at the insane readings on the sensors. Turn back, find the Commander, somehow get her over the line and out of the Empire . . . Live to fight another day . . .

The only trouble with that idea was that James kept seeing Trevanian's face—behind the mask in which the Romulan Prince had gone to meet the fate intended for James. The man was his friend. More than James had known.

And there was really only one answer to that.

There had always been only one answer . . .

James saw the golden ship ahead plunge through a large gap into what looked like nonexistence—and vanish.

He set his teeth and headed the scoutship into the center of nothingness . . .

Then his scoutship started to break up.

James saw the readings and knew the end of the story.

It was like a tunnel of force, inexorably pulling the ship apart.

He tried reversing, but the ship did not even slow.

He had perhaps three or four minutes . . .


The Commander sounded battle-posts.

The Commander-in-Chief's fleet was closing slowly from behind her, not far out of range. But the Doyen's new heavy cruiser, pocket battleships, and fast destroyers were quartering in to get ahead of the Commander's fleet and on the Commander's present course the Doyen would intercept her before the Commander-in-Chief's fleet caught her.

The lone unidentified ship with the improbable power readings had disappeared into the roiling force-clouds of the Null Maelstrom, which the Federation called the Anomaly, and the Klingons called simply: the Mouth.

By any name it was the mouth of hell and Hal Vo Rah.

And Dí'on had just tracked the trail of James' ship straight into its teeth.

The Commander could barely believe what was on her viewscreens. All hell was about to break loose. War.

She turned to S"Tal. "You will cover my departure in the power scout, and evade the two fleets by skirting the Nullstrom for as long as you deem possible with safety. When necessary, surrender to the Commander-in-Chief and inform him that I required you to take this action under bond of personal fealty—while I told you I was obliged to pursue a kidnapper whose success would split the Empire with the Doyen's secession. That should cover you sufficiently to give you some kind of chance to survive. You will then repudiate personal fealty to me on grounds I deceived you in pursuing an independent policy—"

"You know better than that," S'Tal cut in.

"Sub-Commander S'Tal," she said, "that is an order, and I bind you to it under personal fealty. You will not go down with my ships if you—or I—can help it. If there is any chance of my survival, I will need both you and the ships. You will remain in the area for as long as you can stall—on pretext of hunting me as a fugitive. And when you must write me off, you will maintain your innocence to the end. You will save yourself. And you will assume that the kidnapper who went into the Mouth knew what he was doing and expected to survive. You will, therefore, so far as is in your power, pursue the search for my hostage and his kinsman. Should you find either, you will inform Kirk, Spock, or Scott of the *Enterprise* and accept their recommendation as if it were my order—at any cost. You will privately inform the Doyen that I have committed no treason to our private agreement, and that the man she could not control is responsible. If she believes me, she is not to war on the Federation."

"My impression would be that she will not be amenable to an unsupported word in a matter involving the Prince."

The Commander nodded. "Inform her that if you find the kinsman Trevanian, she may have him as an earnest of my good faith. But in that event, I expect her loyalty to the death."

"I cannot answer for the Doyen," S'Tal said. "But there is one source from which you will always have that."

The Commander nodded her head. "I know that, S'Tal."

"Allow me to go," he said.

"No."

She stepped into the scout.

In moments she was free and booting the small ship into the heart of hell.

She found the trail of James' ship.

And another one—converging ahead from a slightly different angle. But this ship had the same strange power readings as the kidnapper's ship. Had the kidnapper doubled back?

Then she received a burst signal, faint and partly garbled " . . . Phoenix One here. The original and friend, hunting with first Fire Dragon. Second dragon is quarry, despite appearance. Follow us in. Gates of hell. Original out."

She looked at the message very carefully. It should confuse the Commander-in-Chief sufficiently. She punched in a reply. "Understood. However same message possible from second dragon. Immaterial since I want him, too. Lead on."

She set her ship to follow the other.

It was a trap. Or it was an impossible alliance, impossibly coming to join her hunt.

Kirk, Spock and—Omne . . .

# CHAPTER XXI

KIRK watched Omne's hands fight the controls of the Phoenix ship. Spock sat in the auxiliary chair, looking like death warmed over, but feeding Omne figures.

It would take the Phoenix ship to survive here, if even it could.

"The entry force-tunnel opens and closes in at irregular intervals," Omne said. "When open it is relatively navigable. This is several degrees tighter than I have known it. It tends to close behind a ship. The traffic is somewhat excessive today."

He was adjusting a vernier control with a steady hand.

Kirk saw the Vulcan's eyes riveted to the tiny shape which was the Romulan scoutship they had just sighted ahead: James.

The little scoutship's right nacelle sheared off and vanished into the force field. The scoutship reeled.

Omne set the vernier adjustment and hit the transporter control. Something whined with the sound of strain. Kirk turned in the navigation seat to look at the transporter reception area.

For a moment the image of James shimmered there. Omne beefed up the power. The image almost solidified. Kirk could see James frozen at the scoutship controls, still trying to wrestle the disintegrating scoutship.

Then the image of James faded out.

Kirk whirled in his seat to see the small shape of

James' scoutship shudder, pinwheel—and come apart in pieces.

Kirk sat for a long moment unable to look at Spock's face.

Finally Omne said, "The power was not equal to the inward flow of force. Possibly if we had reached the field ahead of him—"

He was adjusting the vernier again, and suddenly the secondary viewscreen shifted to a rear view behind their Phoenix ship.

There was another small ship being buffeted where the tunnel was not quite so tight. It was still intact, but beginning to shake apart.

Omne hit the transporter control.

The image of the Commander shimmered, wavered, faded, returned slightly.

Spock reached forward woodenly and fine-tuned a secondary cross-circuit, punched in a cross-connect which Kirk thought might blow them sky-high.

The image shimmered . . .

Suddenly the Commander came through, still in the position of fighting her controls, and crumpled to the platform.

Kirk was there but she was up in a moment, looking into his face.

"Why—did you not—transport *James?*" she grated.

"We tried," Kirk said.

She shook her hair back and took a step away from him, and stood wearing that look which Kirk had seen on Spock's face once or twice.

It was on Spock's face now.

The two matching Vulcanoid faces looked at each other with perfect comprehension.

"The Omne who wears your face is *mine*," the Commander said.

Spock shook his head. "No. He is mine."

"No," Kirk said softly. "Mine."

The Commander turned on him bitterly. He could see the naked grief in her eyes—and the fury.

"*This* is the end product of *your* risk-taking," she said in her throat.

She took a step toward Kirk, and he thought she would explode in violence.

Beyond the ache in his own throat he thought that she was right. It was Kirk's own foolhardiness which had doomed James. How many times had Jim Kirk pulled some fool stunt from which only luck, pigheadedness, or a Vulcan had saved him?

Now James was the natural inheritor of Jim's willful stubbornness, and he had bought the farm which should have been Kirk's.

The Commander saw his pain and something in her eyes relented but did not forgive.

But Kirk felt his eye suddenly caught by Omne's face.

The giant's face was a carved mask of purpose, and the great hands still fought the controls and savaged the accelerator to plunge them faster into the heart of the Anomaly.

Kirk suddenly sank to his knees, gasping for breath. And then he understood . . .

Abruptly Spock was there, lifting him up, the Vulcan eyes dawning with the same comprehension.

"James!" Spock said.

And Kirk gasped and nodded confirmation, then tore away and reeled to grab the back of Omne's seat, bracing himself. "He's alive!" Kirk croaked.

"I know it," Omne said. "No thanks to him." He motioned to the Vulcan but Spock was already moving into the second seat. "Scan for the jettison pod."

"James can't breathe," Kirk whispered.

The Commander was bracing Kirk. He felt blackness closing in on himself, felt the buffeting and tumbling in his own body.

"The resonance?" the Commander asked, her voice barely audible.

"For the first time—since that day," Kirk confirmed, fighting for air. The other identical body reverberated in his own—and it was desperate. James was dying . . .

"Sensors on overload," Spock said. "They will not register the pod."

Abruptly Omne reached back and put Kirk's hand on his shoulder. "Guide me," he ordered.

For a moment Kirk groped, disoriented. James had found him once by using the directional quality of the resonance. But that had been in some other hell—

Then it was as if Kirk did feel some sense of direction and he steered Omne toward it with his hands.

Kirk was slowly blacking out when he heard Spock say, "I have him on sensors."

But the Commander supported Kirk and some thread of consciousness remained. He could feel James' hand still shoving the accelerator of the jettison pod. Forward—

Then there was a tug-of-war of two tractor beams, and Kirk felt James, buffeted and breathless, black out.

Kirk very nearly followed; he was not sure who had won the tug-of-war . . .

After some moments there was a clang. Then something settled into the emergency-handling airlock, and when the pressure equalized the lock opened and the jettison pod's door blew open. A moment later Spock and the Commander were extricating one extremely bedraggled Human, whose Romulan ears were practically drooping.

Kirk felt himself still light-headed from anoxia.

The Commander pounded James on the back, none too gently, making him gasp for air. Jim flinched and gasped, too.

Spock bent over James just as James' eyes opened and saw only the Vulcan's face.

"Then I *did* reach you," James sighed in a whisper. "How is Trevanian?"

Kirk saw the Commander stiffen.

The Vulcan also did not look pleased.

"You were aware," Spock said carefully, "that rescue from your friends was behind you?"

James' face wore the look of knowing that it was useless to deny it. "Yes."

"But you launched the escape pod *forward* to try to reach Trevanian and his kidnapper?" Spock prompted.

James shrugged. "I could not leave Trevanian to die—alone with *you*. When I called to you—I knew you would reach back for me."

Spock nodded. "Of course. Such nobility. You would make quite a splendid hostage. Whom should I ask to come for you?"

James' jaw set. "I know that. But they will come after you in any case."

"Yes," Spock said, very low. "That is true."

Then James tuned in to something odd in the Vulcan face. "Spock?" And as James snapped fully to clear consciousness he struggled up—and saw the Commander.

His eyes widened and finally found Kirk, Omne.

For a moment relief and joy struggled with chagrin in James' face. "Oh, sh—"

He cut it off, laughed, cut that off and realized that he could be in trouble.

He was looking at the Commander's face.

"Um," James said. "Yes. However . . . " He sighed. "Well, there *was* Trevanian . . . " He turned to the Vulcan. "It wasn't as if you—as if *he* wouldn't turn back. No Omne would miss that chance. To take a hostage to fortune against you."

Spock looked at James stonily.

James turned to Kirk. "*You* would understand. I couldn't leave Trevanian to die alone."

Kirk stood up a little shakily and went to stand over James.

"I understand," Kirk said—and it was at that moment that Kirk saw James sense Kirk's blazing fury.

"Jim?" James said, startled.

"But you could leave *us*," Kirk snapped. "You could go charging off out of the frying pan into the bonfire—and from the bonfire into the blast furnace. What did you think you were doing?"

For a moment James looked as if Kirk had hit him. Then the temper they shared flared up. "What would you have been doing? What *are* you doing—with *Omne?*" He saw that that had struck home.

But Kirk was not stopped. "*I* didn't put myself at Omne's mercy, alone," Kirk shot back, and then hesitated. "Well, not if I could help it."

James smiled.

Kirk did not.

"I did not go to the *Other* Omne," Kirk said. "You saw him use Spock's body to come after you and to kidnap a dying man. But you would put Spock or the Commander into the Other's hands. Which of them would not walk in naked and unarmed to go after you if the Other required it?"

"As you would, too," James conceded.

Kirk set his teeth. "Never mind me," he said. "Don't you know that the Other Omne *killed* Spock?"

James' eyes suddenly widened and his face went white. "No," he said. He turned to focus on Spock's face. "The—Phoenix?"

Kirk realized that his anger had made him savage. But he kept seeing Spock's own lifeless face, knowing how easily it could still be lifeless again, forever. He saw the same fear now in James' face. "No," Kirk said. "Omne revived him. Medically."

James shot Omne a look. A trace of color began to come back into James' face. Then he looked at Spock, seeing some of the ravages of the last days written in his face. "My God," James said softly. Then he looked at Kirk with a kind of apology. "I'm sorry." He sat up straight and looked out through the viewscreen. "Then this second Omne is a murderer?"

"Yes," Kirk said.

James looked at Kirk, seeing the long vista and the exact enormity of that. "I could not tell him from Spock—then or now," he said.

And Kirk said: "Neither could I."

The Commander moved to James without a word.

"You will cease," Omne said.

The voice cut through them all.

"Cease," Omne said. "Strap in. We are about to make planetfall. 'Fall' is the operative word."

Kirk saw that their ship was plummeting through swirls of force field toward a planet.

The Commander saw it, too, and knew that there was not time to deal with James. She got him into a chair with a force-belt restraint system.

Moments later, they crashed.

# CHAPTER XXII

KIRK opened his eyes to look into the face of Omne.
Around them was the smoking hulk of the Phoenix
ship.

Omne hauled Kirk to his feet and Kirk could see the
Commander moving, getting James up.

Then Omne took James' arm too, and the Commander turned to find the Vulcan on his feet but falter-
ing. In a moment she was half supporting Spock.

Omne was rushing the open cargo door, his bull
strength virtually carrying Kirk and James and herding
the Commander and Spock ahead of him.

Omne got them all out and away, behind a heavy
projection of rock.

And as Kirk turned to look back Omne pulled his
head down, and the ship blew.

When it was over they were on a barren badlands of
rock, lava flows, gullies, rising to a high escarpment of
forbidding mountains. The flat stretch on which Omne
had skidded the Phoenix ship to a stop seemed to be the
only one for miles.

"What brought the ship down?" James said after a
moment.

Omne looked at him with carved irony.

"*You* did," Omne said.

The others turned to him. Omne shrugged. "How did
you suppose I extracted James from that tug-of-war

with an identical ship—when the other ship had James' own foolhardiness, and the vortex forces, on its side?"

"I *had* wondered," Spock managed rather dryly.

Omne shrugged again. "I blew half the dilithium crystals gunning our ship to get close enough, and most of the other half on power to the tractor beams."

"Why?" the Commander said.

Omne smiled the wolf smile. "My dear, do not accuse me of virtue, if that is your thought. You should know by now that I will not be balked—certainly not by my Other self. Besides, you are all quite useless if one of you is in enemy hands. And as I shall have to make an assault on a base which I myself designed to be impregnable, that could prove inconvenient."

"As inconvenient as losing your ship?" the Commander said.

Omne's jaw set a trifle hard. "We would, in any case, have had to come down with some inconvenience. My base landing method depends on going down into the eye of the vortex, requiring very delicate flying, at best. You have observed that the vortex closes in after the passage of one ship. It is why I chose the base—and why the Other did. He would know that I would have to land elsewhere and come after him by other means. It would amuse him."

"What other means?" Kirk asked, looking up at the mountains.

"Shank's mare, Captain," Omne said. "Afoot. Naked and unarmed. Or nearly so." He surveyed the little party with grim amusement. He himself was half-naked, his shirt missing, his back still showing the half-healed ravages of terrible injury. Spock looked like death. James was barely on his feet. And Kirk didn't feel too well himself.

The Commander was inspecting James critically. She alone seemed to have an endless endurance. James reached for her hand.

She didn't allow it. "I will deal with the matter between us—later," she said.

She turned to Omne. "In this gravity and against

what I would judge to be the planet's extremes of temperature and other local hazards, we have two Human males. They are more vulnerable than you might suppose. And Mr. Spock is not well. I suggest we begin."

Omne was already looking off into the distance to the mountains—rising in one impossible miles-high cliff, looking unbreached and unbreachable.

"Where is your base?" Kirk asked.

Omne turned to him. "The top of the world," he said. "Come."

# CHAPTER XXIII

THE DOYEN opened hailing frequencies.

Presently she had the Romulan Commander-in-Chief on her screen.

She was familiar with the set to his jaw that indicated the immovable object.

She, however, had not been idle, and had a fair claim to being the irrestistible force.

What with emergency shipbuilding and the new alliance she had forged, she had Rovan outgunned—at least here and now.

And none of that would help her with what the Anomaly had swallowed.

"Commander-in-Chief Rovan," she said. "You claimed my Prince from the Commander in violation of custom. Such a claim stakes your honor, and now your life. If he dies, you will not live to regret your haste. Your claim was instrumental in events which have led to his probable death. I am not yet certain what treacheries are involved, nor whose. When I *am*, I will have satisfaction."

"So will *I*," Rovan said. "The Commander is guilty of treason. Your Prince is part of her plan. She will pay. I do stake my honor on that."

Another hailing frequency cut in and the screen split to show S'Tal.

"The Commander is guilty of no treason," he said, "neither to the Empire, nor to you, Doyen. Your Prince and his kinsman are missing through no fault of hers. The kinsman was kidnapped while posing as the Prince to protect him. The Prince went after his kinsman without authorization. The Commander went after both." He turned to address the Commander-in-Chief. "That cannot be treason, since you required the surrender of both prior to her standing trial. Nor could she allow an enemy to invade the Empire to kidnap royal hostages at will."

Rovan shook his head. "Do not dig your grave with your tongue, Sub-Commander S'Tal. Loyalty is admirable, to a point. It cannot save her. I have evidence that the same Federation agents with whom she has twice collaborated before are involved in this—doubtless at her instigation."

He cleared the screen of his image and replaced it with another—a tall, dark man with sleek black hair and pointed ears, in a Federation uniform—an identification shot of one of the relatively few Federation officers known within the Empire. His Vulcan background, among other things, had made him of interest years ago, and he and his ship and his Captain had twice tested their steel on the Empire, to the Empire's cost. The Doyen knew the face: Spock of Vulcan.

Then in live action, slightly blurred by security cameras, she saw the face of Spock and the face which no mask could conceal from her.

The Commander-in-Chief offered no soundtrack with it, and she wondered what he wished to conceal. But she would have the recording and would reconstruct such sound as the lip movements would reveal.

Then she saw the shot fired by the guard, saw Trevanian hit—and then saw the other one coming, James. And on James' lips she could already read the single damning word, and the look of welcome: "Spock!"

She saw Trevanian cry some warning, but could not read it. James went for the phaser.

Then Spock beamed out with Trevanian.

And a moment later James beamed to the Commander's ship.

The Doyen turned to her Fleet Sub-Commander. "Maroc, answer the communication from the new Lord Regent of the Dynastic Hegemony. He should be inaugurated by now, and his plans for secession well-advanced. Inform the Regent that barring an immediate return of my hostage and his kinsman I will declare war on their Federation kidnappers. I will do this with or without the Regent, but in alliance with him, if he chooses."

S'Tal cut in. "Doyen, the Commander has instructed me to inform you that she has committed no treason to you—and in earnest of that, should he be found, I am to return the kinsman Trevanian to you."

The Doyen felt her lip curl. "I had thought the Commander was an honorable woman. Inform her that she is a dead one."

S'Tal's face was bitter. "I believe that she knows that," he said. "She has gone into the Mouth for her honor and your hostage."

S'Tal turned to the Commander-in-Chief. "My Commander has escaped your grasp. I have registered the destruction of two scoutships within the Maelstrom. I assume that one of them is hers. However, I propose to stay here and explore all means of penetrating the Maelstrom, until I have exhausted the possible, and the impossible. If you wish to arrest me, sir, you will have to contend with that."

"If I wish to arrest you," Rovan said, "I will. However, it is also my intention to exhaust the impossible. There are two ships in there which may have survived. They can only come from the Federation, and they have capabilities which we do not understand. They have violated Romulan space. Doyen, you will not, of course, be permitted to secede. But if your wish is war with the Federation, you may find a closer ally."

The Doyen shrugged. "I need none. Nor do I need permission. Exhaust the impossible to return my Prince and kinsman, or you will find a closer enemy. Out."

She switched off.

She punched up the recording of the moment of the shot. Trevanian's wound was mortal.

The Doyen's Sub-Commander Maroc came and stood at her elbow, communicating silent sympathy.

Then Maroc said, "We have a reading on a starship approaching from Federation space. The only starship known to be in the sector is the *Enterprise*."

The Doyen turned to Maroc slowly.

"The *Enterprise* is mine," the Doyen said.

# CHAPTER XXIV

SCOTT sat in the command chair.

"Mr. Scott," Uhura said. "I am picking up sub-space traffic from Romulan ships near the Anomaly. It's faint, but I think I'm getting it on recording."

Scott turned. "Play it back."

She nodded, working. "I'm picking up readings from a number of ships you wouldn't believe, Mr. Scott. A fleet—"

"I'm afraid I would, lass," Scott said without pleasure. Chekov had just given him readings on power sources ahead.

"Fleet?" McCoy grumbled looking over his shoulder. "It's an *armada*."

"Aye. Two or three of them," Scott conceded.

The screen lit with a three-sided transmission. Sub-Commander S'Tal. A strange woman. The Romulan Commander-in-Chief. Scott watched it through. For a moment as the security cameras came on with the impossible image of Spock, Scott had the impulse to cut it off. He knew that he did not know the whole story, but he knew still more that this was some part of the story which had started at Omne's Black Hole planet the day the Captain died.

And Chief-Engineer Scott, in acting command, knew that even the bridge crew was not to know that story.

"It's *Mr. Spock*, sir," Chekov said.

Sulu merely caught a breath, and Uhura made no sound.

But when it was over and the translators had obligingly rendered the Romulan arguments until the Doyen switched off, it was Uhura who spoke.

"Mr. Scott, I'm trained to read lips, you know."

Scott turned to her inquiringly.

"The second Romulan who came to the rescue of the wounded one said: 'Spock!' But the dying Romulan said 'James, it's *Omne!*' " Uhura took a breath. "How can that *be*, Mr. Scott? Mr. Spock was here when we got the Commander's coded message from the Empire. And—Omne was here. And—who is a *James* in the Romulan Empire who would know Spock?"

Scott nodded. "Aye, Lieutenant, I can't answer those questions, either. But I intend to *get* some answers. Meanwhile, we have had our share of experiences with imposters. These could be intended to bring war on the Federation, which it appears they will do, unless we find a way to head it off. Uhura, take the con. No word of this to anyone. Doctor, come with me."

In the elevator Scott turned to McCoy. "Doctor, out with it. I'm not appealin' to y' as a friend. I am orderin' y' as the commander of this ship in a battle situation. The whole thing. Start with: Who is *that* Spock? And in God's name: *Who is James?*"

For a moment McCoy looked stubborn. "As a friend, I'm telling you, you don't want to know." But he put up a hand, warding off Scott's glower. "As the commander you have to know. About that Spock—*I* don't know. But about James . . . "

McCoy looked suddenly very tired. "I suppose he is dead, now, finally. Oh, hell, Scotty. You know it. He is—he was—the Captain."

Scott found himself standing very straight. "Then— the Captain *did* die that day."

"Not quite, Scotty," McCoy said. "But he did come back from hell. In duplicate. Come on, I'll prescribe a drink again. *I* need one."

"That makes two of us," Scott said, taking McCoy's

arm and steering him toward Sickbay. He could feel that McCoy was shaking.

And that made two of them, too.

Scott was seeing the whole story. Two of the Captain. A charred body had been brought back from Omne's planet, and the body was indisputably that of James T. Kirk. But Kirk came back alive. And after Kirk had said that Omne was dead, Omne had appeared that day on the *Enterprise*. Scott had known without words that Omne had died again on the *Enterprise*. Only to return . . .

Omne *had* died. And now he lived.

Sweet mother, what a piece of engineering it must be . . .

Scott parked McCoy at his desk and poured him a drink. But Scott did not take one.

He had never needed one more.

Kirk found himself roped in between Omne and Spock. James was roped between Spock and the Commander. Omne had made the ropes from the snake-arms of a giant Medusa plant.

They had climbed up god-playground slopes where single rocks were the size of temples.

Now they clung to minute projections of rock on a vertical cliff face 500 feet above the god-playground.

Kirk had done the obligatory survival climbing at the Academy. It had not become his favorite pastime. Certainly not in more than one and a half gravities.

The leaden feeling was insidious.

Sooner or later Human muscles would fail to answer at some critical point.

Allegedly Kirk was belaying Omne now with a turn of rope around a rock. Even so, if the giant fell, Kirk doubted that he could hold him. He had visions of them all being ripped off the mountain like a chain of beads. Pop, pop, pop . . .

Omne reached the other side of the dangerous traverse and wedged himself in a chimney, belaying Kirk and all of them.

Kirk set his teeth and climbed, using the semi-imaginary hand and footholds he had seen the giant find.

The vision of popping beads vanished. Omne was like an anchor set in rock.

At the end of the traverse Omne reached out a hand and pulled Kirk in.

It was luxury to rest in the chimney, still clinging to rock over space, but safe there now, for the moment.

After a moment Omne gathered up the slack and belayed Spock, then the others.

Spock was climbing with effort but with that set of Vulcan will which would carry him as long as he was needed. James looked ready to drop.

Curiously Kirk noticed that he was no longer feeling the resonance with James. Perhaps Kirk had involuntarily withdrawn inside his skull again after the crash-landing of the Phoenix.

Or perhaps it was that Kirk and James were no longer identical, in mind or body. They were becoming, in truth, different men—diverging in memory and even in body since the day of the Phoenix. The difference had eroded the resonance almost totally. Kirk suspected that the one last burst, as James was close to death today, had finished the resonance forever.

Kirk helped Spock haul James up into the chimney, and felt for the first time as if he touched a stranger.

Then he looked at the still identical hands locked around each other's wrists, looked down into the eyes which knew too well what was behind his own, and felt again the full impact of the fact of the Phoenix.

James grinned tiredly, as if reading Kirk's thought, then swung up in a last scramble and half-sagged against Kirk. "Remind me not to take this up for our health."

"If you need a reminder," Kirk said, "you're not the man I think we were."

Then they turned to belay the Commander.

Kirk noted with what care James checked the belay and took up the slack himself as the Commander climbed. With more than characteristic caution, James payed the rope back to Spock as a second line of safety.

The Commander was the only one of them who looked as if the climbing were for her health. She moved lithely and found a quarter-inch toehold or fingerhold with ease, and her endurance seemed inexhaustable.

Omne called her up now to where he stood.

"The only rock face out of here is crumbling," Omne told her. "There is no chance that it will take my weight. There is no guarantee that it will take yours."

The Commander surveyed the traverse. "Guarantees are in rather short supply." She started to ease out of the chimney. "Pay out the rope."

James and Spock started to protest and Spock said, "I will do it. My reach exceeds yours."

The Commander looked back with a faint smile. "Your reach also exceeds your grasp at the moment, Mr. Spock. Have you seen your face lately?"

In a moment she was out over space.

Omne braced the line. There was no projection he could belay it around. He wrapped it around his body in a body belay, and braced his legs against the chimney.

Kirk saw the line settle across Omne's back. One jerk and it would cut the tissue-thin new skin.

The Commander climbed with painstaking care, testing footholds and handholds as if they were made of eggshells—which was approximately the case. They crumbled under her.

Kirk found that he was not breathing. Then he began to feel tight bands around his chest and knew that the resonance was not, after all, quite gone.

She fell.

A sheet of cliff face simply crumbled away under her and she dropped like a stone.

The Medusa rope slid through Omne's hands, biting into them, then cut into the new skin of his back.

Omne didn't move, just clamped down on the rope and brought it to a stop as it smoked through his hands.

But she had been twenty feet out and she swung like a pendulum to slam against a rock.

She lay there, very still, and James started to go over the edge to her. Spock flung him back and went over himself.

Kirk set himself to brace Spock.

But the rotten rock crumpled under Spock even before he could climb down. The Vulcan slid down rather slowly finding partial holds, with Kirk slowing him with the rope and James bracing Kirk.

Rocks crashed and fell on the Vulcan with the force of the planet's gravity. Kirk doubted whether he or James would have survived.

Somehow Spock reached the ledge where the Commander lay. They saw him check her pulse.

"Alive," Spock said.

Then Kirk saw Spock check for injuries and finally gather her up into an arm.

Kirk turned to Omne.

The giant's hands were bleeding and there was a deep, raw rope burn across his back. But he remained focused on the scene below.

The Commander opened her eyes. She looked up into the Vulcan's face.

And after a moment: "This wasn't exactly what I had in mind, Mr. Spock."

"Nor I," he said.

In due course the Commander found that she could move. Spock attempted the cliff but almost any projection he tried crumbled under his weight.

Twice he skidded back down to her ledge in a hail of rock. Finally it was the Commander who followed the ledge out to a cliff face which looked perfectly sheer, and somehow proceeded to climb it.

By the time she reached the solid ledge which had been her original objective, any fall would let her swing at the end of forty feet of rope.

She did not fall.

She anchored the rope. The others went across the

easy way—hand over hand—and it was still not recreation.

They went on until they were following a ledge in blindest night, and Kirk did not think that he could move one more foot in front of the other.

Then Omne handed him around a corner into a coruscation of light.

It was the mouth of a cave.

In a moment they were inside and in various states of collapse.

It was an enormous cavern, shadowed with unearthly shapes and lit by a slow light which swirled in a visible pattern through the air like some impossible aurora swirling in a circle of power.

"The Vortex," Omne said. "Certain gases make it visible in the cave."

Then he produced from his belt a small tablet which ignited as he put it down and burned with the warmth and cheer of a campfire.

"An hour's rest," Omne said. "It will pay in the long run."

For once Kirk found no argument. He couldn't move. He stretched out, easing the muscles which complained bitterly about the gravity, and saw James do the same. The Commander saw them settled and then moved off a little way as if to investigate something.

Omne and Spock sat up over the fire, by tacit consent keeping a joint vigil.

Kirk did not intend to sleep, but he caught himself sinking down into exhaustion. Strange, distant nightmares came to him, a haunting feeling of sadness, some sense of an ancient time when this world had lived. He could not quite see the inhabitants, but it was as if he saw their long struggle up out of these caves, and then their long fall, in which a few shattered survivors returned to the caves again, but now bereft of hope.

Kirk struggled to escape the dream.

Once he thought he heard Omne say: "The Vortex forces are inimical to intelligent life, creating disorientation, distortion, and progressively more primitive behavior. Animals which live in the caves are mutant forms, large and belligerent. Our hours here are numbered."

It seemed to Kirk that he heard Spock name a number. But that must have been a dream.

And once he did hear Spock and Omne softly talking: "You understand, of course, that you are the last man in the galaxy who should have created another self?"

Omne chuckled. "I knew that. But the temptation of your perspective was too great, Mr. Spock. I am the last man not to try the last challenge. Including the challenge of setting a trap for myself. However, I suspect that I underestimated both myself and my Other. He is your Other, too. And that, or the destruct, or both, may have made a difference in him which I cannot disown. If so, I will pay for the mistake with my life. It is the going rate."

"Yes," Spock said. "It is. The Phoenix would not work for you here?"

"No. We are on equal footing here, Spock. Do you wish to take up where we left off on the Black Hole planet?"

"Not until I have dealt with your Other—and mine."

"I don't believe I thanked you for your honor, or my life."

"Nor I you."

"I did not do it for you, Spock."

"Nor I for you."

Kirk slipped down into dream, and now the dream was of a game in which the master player played his opponent to an impossible losing position, then reversed the board and played from his opponent's hopeless position—and won, demonstrating the ease of doing it.

Kirk looked up from the dream game board, where he was one of the pieces, to see the face of the master player, and it was Spock's face.

But the eyes were Omne's.

Kirk awakened and the eyes from the dream looked

down into his. But this time the eyes were in Omne's own face.

Omne was shaking him awake. "Time to go," the giant said.

Omne led them off through the tunnels.

The uncanny light of the vortex played tricks on the mind, shaping monsters at the edge of vision, then turning them to stone. A cave-bear was a stalagmite. Then a lizard-cat leaped from around a turn and revealed itself as a crouching rock outcrop. At first it was merely a trick of the light, then a trick of the mind.

Kirk fought to see through the illusion, to find that angle of sight which would turn the hulking danger to harmless rock.

He saw that none of their party were free of the illusions—not even Spock or Omne. How many times had the Vulcan's ability to penetrate illusion saved the day? Omne would have that Vulcan power now, too. But it was not sufficient.

Still, Kirk saw that it was Omne who saw through the false appearance first, even before the Vulcan.

They all followed Omne more and more closely. Spock and the Commander formed a rear-guard. The illusions became more spectacular.

"What makes the effect work?" Kirk asked.

Omne did not look back when he answered. "The Vortex is, among other things, a swirl in those psychic fields which are related to the 'emanations' which the Phoenix records. That was one of my clues in inventing the mind-recorder of the Phoenix process. The Vortex affects the brain, or the mind, directly. I have seen it do this. The illusions the Vortex creates will get worse as we penetrate nearer to the center, and spend more time in the caves. Also, our judgment will get worse. And one or another of the monstrosities we see will be real."

They turned a corner and there was some large animal, gray and shapeless like a rock. A giant sloth, was the image which came to Kirk's mind. More than twenty feet tall, shambling, with great digging-claws which could disembowel. There were fossils of such giant sloths on Earth.

Kirk blinked, trying to see through the illusion to the innocent column of stone—

The monster shambled forward.

It shambled suddenly with awful and unmistakeable speed, swinging the disemboweling claws.

This time Omne moved with the knife from his belt.

It was shocking to see the giant look puny, dwarfed by a gigantism which was not even of the same order of magnitude.

Kirk saw that Omne had no chance. The thing was bigger than a tyrannosaurus, and faster.

Kirk ran forward along the opposite wall, yelling, drawing the sloth's pig-eyed attention. The sloth's great arms swung down toward him and Kirk jumped without looking, without time to look. A claw ripped his shirt and raked across his chest. He found himself landing on a narrow ledge with a shaky hold on a slender stalagmite, and he clung there over space.

But he saw that he had given Omne a chance to strike home with the knife.

It had found a major vein in the animal's body and the creature's life blood was pouring out as the Medusa venom Omne had put on the knife poured in. The animal was dead. But it would be some time before it would know it.

The sloth's arm had caught Omne up and was lifting him toward the ratlike teeth.

Kirk yelled, but it was James now who jumped in from the other side with a banshee whoop.

The sloth looked down dimly and raked out at James with the paw which still held Omne. James jumped on the paw, trying to dislodge its hold on Omne, but succeeded only in being lifted up himself twenty feet toward the mouth.

"Jump!" Omne ordered, but James was at work with the small ceremonial knife which belonged on the Prince's jeweled belt.

Spock and the Commander had closed up the distance, but they were weaponless. With one accord they jumped for nerve centers in the animal's spine.

Then Kirk yelled, drawing the sloth's attention, and it shambled toward the edge of the chasm which separated it from the ledge where he clung.

It reached for him. But the edge of the chasm began to crumble under the sloth. It was feeling its death now, and falling.

"Jump!" Omne snapped again. He flung the Commander off her hold and back from the edge, and tried to reach to fling James off.

At that moment the ledge split and a chunk of it plummeted down, taking James, the animal, and Omne.

Kirk watched it happen as if every instant were recorded separately.

The animal and James slid down a steep breakaway slope in a mass of rubble.

Omne somehow wrenched himself out of the animal's paw and caught a small ledge by one hand. He hung there, clinging by a rock outcrop, half-conscious from a mauling which would have crushed anyone else.

And at the same moment Kirk felt his own ledge, undermined by the rock-fall, breaking away.

Spock reached out toward Kirk, but the crumbled edge opposite him was twenty-odd feet away now. Kirk couldn't have cleared it with a running jump, much less a standing one.

He looked down at a straight drop and felt the ledge shearing off.

Then Omne shouted, "Jump to me!"

Kirk looked down and across at the giant's one-handed hold. "I'd pull you off with me."

Kirk saw crackling fury in the giant's eyes. "I said *jump!*"

Kirk felt the ledge go, and in the last instant he felt himself jump, not with conscious decision, but with instinctive trust.

At the last reach of Kirk's jump, Omne's hand caught his wrist.

Kirk thought that the force of his momentum must

snap Omne's single hold on the rock above. But the giant was steel. He held on. And slowly he began to draw Kirk up.

Then the rock snapped.

It was death—

They were sliding on Omne's back down the near-vertical slope. Kirk suddenly realized that the slope was not quite vertical, and was growing slightly less steep.

At some point Omne was able to dig in his heels and work toward the edge.

Then they hit something and Kirk went out—not certain whether it was unconsciousness or death.

The Commander and Spock looked over the edge until they could see nothing.

Then Spock stood up and began to uncoil the safety ropes they had carried wrapped around them.

It was not a descent they could make. It was near-vertical, over the worst kind of crumbling rubble, with no equipment but inadequate, half-poisonous ropes.

But it was not a descent they could not make. Presently they went over the edge, with the Commander testing the rubble and Spock anchoring.

They said nothing.

She climbed steadily downward.

Once when Spock joined her on a ledge, he steadied her against him.

At the bottom they found the animal. That was all.

Was it conceivable beyond all hope that something besides the inevitable had happened?

Spock looked at her and she knew that they could not reject the hope.

They started a foot-by-foot search in a logical pattern around the body of the animal.

There was no sign of James, Jim, Omne.

Spock was making his way across the pile of tailings from the slide.

"I saw Omne trying to work out of the slide to the right," Spock said. "It did not seem possible. However—"

The Vulcan stopped suddenly and bent to inspect something.

Something in the rigidity of his shoulders suddenly struck the Commander and she scrambled across the rubble to join him.

She looked down into a patch of soft dust and saw the print of a regulation Star Fleet boot—the shape of the toe, the heel, unmistakeable.

Then she looked more closely and knew that the print was longer, narrower than Jim Kirk's.

Spock turned to her. "We are standing in my footprints."

She nodded. "And *you* have not been there."

They both turned to follow the trail, and in the next patch of clear dust they saw the same footprint and beside it another.

She did not have to look twice.

"It is the soft-boot I had made for James," she said.

Spock turned to her. "James is alive, and he is with 'me.'"

She nodded. "At least—we must assume that he thinks so. How long will James believe it?"

Spock's jaw set. "Until the Other wishes to reveal himself."

# CHAPTER XXV

JAMES had awakened to find Spock bending over him. "My God," James managed, astonished to be alive.

His last memory was of falling, somehow entangled with the giant sloth, sliding.

Spock was gathering James up off the body of the sloth, and finally James understood how he had lived. He had made some effort to ride the body down, and he must have clung to it even after he had smashed against something and lost consciousness. The body had broken his fall.

But the others—

"Alive," Spock said finally. "Undamaged. Can you stand?" The Vulcan was setting James on his feet. James swayed experimentally, found his balance.

"Yes."

"Come with me."

James finally asked, "Where, Spock?" He struggled to walk beside the Vulcan along a narrow downslope corridor.

The Vulcan took his arm to support him. "A place of safety. The Commander is safe." He looked down at James. "I wanted to come for you myself. It is the first moment we have had." The Vulcan looked back toward the place of the fall. "That was very nearly your last. James—" The Vulcan slowed almost to a stop. "How is it for you? In all truth, between the two of us? The Commander? The path you walk? In a warrior empire where you cannot fight? In the boots of a Romulan Prince?" Then the Vulcan did stop for a moment and his look was very grave. "I let you go into that. Do you want—to come home?"

James looked up into the Vulcan face. "Part of me always will," he said. "There are nights, hours, moments when I think—it is still all of me."

"What stops the moments?"

"She does."

"And can you bear that?"

"No. But I cannot leave it." James found himself smiling slightly, ruefully. "Sometimes I wish I could bend *her* stiff neck for her when she needs it. Almost always I wish that she could not bend mine. But she has stayed her hand on the one thing I really could not bear. She wanted the deep link, to be able to trace me. But it was as if that capacity in me had been burned raw, torn up at the roots."

The Vulcan nodded and moved on slowly. "It was."

"Did you—try it with Jim?" James asked.

"The tracing link—yes. That was tried. There was still the danger of Omne. But in this case the incapacity was not Jim's. A Vulcan cannot tamper with that capacity lightly. The attempt cost severe psychic shock to Jim."

James looked at Spock thoughtfully. The Vulcan had not said what the attempt had cost *him*. "Perhaps there is some healing we could do together," he said carefully.

"Perhaps. It would be dangerous for you. Do you require healing?"

"I think—*you* do," James said. "What will you do on the day when Jim is taken hostage and you cannot find him? And what will *he* do?"

"And for yourself?" the Vulcan said.

James was silent. Then he said, "The deep link would be the last seal on my allegiance to her—and the last bridge burned behind me. She has burned *her* bridges. The next time she reaches for it, if we both live, I will reach back—whatever the cost."

"That is what I wanted to know," the Vulcan said.

"Do you love her?"

James moved in silence for a long moment.

"Yes," he said simply.

"That, also, I wanted to know," the Vulcan said softly.

They had reached a place where the coruscating light of the cave seemed to whirl down into a tight spiral.

James looked at it with some astonishment. Surely it could not be the center of the Vortex?

And yet he felt curiously light-headed.

No sign of Jim, Omne. And where was the Commander?

James looked up at Spock and for a moment caught an odd flicker of expression, something fathomless in the dark eyes.

James found himself swaying, almost falling. The doubt hit him in the pit of the stomach and poured through him as shock.

"Omne," James said, and the Other's dark eyes flickered with the pleasure of being recognized, now that he had allowed it. "The Other—"

"The Other?" the Vulcan's mouth said. He shook his head. "It is still Omne. Although I am, in some sense, the Other of your Vulcan, too. You may call me the Other for purposes of reference, if you wish. My congratulations. You were able to recognize *my* look in *his* eyes. But only when I permitted it. That, also, I had to know. The Phoenix process is perfect. The galaxy is mine."

James scanned the circular chamber of the cave for a way out. There was only the tunnel they had come by.

The Other shook his head. "This is the only place within the caves from which it is possible to transport to the base. We will go now. Mr. Spock will come for you when I call him."

James broke for the tunnel.

But the Other was on him. The steely Vulcan arms stopped him cold, and there was no mercy in them now. James lashed out and made no impression. He lunged, tried to roll, and was held, his arms pinned from behind, a near-stranglehold stopping him.

There was no appeal and no recourse, neither to strength nor to mercy.

This was the body which had beaten even Omne himself, once, and brought him down to his death—the man who hated death. And the body still included the mind and will which had done that: Spock's—and the mind and will which had pulled the trigger on itself rather than yield to that defeat: Omne's.

But this dark child of the Phoenix was neither of those men: This was the Other, an immortal born under sentence of death, and now prepared to murder. First of all, to murder Spock.

Finally James stopped struggling against the steely armlock which held him with an arm locked around his throat from behind. He straightened slowly and fought for breath to speak. "I'll—go with you. Only—leave the others free. And—don't use *that* body to harm me."

The Other released the arm across James' throat, and turned him slightly until James could see the Vulcan face.

It did not smile, but it was more Omne's face than the Vulcan's. In truth, it was neither. A new being—

"What body would you suggest that I use?" the Other said.

"Just—not that one," James said and was surprised to hear his voice drop low. "Jim faced you and fought you in the body of Omne. I could take that. Spock could. But if he knew that you fought me, wearing his face, his flesh—"

"You have no bargaining position, James," the Other said. "Whatever I wish to do, in whatever form, I can do. I have proved with you that the identity is without flaw, even against perfect knowledge and aroused suspicion. If I wished, I could appear as Spock of Vulcan, even on the *Enterprise*—or on Vulcan. As Vulcan goes, so goes the galaxy. And if my imposture will work even against you, so it will against anyone. The galaxy is in my hand, and so are you. And therefore, shortly the

Vulcan will come to me, for he will be in no position to bargain, either."

James felt the chill close a fist around his heart. "Don't kill Spock," he said. "I *do* have something to bargain with. I will make you the offer I made you as Omne. You wanted a thousand-year hostage. I will stay with you until we settle with the questions of death and immortality. You will own the unownable. Let the others go safely."

The Other looked at him with interest. "Do you bargain even for Omne?"

James considered carefully. "I owe him a debt. Spock's life, mine, the Commander's, even Jim's, I suppose. I would not have you kill Omne, although we will have war with him again if he lives. But I cannot bargain for him. He would not stand tied for it. I would *ask* you to let him live. But I doubt I am hostage for him."

The Other's eyes laughed without disturbing the Vulcan face. "You understand that Omne would not permit you to keep that bargain. He considers that he created you, and owns you."

"He did create me. He does not own me."

"No. *I* did. And I *do*. I do not require your consent." The Other's face went suddenly hard. "I do not have a thousand years. I do not have a thousand minutes. I have one, possibly two, chances to live, and for that I shall require Omne, and Spock. The Commander I have so embroiled in trouble within the Romulan Empire that she could not do much damage even outside the Anomaly. *Her* I might possibly release, for a price."

James straightened and lifted his head. "Let her go."

The Other smiled fractionally with his eyes. "Same offer?"

"Yes," James said, "but know that I will still kill you if you harm Spock or Jim."

"Done," the Other said. "I have told you that that will be little more than an inconvenience."

"The automatic machinery set to reconstruct you?" James said. "Is the Phoenix machinery here set for me again, too?"

The Other nodded. "When we reach the laboratory. Death will be no exit."

"You will return the Commander safe to the *Enterprise*," James said. "With Trevanian and Jim."

The Other laughed silently. "The asking price was the lady. I do not throw in extras—certainly not the catalyst of a perfectly good war, or another thousand-year hostage. It is rather convenient that you and Jim are hostage for each other."

"Not if you kill Spock," James said. "There is no question of bargains or mere enmity then, no honor, no amnesty. Then it is war to the knife."

The Other nodded slowly. "I shall remember that, James. Come."

He turned James toward the center of the chamber where the Vortex forces swirled down into a deep depression, as if they vanished down into a drain. James saw that several steeply slanted shafts decanted into the chamber and almost into the mouth of the drain, as if some inconceivable force had sucked solid rock out of them—as if they were straws, leaving tubes as smooth.

They walked around the end of the nearest shaft and James saw Omne and Jim, entangled as if they had fallen in a heap.

For an instant James thought they were dead. Then he saw their eyes.

The Other took a small object from his belt, pointed it at the shaft and pressed the trigger. An energy beam shot out and dissolved what must have been a stasis field holding the two motionless.

Omne stirred. In a moment Jim moved slightly. Omne got slowly to his feet, bringing Jim up with him and bracing them both against the crackling vortex forces still flowing down the shaft and around them.

"It is—war to the knife—between us—*now*," Omne said slowly, even his voice betraying effort.

So, they had heard.

"I shall remember," the Other said.

Then he motioned with the small energy weapon. "Into the center."

"If you have not calculated the transporter field equalization correctly," Omne said, "we will fall through into the other side of the Vortex. You know that I—or *we*—have never been able to bring anything back alive."

The Other shrugged. "When have you—or we—failed to calculate correctly?"

Omne nodded toward Jim and James. "On the day of the Phoenix."

The Other smiled. "A slight case of unknown variables. But in fact, it was one of 'our' more brilliant solutions. Vastly entertaining. And in direct consequence, I exist, and I have used our entertaining and noble variables to create galactic upheavals on a far wider scale, and much faster than you had planned."

Omne inclined his head. "For me a miscalculation on my part. A serious one. These two noble variables are merely a dangerous but serendipitous combination. Fatal, but fascinating. Also useful. Through them you have certainly moved events swiftly, not to say precipitately. My congratulations. Although you have diverged somewhat from my design. I would have split the Federation first—at that conference at which you so thoughtfully intervened, breaking the momentum I had built up for secession. Then it would have been easy to split the Empire—the Doyen to rally to the Commander against the Commander-in-Chief, say. After which the four sides might or might not have been too busy to have general war for the next several decades. Your solution is spectacular, but lacks subtlety."

"I am not a subtle man," the Other said. "You saw to that. I have no time for a waiting game. I will see results before I die—*if* I die. And I have brought you to me in time to prevent that. It would be interesting to speculate whether the galaxy would have been big enough for both of us, even if you had not murdered me before I was born."

"One cannot murder a fragment of self," Omne said. "If I had set aside a level of consciousness to learn a language while I slept, I would not expect it to rise up to slay me. Your memories would have been preserved in me—and will be, if I am able."

"Generous of you," the Other said with a tone of irony. "Tell that to yourself when your memories are preserved in *me*. By the morality of your own argument, you should have no objection."

Omne bowed slightly. "You are right. I should have understood that you would not be a fragment, nor consider yourself so. Nor could you. Nor can I. It is, in a way, the problem which Jim and James faced—or the two Residents of Razar. Jim and James solved it. It would behoove the two of us who are the creator of the Phoenix to do the same. There is one thing which I am prepared to negotiate before it is Armageddon between us. The galaxy is *not* big enough. But we know of certain alternate universes, certain ways, although with difficulty, to reach them. I will give you a universe. But not this one, nor anyone in it."

"Generous," the Other said bitingly. "What man has been offered a universe—and turned it down? I will make you the same offer."

"Same answer," Omne said.

"You see," the Other said, "it is *this* universe which is ours. Neither of us will give that up."

Omne nodded. "But *I* am not dying."

The Other gestured with the small weapon. "I'm afraid that you *are*. Rather suddenly. I shall require the medallion and its code."

Omne shook his head. "You know that we have a deadlock. If I give the code to you, you will certainly kill me. If I do not, you will at least keep me alive until your time runs out—and, at worst, die with me."

"There are alternatives," the Other said. "However, I am prepared to break the deadlock. And I urge you to believe that I will kill you where you stand, if I must. However, I might merely start by shooting someone in the leg. Not necessarily *you*. Step into the center."

Omne hesitated for a moment. Then he moved, steering Jim toward the center. Jim started to balk. "Once he *has* us—"

"He has us now," Omne said. "Be still."

Jim looked at him oddly but shut up.

The Other steered James after them by an arm.

They all moved down into the Maelstrom which whirled in the center depression.

James felt as if electric currents crawled over his body—and through it, scrambling neural signals, making his body refuse to obey. He could barely stand or move, and the Other's hold on his arm became a support.

The little weapon had never ceased to cover Omne, whose strength was bulling Jim through the crackling hold in the same way.

Even Omne and the Other were very nearly stopped by the field.

James focused every ounce of discipline he had ever learned—from Spock, from the Commander, from whatever inner resources he had ever had.

He lunged once, swinging his weight to throw the Other off balance, throw the weapon off aim, give Omne his chance.

Omne moved in the same instant, as if by telepathy. He launched himself at the Other and Jim managed to lurch toward the center of the fray.

But the Other brought the weapon back and fired at Omne's legs.

There was no visible result, but the giant's legs ceased to carry his weight, and white shock registered in his face.

Still Omne crashed into the Other and locked with him, trying to use sheer mass and momentum against the lighter Vulcan body.

James swung his legs against the back of the Other's knees and tried to bring him down and Jim crashed into the Other from somewhere.

The Other went down.

But he was still two of the most formidable fighters in the galaxy. And he was not half-paralyzed by the weapon, like Omne, nor almost wholly incapacitated by the Vortex field like the two Humans.

The Other shoved Jim and James away as if they did not count and focused on Omne. It was still close as Omne held the weapon off and tried for a nerve hold. But Omne's paralyzed legs dragged him down. The Other got in a chop, then had the weapon at Omne's throat. "You first," the Other snarled, "then those two."

Omne strained for a moment, then stopped. "All right."

The Other kept an arm locked around Omne and moved him through the last swirls of the field to a clear center in the eye of the Vortex.

The Other's casual shove had already carried Jim and James half into the eye. The Other gestured to them and they slowly pulled themselves into the center and finally to their feet, bracing each other, and came to him.

James could feel Jim debating it with himself, even now. One more rush . . . But that would give the Other little option but to shoot Omne, or them, or both. And they needed Omne.

James knew without looking at Jim that they had reached the same decision.

Omne was still their only chance to get Spock out of this. The Commander the Other might spare. But not the Vulcan. With one mind James and Jim kept their hands down and came to the Other.

The Other touched what James suspected was both a dead-man switch and a general transporter control on his belt, bracing Omne on his paralyzed legs for a moment to do it.

James took a last look back.

There was no sign of the Commander or Spock.

Then the transporter took the four of them out of the eye of the Vortex.

When it released them, James saw that they were in a base which could only have been designed by Omne.

The Other heaved the original Omne off the transporter and parked him against a bench, almost standing,

propped on the rigid legs. And then James saw the
Other switch on a small stasis field and lock Omne's left
hand into it. The giant might as well have been imbed-
ded in stone. The Other stripped off Omne's survival
belt, Jim's uniform belt, and inspected James for weapons or other dangerous items.

James looked at the sweeping expanse of the main
control center. Every line spoke of the precision of
thought, the design for perfect function, the integration
of both luxury of material and economy of effort which
were the hallmark of Omne's design. James could well
believe that the base was impregnable. Here was the last
Omne stronghold, which would last for a thousand
years.

It was here that James would keep his bargain, pay,
as Jim had once paid, for Spock's life, the Commond-
er's, James' own.

This time James might not even save Spock, perhaps
not even the Commander. But every moment he could
buy while they stayed alive and free was a moment in
which some tide might turn.

James turned toward the Other.

It was still impossible to look at the Vulcan body and
not see Spock. That would be the worst of it.

James saw Jim also turn to the Other with the same
idea forming on Kirk's face.

"No, Jim," James said. "This one is mine."

James moved toward the Other, rising a little on the
balls of his feet.

The Other laughed. "No. But the converse is certainly true. You are created life. Engineered by my
hand. Mine."

"By that argument," James said, "you are the possession of Omne—the original Omne." James nodded toward where Omne stood propped on numb legs.

The Other sobered. "*He* is not the original—no more
than I am. The original Omne died, thanks to your Mr.
Spock. The first immortal who rose again was no longer
merely Omne, but an alloy of Omne and Spock. That

was the real second Omne—and he was killed by the first Kirk." The Other looked at Jim. "If you have forgotten that, Kirk, I have not. Nor has the one you call Omne. But he is *not* Omne. He is merely Omne the third. In truth I am Omne the fourth—still Omne as much as he, but with perhaps a slightly stronger dash of the Vulcan since I have his body, and I have lived his life."

"When?" Jim said. There was a flat tone to his voice which did not indicate surprise—but a question which had been lived with, too long.

James looked at Jim in surprise.

"I will not answer," the Other said. "I was on your ship. You never knew when, nor did Spock."

"That first night—the night of the Phoenix?" Jim said tightly.

The Other smiled. "Or of the Fire Dragon? In either case, the memory is mine."

Jim put a hand on James' arm. "Move over, James. I have a prior appointment."

They both moved toward the Other, but he merely looked at them with a mild, almost Vulcan amusement. He reached to a panel and flipped a switch. A bank of viewscreens behind him filled with images from the caves. Monsters, cliffs, tunnels, glowing swirls which were the Vortex forces.

And on one screen: Spock and the Commander.

They had found the tube where a skid-path through the rubble must have marked Jim and Omne's fall. A few feet below that the camera showed a vertical drop-off from the path they had been sliding on. Omne must have known of the smooth slide-tubes and managed to throw himself and Jim into one.

But the Commander and James could not know where or how the slide-tube would come out. Now they were dividing the fibrous rope into thinner strands to make a rope long enough to attempt the shaft. It was a smooth, glassy rock, like basalt, and much too steep to climb.

"Spock," the Other said in the Vulcan's own voice. Spock and the Commander whirled to look in the direction of the camera.

"That's right," the Other said encouragingly. "Did you find the footprints I left for you?"

"Yes," Spock said. "Is he alive?"

"James? Oh yes."

"Undamaged?" Spock said tightly.

"For the moment."

The Vulcan's face went gray. "Once I stayed my hand and did not kill you for what you had done to James and to Jim. No more."

"You did not stay *my* hand, Mr. Spock, and you forced me to call your raise by cashing in all my chips. You wanted to deprive me of a memory. Now I have taken all of your memories, and you have some I have given you which are not, in truth, real. *I* lived them, not you. I planted them in your mind."

"Where is James?" Spock said obdurately, refusing to be drawn. But James could see the strain in the Vulcan's eyes.

"Here," the Other said. "Mr. Spock, let us not haggle. The price is the usual. Your soul, your honor. This time it may include your life. I promise you nothing. Not even the merchandise. You will nevertheless come at once. Otherwise I do promise damaged goods."

"Spock, no!" James snapped in the tone of an order. The Other grabbed James and locked a hand over his mouth. Jim started to come at him and the Other tripped a switch. Jim's feet were suddenly bolted to the floor by a stasis field.

The Commander stepped forward. "I will come. He is mine," she said.

"Not satisfactory," the Other said. "You are welcome, of course, my dear. But you are not my price. Tempting. But that is the personal. Politically I do not need you. And at the moment I have a much more urgent need which is ticking away toward finality. For that need I require Spock. Mr. Spock, you will simply slip over the edge and slide down the shaft."

"It would kill him," the Commander said.

"Perhaps that is what I require," the Other said implacably.

"Spock is no threat to you here."

"No."

"Then let him go. Him, James, Trevanian. If you do not want me to stay, I will go—which should stir up any amount of trouble for you. That is a value."

"An amusement," the Other said. "The value I already have. Without Trevanian there will be war. You may go, my dear. It is a bargain I made, for an offer I could not refuse."

"James!" the Commander snapped.

"Proceed, Mr. Spock," the Other said.

She caught Spock's shoulders. "Don't go. The Other has tried once to kill you. He will not let you live wearing your body, which he has taken. He will kill you. And then he will do whatever he is going to do, anyway."

"If I do not go," Spock said, "he will do that wearing my body and my face. James will take a beating, at my hands."

"He has taken beatings before, Spock. For you. Even more or less at your hands—imposters, strange states . . ."

"Not in this way," Spock said. He turned toward the shaft.

The Commander seized Spock's arms and her hands bit into them. "One step and you are doomed. Jim may still be alive. You have not felt his death emanations. Will you leave him alone?"

"I doubt if he is alone *now*," Spock said. "If Jim lives, the Other would have him, too. But it is enough that the Other has James." Spock unlocked her hands from his arms and moved toward the edge.

For a moment James could see the poise in her body of considering stopping Spock by main force.

But she was caught by the same argument. It was unanswerable.

Then Jim spoke: "Mr. Spock, don't come. That is an

order. Remain free for a thousand minutes. The Other told James that is longer than he has before the destruct deadline."

Spock looked around, stopped for a moment. "Jim!" Then he shook his head. "Too long."

Spock reached down and levered himself over the edge. He slid out of sight.

Without hesitation the Commander anchored as much of the unravelled rope as they had finished and went over the edge herself, rappelling down on the rope, bouncing on her feet against the smooth wall.

It looked, and was, more cautious than the Vulcan's rifle-shot descent, as she would doubtless point out.

What she would not point out was that it was almost certain that the rope would end before the shaft did.

And then she would be in much the same position as the Vulcan, and sliding on the same anatomy.

But whether it was toward immediate death or merely capture, James did not know.

# CHAPTER XXVI

SPOCK plummeted down the tube.

He was all but unconscious from the batterings and from the Vortex forces when the shaft decanted him into a whirling central vortex of force. It buoyed him up almost like liquid, whirled him to a center and deposited him in an eye of safety.

He lay there unable to move for a long moment.

Then he pulled himself up by main force and was on his feet when the Commander shot out of the tube.

He walked a little to the whirling wall of force and caught her out of it and into the center.

In a moment she lifted her head and looked at him.

And she looked as much like an aimed bullet as he felt. Both had a single target.

If they died in the next moment, that also was an exchange which was permanent.

Spock held her as the transporter took them.

The Commander emerged and turned away to see Jim, James, Omne, the Other.

She and Spock moved directly and of one mind off the transporter and toward the Other.

She did not much care what plans he had to stop them. They were in his hands, in any case, and she only wanted to get hers on him.

They got within a few feet. Then the Other displayed a small, nasty-looking weapon.

"Paralysis," Omne himself said from behind them. "But frequently fatal to Vulcanoids."

She stopped and after another step so did Spock.

"Excellent," the Other said. "Excessively noble, but impressive. Commander, you may make yourself useful by putting these on Mr. Spock."

She inspected the empty handful of air which he tossed her and which she caught. She felt the shape. Stasis cuffs.

"Hands behind your back, Spock," the Other said.

She hesitated. Once Spock was incapacitated, the Other could do what he liked with Spock or anyone else.

But the weapon was decisive. The Other had a Vulcan hostage against her—and the two Humans whom he could smash even without the weapon.

Spock put his hands back and she locked the cuffs on him.

"What do you want with Spock?" she said.

"Perhaps I want to punish him for making me die."

"Your choice," she shrugged. "He did not kill you."

"No," the Other said—and looked pointedly at Kirk, who had.

"Very well," the Commander said to the killer. "You have us. To what purpose? You are not Omne."

"The enduring purpose is perhaps the same," the Other said. "But the fragile ideal is yet more fragile in the face of my immediate problem. I do not propose to die. Omne does not propose to have me alive in the universe which he regards as his—for the excellent reason that I regard it as mine. That is stalemate. Therefore there must be a way to sweep the board clean. You would call it thinking outside the phalanx. The Captain speaks of changing the name of the game." He turned to Omne. "All right. New game. I will name the playing pieces and the rules. You have said, or *I* have, that the man without love gives no hostages to fortune."

Omne shrugged. "We have said it."

"We have altered the nature of hostages," the Other said. "There is a level of enmity which is perhaps more binding than love. The two of us are known now only to our enemies, and to each other. We have found no steel worthy of our sword but what is in this room. Spock has beaten us. Jim Kirk has killed us. James attacked me just now to give you your chance—after he had offered a price for the Commander's life. For those things there is a price, but each of us wishes to exact it himself. For that purpose you, who hated death and now could be immortal, have risked your life more than once. And even I, who rage against the dying even more, have taken certain risks to draw you all here and keep you alive. Now that you are here, however, I am under no such constraint. You have a galactic purpose. I have. In many respects they are the same. In others, not. And in truth there is little enjoyment for either of us in carrying them out against a galaxy of lambs who do not know the wolf, let alone have the capacity to stand against him."

Omne inclined his head. " 'Know thine enemy,' " he said. "It is a proverb which is particularly relevant to our case. There is another: 'Know thyself.' Very well, I know you and your point very well. We have a unique collection of enemies and in a number of ways each of them is a key to aspects of our galactic purpose. We have lost to them, twice. However, I do not see how that helps your problem. Or mine, for that matter."

"You do see," the Other said. "You merely do not wish to face the logic of the situation."

"You wish to use us to force Omne," the Commander said with sudden certainty.

The Other turned back to her. "Yes. Of course."

"What do you require?" she asked.

"Let us begin with what *you* require," the Other said. He crossed to a control panel and pressed a switch. A sliding panel opened to reveal Trevanian.

He was stretched out under a sheet, his eyes closed, the startling profile pale and pure.

It looked like death. Then the Commander saw the slight rise of his chest.

At his waist was a life-support system. Tubes were hooked to a cuff on his wrist.

The other touched a control and a spray hypo attached to the cuff sprayed, then disengaged with the tubes. Trevanian's breathing altered and his eyelids flickered toward consciousness.

"He can survive for limited periods on the portable belt unit," the Other explained. "But the wound is lethal. The internal damage affected almost every vital organ. It is beyond surgery. I have done what can be done."

"But the Phoenix—" James began.

The Other turned to him. "There is that possibility. It would require his death."

James caught his breath. "We still forget—all the implications."

"Yes," the Other said. "But I have required myself to remember. There is more. I could preserve Trevanian's consciousness, but at the cost of putting him in another body."

"Why?" James managed.

"The body cannot live," Omne said. "There is no value in duplicating it. I have no transporter pattern of his own undamaged body."

The Commander moved past the Other and James followed her to look down at Trevanian.

It was not possible to think of the beautiful face as doomed, the body which was sculpture in life, committed to death. Of what use was immortality if it could not preserve this?

Then the Commander pulled herself together. Of course immortality was of use. *Life* was of use, and the consciousness behind the face. He could have another body.

And yet she found that she could not breathe properly. She was thinking of the Doyen . . . If it had been James . . .

# CHAPTER XXVII

TREVANIAN opened his eyes and took in their presence, and he must have seen the expression on their faces.

But the sum of his feelings added up to his peculiarly radiant smile. "My lady. You came. You should not have. James." His eyes blazed. "You were not to come."

"*You* were not to go charging out to take on my personal devil," James shot back. "You know I would rather have gone myself."

"I know," Trevanian said. He shook his head. "But he was my devil, too. Do not take it so much to heart. Either of you. For myself I would do it again." He looked up at the Commander. "My lady, I am sorry. It was unforgivable to risk your word to the Doyen, and to lead James—and you—into a trap."

She nodded. "Yes. It was."

"The Doyen?" he said.

The Commander shook her head firmly. "We will deal with that when we have dealt with this. The Doyen will be all right in any case. Whether the galaxy will is another matter." She reached down and took Trevanian's hand. "At the moment, you are the problem. How much has he"—she indicated the Vulcan figure of the Other—"told you?"

Trevanian shook his head. "That we were both dead

men, but it was not necessarily an irreversible condition."

She held Trevanian's hand tightly and turned to the Other. "Explain."

He nodded. "There is the option we discussed. Another body."

"There is more," she said. "Or you would not be talking."

"Astute, my dear. Yes. There is the refinement of the Phoenix on which my—predecessor—and I were working before the first trial. But the improved model required a power source which we could generate only with the Vortex. It is one reason I came here. I have made some additional improvements."

He flipped another switch, and a lighted cubicle opened to show half of a plant leaf, cleanly cut down the center. The Other adjusted a dial and a ghostly pattern of the missing half of the leaf appeared.

The Commander shrugged.

James also did not look too impressed. "It's the old Kirlian effect—persistence of the other part of the living pattern. It's been known since the twentieth century."

"Yes," the Other said. He pressed an energize effect. There was a slight shimmer.

The Commander watched. In a moment the Other reached into the cubicle and turned to put the result in her hand.

It was a whole and perfect leaf, a true completion and reconstruction of the leaf when it had been whole.

James took it out of her hand. "My God," he murmured. And after a moment: "If Dr. McCoy were here . . . " He looked at the Other and for the moment the look was tribute.

"Yes," the Other said. "It is not merely the defeat of death. It is the end of medicine, and its final triumph. Reconstruction. Regeneration. The completion of the continuity of the pattern. The special scanner reads the intact part and the remaining indication of the pattern, down to the original DNA and RNA codes. The integrating computer fills in the pattern for what is missing or damaged—from a minor wound to a blasted heart."

James turned to look at Trevanian, and back to the Other.

"Then do it," James said.

"At what price?"

The Commander thought that James would go for the Other. She put out a hand in restraint. But James mastered the rage. "What price do you want?"

"The only one which will do me any good," the Other said. "It will save my life, and, incidentally, Trevanian's. Omne holds it: the medallion, which he must code for use. It will permit reconstruction of the original pattern of my body, without the fatal self-destruct flaw, which Omne keyed into it. The medallion and the regeneration machinery will allow the reconstruction of Trevanian's body. It permits the life-to-life transmission of our mind-recordings into the reconstructed bodies— without death."

"Otherwise—Trevanian must die?" the Commander said.

"Yes. It is not an experience I can recommend. For myself, even death is not an option. I cannot use the Phoenix without the medallion."

"For you there is no hope without the medallion?" she asked.

"There *is* one," the Other said, "but it is not a hope for you or for anyone else here."

He turned to Omne. "I would prefer not to name that hope," he said. "I will ask you to set the medallion now. I can offer you no amnesty or victory. I will make you my best offer. We know that the Anomaly is, in part, a gateway through the Vortex to an alternate universe planet. The planet is inhabitable for class-M life. The animals we sent through wearing dead-man switches found air, water, food—before they died and the switches returned them through the transporter tracer."

Omne nodded rather grimly and shifted almost imperceptibly as if testing the paralyzed legs. "Also, certain things found *them*. They did come back on *dead*-man switches."

The Other shrugged. "Tough universe. I never promised you an Eden. And Eden would bore you. That happens to be the only universe I have to spare at the moment. I could merely kill you. It would be my safest course."

"With the medallion you could do more," Omne said. "You could attempt to merge minds with me and take over. You would have my recent memories to gain, and the body which was once yours. It is not a negligible asset."

"I *am* tempted," the Other said. "It is my body. The memories would be of interest, and there would be a certain justice in it, since you have claimed the right to repossess mine. However, I have not time at the moment to fight you for control. There is a fast-moving galactic situation. This body is adequate to my purposes for the present. For certain things, it is even useful and interesting. Spock of Vulcan and of the *Enterprise* can go certain places, do certain things, influence certain decisions which Omne's body cannot do. Besides, I have begun to become accustomed to it, and a part of me is quite at home. The Omne body is recorded and I could reclaim it at some time through the Phoenix. But the life-to-life transfer process will serve me much better now. The continuity process will reconstruct this body in its original form, without the destruct. That will suit me."

"Even presuming that I would believe you," Omne said, "why would I agree?"

The Other hefted the little weapon. "Consider the alternative."

"Death?" Omne said. "Now that the base dead-man switch tracer has picked me up, the automatic Phoenix machinery would operate. Death would be no more than a serious inconvenience."

"There is the override," the Other said. "I could

leave you locked in the machine. It is a considerably smaller prison than a universe."

"Why would you not do that in any case after I gave you the medallion key?" Omne said.

His Other smiled. "Are you saying that we are not a man of honor? I will not strain your trust," the Other said, "nor trust you unduly. You will have to set the medallion key to work properly for Trevanian. I will use the same setting. And at the same time I will set the transporter circuit to send you off. You will be able to see that the transporter is set for the Vortex, not for death."

Omne smiled. "I have no objection to the existence of Trevanian. He is decorative and enterprising and appears to have possibilities as an enemy. But why would I go to such lengths for him?"

"Your actual plan for the Empire depends on the Doyen. You would prefer to use her as a political force, rather than a berserk machine of vengeance for a lost Trevanian. However, that is not why you will do it. Do you not know why?"

"Name it," Omne said with sudden ferocity. "I will not name it for you."

The Other turned away from Omne and went to face Spock, who was standing beside Jim. "Mr. Spock, have you wondered why I brought you here?"

"I had wondered why you kept me alive," Spock said, "when you had killed me at the reception. However I believe that is becoming much clearer to me."

The Other smiled the wolf smile with Spock's face. "Indeed, Mr. Spock. Explain."

Spock straightened and met the identical eyes levelly. "You killed me because you could not fight both your own selves at the same time."

"Excellent, Spock."

"And perhaps—you had a use for a recording," Spock said, a little hollowly.

"Even better, Mr. Spock," the Other nodded.

"Then you *are* a murderer," the Commander said with finality, turning on the Other.

"Am I?" he said. "Is it murder to make a recording? Perhaps it is merely conferring the benefit of immortality. You see, the Phoenix changes everything—even the morality of murder."

"It is still murder," Kirk said.

"You are the man who set a trap for me, and killed me," the Other said. "Was it murder?"

"No," Kirk said firmly.

The Other shrugged. "It was death. My second death which you intended to be final. You planned it in cold blood, almost an execution. Neither the current Omne nor I have settled with you for that, and I do not advise you to give him a chance."

"Nor you?"

"Nor me. But I will not give you any option. However, the nature of the Phoenix has altered the nature of your act, and of mine, irrevocably. It is now possible for a man to come back to punish you for killing him. And it is now possible to kill a man without wishing him dead—nor keeping him dead. That is war. But is it murder?"

Kirk looked into the Vulcan eyes which held the soul of Omne. "What has stopped me is that I did not think the man who had been Omnedon would be a plain murderer. A warrior, yes, perhaps responsible for death, as I have been, too, and even in ways which I would not condone. An outlaw, but one who would claim a hell-busted ideal or two, and a purpose of freedom. The wolf, but not the wolf in sheep's clothing. Not hiding. Not striking by night without warning, against a conference of lambs. You are Omne, and part of you is even Spock—and yet you did kill Spock. Are you saying—*you made a recording?* That was why you did it?"

Jim's eyes were wide.

The Other shook his head. "As it happened, Omne transported him into the force field just before the moment of death. But that was my intent. Mr. Spock is far too interesting to destroy irrevocably, unless as a last resort."

Jim straightened. "I do not begin to forgive you

Spock's death or that risk. But I do see that you have a certain point. The Phoenix alters every morality we have had about life and death. You killed the Old Hegarch, but he did not die, finally. You knew he would not. He has a new life, and his grandson a new lease on life. Is that murder? Spock forced you to kill yourself. I killed you. Omne put you under the gun of a death sentence and thought he could reabsorb you. None of us are dead. If you did not intend irrevocable murder of Spock, I do not forgive, and I do not wish to share the universe with you, but I might not shoot you out of hand like a mad wolf."

The Other bowed mockingly. "Thank you, Captain. I cannot tell you how that relieves my mind."

"Accept your own offer from Omne," Kirk said firmly. "I believe he would gladly cancel the destruct if you accept exile."

"And you would gladly share the universe with *him?*" the Other said.

"No," Kirk said. "He is far too dangerous, but not so lethal as you have been. He has only to wait while your time runs out. You may kill him, but even that, here, is not irrevocable, and it does you no good. You need the code from him. He is as stubborn as you are, and he has everything to lose. So do you. But you have no options if he does not yield."

The Other shook his head. "I have one." He looked at Spock. "I believe your logic has arrived at it, Mr. Spock. Would you care to name it?"

Spock looked at him bleakly. "You believe that the resonance of our bodies and the similarity of a portion of our minds will make it possible for you to subdue my consciousness and take over my body—by mind link, without need for the medallion or the equipment."

"Spock!" Jim said and James turned slowly to look at Spock.

The Commander could feel the sudden metaphysical horror spreading through the room, and she knew that they all believed it—that even Spock believed it was possible.

She stepped closer to Spock, between him and the Other. "You will do it over my body," she said.

"And mine," Jim and James added in one voice.

"That can be arranged," the Other said flatly.

He turned to Omne. "That is why you will give me the key. If not, I will systematically see to it that some or all of your hand-picked enemies are in no condition for the roles in which you, or I, have cast them in the galactic scenario. And in the end, if you do not see reason, I will trade this dying body for Spock's living one and he will cease to exist as an independent entity. Is that murder? Probably that is murder—of a totally new kind. Under your sentence of death, I do not know, nor much care. In any case that act will alter irrevocably all relationships of honorable enmity for me, but also for you. We will be dealing with berserkers. You and I now plan on a scale of a thousand years. Exile is not irrevocable. But final cessation of an entity is. There is justice, Omne. Absorption is what you planned for me. If I do it to Spock, it will be on your head."

"No," Omne said. "What will happen will be on your head." The original Omne lifted his head and bowed faintly to all his enemies. "I will set the key for the medallion," Omne said.

# CHAPTER XXVIII

TREVANIAN saw Omne begin to set a code-combination on the medallion.

"You surrender?" the Other said. "It is rather sudden, my other. Not really in character. What plot are you hatching?"

Omne smiled. "If any—that is for me to know. You have named a price which I will not pay. Mr. Spock I will settle with myself in due course. That is my right. Exile—I could pay, if necessary. Here are my terms. You will give Trevanian to the Commander, alive and well, and free her. You will not kill or absorb Spock— nor 'record' him. You will take the entire party out of the Anomaly in the Phoenix ship. Now that you will have time, I suggest you concentrate less on war and more on splitting Federation and Empire. However I recognize that I cannot dictate to you in that."

"No."

Omne finished with the medallion. With effort he levered himself on his hands to try the paralyzed legs. They would not take the weight. He almost toppled, and Jim instinctively put out a hand to steady him. Omne half fell against him for a moment and leaned on him, bending down to him, then rocked back and leaned against the bench again.

The Other reached with a force key and unlocked Spock's stasis cuffs. "Mr. Spock, you will assist Omne to the transporter. It is still set to the Vortex. You will trip the yellow switch which opens the route *through* the Vortex."

Spock surveyed the possibilities, but the weapon was firm in the Other's hands, and the distance was not possible. Spock moved and did as told.

Jim held Omne's arm from the other side and they helped Omne to the transporter and braced him there. Omne tossed the medallion to the Other, who caught it.

The Other came to the console beside Trevanian.

For a moment that manner in which the Other had attended to Trevanian like a physician or a healer came out. "This is life, Trevanian. Or possibly death. The two of us are in the same lifeboat. Do you want to risk it?"

Trevanian managed a smile. The drug was fading, and the pain was with him again, threatening to rise to blackness. From somewhere out of the darkness, the Doyen's face kept forbidding him to die.

"Do we have a choice?" Trevanian said.

"No," the Other said steadily. Trevanian must have been the only one who saw the wave of wrenching distortion—as of threatened dissolution—go over the Vulcan features of the Other. Trevanian had seen the look with increasing frequency the last few hours, but never so strongly.

So it was that close. The destruct mechanism must be very close to finality.

Should Trevanian warn the others? But the knowledge might lead them to some foolish attempt, and the Other was still able to shoot.

The Other plugged in the medallion and settled a headset on Trevanian's head and his own.

"As it happens, Trevanian, I will not require you to go first."

The Other had no time for that, Trevanian thought. If Omne had set a trap, they would both be caught.

James came toward Trevanian to be with him.

The Other gestured with the weapon. "Jim, step down." Jim stepped off the transporter platform and near to the big control console. Spock remained with Omne. The Other set a tangle-foot field of partial stasis to trap all their feet as if in ankle-deep tar. He set a timer on the transporter. It would take Omne into exile in the other world.

The Other stepped to a special equipment position at the head of Trevanian's platform. He put a curiously gentle healer's hand on Trevanian's shoulder—or perhaps merely the hand of a fellow voyager into the unknown.

Then the Other tripped the switch for the both of them.

Trevanian felt some unknown effect sweep down his body, and he began to lose consciousness.

But suddenly his attention was riveted by movement. Jim lurched and stretched out in an impossible dive and reached a red switch on the console.

Trevanian felt the Other stiffen, but the Other could not move now. A kind of current flowed around them both, immobilizing them.

Omne said: "I warned you. We are not a man of honor."

Then Jim was leaning across onto the transporter platform trying to get Spock clear, heaving to get the Vulcan away, half-bracing himself against Omne. Omne caught Jim's arm—and threw the Vulcan clear.

By Trevanian's side, the Other vanished, and Trevanian knew that Omne had set a trap with Jim to throw the switch to lock the Other away in the machinery—as a recording. The timer activated the transporter and it caught Omne and Jim. Spock tried to throw himself into the transporter effect after them, but he was too late.

The Commander moved to him. "You can't go. You must take the ship out to prevent war."

Spock turned to her—almost turned on her. "Omne planned this—to take Jim with him into exile—into a world from which nothing has returned alive. He planned all of this. How did he plan to penetrate his impenetrable stronghold? Answer: get himself taken in. He played this game against himself and used us as pawns and pieces against the Other."

Spock smashed a hand down on a table, and it split. "I have been a *fool*. Omne has been one step ahead of us from the beginning."

"Spock!" the Commander said fiercely. "Omne is alive, or his dead-man switch would have brought him back. They're both alive."

"I know it." Spock's voice was still hollow.

James came to join them, put a hand on Spock's arm in an effort to reassure. "Jim will be all right."

Spock turned to him slowly. "No, he will not. At best he is hostage for us to come after him—giving Omne his chance to return to this world—if that world does not kill both of them first. And *if* we make it back. But Jim would order us to go. He would say that the war must be stopped. It is his ship, his job—and if this goes down, it will go down as his war. It will split Federation and Empire into fragments for centuries."

The Vulcan's jaw set in the discipline of duty. "All right. There is no time. There is no one we can leave here. James must appear as your Prince." He strode down the room to Trevanian.

"What is your status?" The Vulcan said without preamble.

Trevanian reached down and stripped off the life-support cuff. "Functional," he said, and then, as he moved: "Reborn."

The Vulcan nodded, but could spare nothing more for it. "Come," he said and gathered Trevanian up with an arm under his shoulders. The Vulcan started to lift him, but Trevanian turned and found his feet.

"Jim was your friend?" Trevanian said.

"Yes," the Vulcan said.

Trevanian looked toward James.

"I understand," he said.

# CHAPTER XXIX

OMNE found himself materializing on solid ground—the transporter feedback-adjust saw to that.

The only difficulty was that the solid ground was a narrow ledge over an abyss. It was a cave ledge—of some different rock, swept viciously by crackling Vortex forces and crumbling under his weight. Kirk teetered half over the edge and Omne grabbed him instinctively.

But Omne's own legs were crumbling under him. They were not quite as useless as he had made them out to be at the last, but they would not take his weight—and Kirk's. Omne crashed to his knees.

The ledge gave under their weight and they went down. Kirk crashed against the wall and went limp. From somewhere Omne's hand found a hold. The force nearly took his arm off.

It was an impossible hold on a fingertip-wide ledge. Omne held on.

In some manner he raised Kirk to his shoulder and found a grip with the other hand.

Omne hung there by his fingertips and laughed.

He was well-pleased. That had been the one insuperable danger. A one-way drop into an abyss. Even so it would merely have been death.

Ultimately Omne worked his way along the ledge until it widened. He managed to heave Kirk up onto it and himself up after, and then he crawled. He dragged himself with the strength of his arms and reached back to haul the Human along.

By the time he reached a solid tunnel his legs were leaden and searing, but not quite useless.

When he saw daylight he hauled himself to his feet and lifted the unconscious Human up into his arms.

Omne could not walk properly, but he would see a new world on his feet.

Omne stepped out into the sun.

The world lay before him.

It was not the barren, blasted world of its Vortex twin.

This was a living world, a lush and fatal paradise.

Even from this height Omne could see mountain, forest, jungle, beach—and everywhere the game trails and signs of exotic wildlife and the large predators which would prey on it.

Omne nodded. He had gambled again and again won. It was the world his studies had led him to hypothesize, improbable as it was. And therefore somewhere here, if he lived through the predators, would be the plant he needed.

Perhaps it was the sun or the taste of fresh air.

Kirk's eyelids flickered and then opened.

He looked up into Omne's face with a slight frown of puzzlement.

He looked out and saw the expanse of blue-green and red-gold world.

"The other side of the Vortex," Omne said.

Kirk looked up, puzzled. "Vortex? Who are you?" Kirk said.

Omne looked down at him in astonishment. "You do not know me?" It was the one thing he had not expected.

Kirk grimaced, indicating his position. "It would seem that I should. Why are you carrying me?"

Omne nodded. "What is your name?"

The Human began to look alarmed. He fought it

down, but the shock stayed just under the surface of his face. "I—*don't know*," he said with effort.

"All right," Omne said quietly. "It is not important. You hit your head. The amnesia is almost certainly momentary. Don't trouble yourself. I will take care of it."

He moved toward the edge of the ledge, where a short rubble slope led to level ground.

"But who are you?" Kirk said, making a move to get down. "Why are you taking care of me?"

Omne shook his head. "That also does not matter now. Be still."

He skidded them down the slope on his still-wooden legs, but kept his feet to reach the jungle floor.

He found shade under a tree and a bed of cool blue moss.

He put the Human down on it and sank down beside him to explore the head injury.

Kirk seemed to sense the skill in the hands and submitted to the examination without protest. There was a severe bruise and some smaller ones, perhaps from the earlier fall.

"Grip my hand," Omne said, "hard. Now with your other hand." The grips were firm, even-handed. Omne ran the other simple tests for neurological damage. He found no clear signs of severe or fatal damage, although they might develop later. There were signs of shock, probably both physical and emotional.

At those levels of memory which had been blocked Kirk would know that he had been sent off to a world from which he could expect no return—with the man who was his most dangerous enemy.

In truth it had always been their single swords which were crossed: the true son of moral certainty, and the black wolf born on the day when certainty, and a world very like this one, died.

"What is your name?" Kirk said. "Doctor—?"

Omne looked at the world again and into the now-innocent eyes of the son of certainty. The answer came unbidden to Omne's lips. "You have been known to call me Omnedon."

Kirk's eyes flickered with a spark of interest, seemed to reach for some memory. "My lord?" He looked puzzled. "Is that right? I seem to have some memory of saying that. Was it to you?"

"You have said it to me," Omne said.

Kirk struggled to sit up and Omne gave him a hand. For a moment Kirk looked down at the hand, then up into Omne's face. "I do not know you, and yet I feel that you are my benefactor. I owe you my life, do I not?"

Omne nodded. "A few of your lives."

"Then I am right. Thank you, my lord Omnedon."

"You are welcome." Omne rose on one knee and looked down at the Human and smiled at him almost gently. "Take great care," he said softly. "If memory serves you better than you wish me to know, and you still play the game of galactic confrontation—do not try it. If this is a ploy, you will pay the price."

"Ploy?" Kirk said in a tone of puzzlement as Omne rose to stand over him. "Confrontation? How would I need a ploy? If you are my benefactor, are you not my friend?"

"No," Omne said.

Kirk struggled up to his knees. "What then?"

"Your enemy." After a moment Omne added. "And here, your *Ahn'var*."

"What?"

Omne reached down and raised the Human to his feet. "An ancient word from a certain world. It is not necessary for you to understand, if you do not. The simplest meaning is that I require your obedience. Whether you are this new innocent with no yesterday, or my old enemy with no tomorrow, in this world my word must be law. That will be the price of your life."

Omne turned and directed the Human's eyes to the presence only Omne had sensed gathering in the tree above them. It opened its mouth, and its breath was flame.

Kirk's eyes picked out the fire-python's natural camouflage—with difficulty—and understood that the creature had arrived without alerting any sense Kirk owned . . . while Omne had always known.

Omne guided Kirk slowly, quietly out from under the tree.

"Um," Kirk said, "is that the local serpent?"

"The official local variety," Omne said. "Welcome to Eden."

Kirk grimaced. "That snake must be a hundred feet long. What are the local *apples* like?"

Omne chuckled. "We are about to find out." He touched his waist. "The Other perhaps contemplated this when he took our survival belts. This time it is bare hands and knowledge." His glance indicated: against the jungle. "Chiefly mine." Omne said. "Come."

Kirk looked at him and for a moment Omne thought that he saw the starship Captain flare up in the Human's eyes. But then the man looked up at the dangerous dragon-snake. "I didn't see it," Kirk said. After a moment he bowed his head slightly.

The slight bow of the head somehow reached Omne more than he liked to know.

It was the acknowledgment he had wanted from this man and the others on the day of the Phoenix, when he had come back from death—something more even than recognition of what he was; a kind of sanction, tribute, honor.

They had refused it. Stonily. And properly.

And for that he had wanted to destroy them.

Now this innocent looked at him with the look which Omne had wanted to see on that face: simple tribute to what Omne, after all, was.

Omne inclined his head stiffly in acceptance—and then set the feeling savagely aside.

"Come."

Omne turned and the man who had been James T. Kirk followed him into the jungle.

# CHAPTER XXX

SPOCK sat at the control panel of the Phoenix ship. It was shaking itself apart.

The ship would not survive the trip out of the Anomaly, let alone the trip which must be made back in.

But the trip *must* be made, and in this ship. There was no other.

Spock focused the whole of his mind on the Omne and Omnedon memories from that terrible link which had led to Omne's first death. The memories were there, but not clear. They required the Vulcan technique of total recall. Spock must bring back any scrap of help from the inventor of this ship.

He let himself sink into the recall-trance so deeply that the Commander was left to fly the ship.

But Spock found himself sinking into the giant's earlier Omnedon memories—of a lost world—and for the first time he began to understand Omnedon's rage and grief, which had created Omne.

Spock pushed on, pursuing the trail of Omne's later memories, tracing the workings of the ship.

They were obscured, remote.

He fought for the details, fought to clear his mind of the compelling emotions. Since that last link parts of Spock held far too much of Omne.

Suddenly Spock found the key he was looking for and came up out of the deep-search. He reached forward and programmed a control sequence and abruptly the ship's shaking apart eased slightly.

"We will make it now," the Commander said, reading the instruments.

"*Out,*" Spock said.

She turned to look at him. "It is not the direction you want to go."

"No."

"I will come back with you."

He lifted an eyebrow at her. "Illogical. That would be the ultimate confirmation of your treason."

She sighed. "Mr. Spock, I cannot tell you how tired I am of logic." Then she looked at him gravely. "He will be all right, Spock. He is not Jim Kirk for nothing."

She looked at James, and Spock knew that she spoke from knowledge.

It did not help.

Spock knew Jim Kirk. But he also knew Omne.

Spock wrenched the controls and they broke out of the Anomaly past a Romulan fleet with weapons aimed down their throats.

A second Romulan fleet, headed by a heavy cruiser, faced off against the first.

Between them, surrounded, was the *Enterprise.*

"Spock to Mr. Scott and all ships," Spock said. "We have proof of imposture and war-making treachery, and of our own innocence. No Federation officer penetrated the Empire or took captives."

The heavy cruiser turned and fired at them.

"The Doyen," the Commander said. She opened a hailing frequency. "Doyen, I will return the kinsman of my hostage, as promised, in token of good faith."

The screen lighted with the face of an impressive woman. "Return his body?" the Doyen said with effort. "Yes. Do that. Then I will return Spock's body to the *Enterprise* before blasting the ship out of the sky."

"Doyen," the Commander said, "my word is my bond."

She reached back and drew Trevanian into range of the camera pick-up.

The Doyen stood transfixed.

Then she said slowly. "You spoke of imposters?"

The Commander met her eyes. "You may verify the reality by any means you choose. I give you my word, this Spock is as real as your kinsman, and as innocent."

The screen flickered suddenly and was full of the Romulan Commander-in-Chief.

"Spock's innocence, if any, confirms your guilt, Commander. I arrest you."

"You are wrong," she said.

The Commander-in-Chief gave an order and his dreadnought flagship turned its guns to bear on the Phoenix ship.

The *Enterprise* shot forward suddenly to put itself between the dreadnought and the Phoenix ship.

The Commander's own flagship began to move with a similar idea.

Then the Doyen's heavy battle cruiser turned on the Romulan dreadnought.

# CHAPTER XXXI

OMNE walked warily; taking the path along the cliff-ledge was a calculated risk. There was no anticipating a predator around a turn, and no retreat.

He had outfitted the party of two with a heavy club, which he carried, and a light jointed-chamber spear which the Human had compared to sharpened bamboo, and carried now at Omne's back. Omne had found a long flinty piece of stone and chipped a few quick flakes from it to serve as a knife. With it he had carved great sheets from the leather-bark trees. One served him now as pack, and the others he would use, when he had a moment, to fashion various amenities. He had found fruit and food, in plenty.

But not the nepenthe plant. He would find it on the cliff by the caves.

Then Omne heard the padded feet, the claws. "Get back!" he shouted to the Human.

Then the vorlat was on Omne.

It was all claws and teeth, and half again his height—the saber-tooth which the Human would see as cat or bear.

Omne moved in and smashed with the club, stabbed with the stone knife.

The vorlat's claws raked his back and its arms closed around him in a deadly bear-hug.

Omne jammed the club into its teeth, stabbed, bunched the muscles of his back and broke the animal's hold—and the knife. Then he was around the vorlat and clinging to its back, seeking a Vulcan nerve hold or a chance to snap its neck with his own strength.

Suddenly Omne saw Kirk coming with his light spear.

"Get back, Jim!" Omne yelled. *"Get back!"*

But the Human kept coming.

Kirk drove the spear into the vorlat's chest with all his strength, but he had not reckoned with the beast's undying vitality. It staggered forward and pinned him against the cliff.

It's saber-teeth were shearing through the club Omne had jammed between them. In a moment the vorlat's jaws would be free and the Human would be dead.

In that moment Omne found the strength. He locked his arms around the neck and twisted it. The neck snapped with that peculiarly terrible sound which could be nothing else.

The animal collapsed on the Human and Omne for a moment collapsed on the animal. Then he pulled himself together and hauled the Human out from under the vorlat.

Omne found the vorlat's snarl on his own face. "Who asked *you* to get into it? I ordered you back!"

"My God!" the Human gasped. "It was killing you!"

"*I* was killing *it*. But if I were not—you were still to stay back."

"And let you die?"

"If necessary."

"I could not do that, my lord."

"You will, on my order. And if it should happen, you will wait, and stay alive. I will come for you."

"Back from the dead?"

Omne laughed. "Of course."

He looked into the Human's puzzled eyes and wondered whether in truth Jim Kirk remembered nothing of immortality, nor of Omne. He saw Kirk look at the animal and then at him and Omne knew that the Human was seeing the strength which had met the predator with bare hands.

"I do not think I would care to be your enemy, my lord," Kirk said.

Something clicked in Omne's mind. "But that is it, isn't it?" Omne said under his breath. "That is why you cannot remember that you *are!*"

"What?" Kirk murmured.

Omne reached out without warning and put hands on the Human's face in the position of the Vulcan mind touch.

It was sudden, but if Omne had expected to trap the Human into an instinctive recoil—from him or from the agony of any mind touch since the psionic burnout, he had not succeeded.

The Human looked at him with mere puzzlement. "My lord?"

"If you *are* ill," Omne said, "I could heal you with a link. If you are not ill, the link would quite probably kill you. But I would *know*."

No flicker of reaction to that either. "Must you?" the Human said with a look of trust. "You have said that we are enemies. I think it is better forgotten, my lord."

Omne looked closely at Kirk. "Amnesia," he said, "is not more than brief unless there is something which it is unbearable to remember."

Kirk still looked at him with trust.

"Once," Omne said, "I defeated you, badly, and broke you down to tears, for the first time. I had not believed that you do not remember. But I see now that your mind would have taken this chance to wipe that out. You do not want to be my enemy here, nor to live with that defeat, and this one as well. Therefore, your mind has blocked out your enemy, and remembered Omnedon as your benefactor."

Omne unlocked his fingers from the position of the mind touch.

"All right," Omne said. "I will not force you to remember, nor risk your mind or your life to know whether I am right, or whether you are still fox enough to be faking it. If I am wrong, you still are in my power."

"Yes," Kirk said. "You speak in riddles, my lord, but I—almost—understand."

Omne laughed. "Rest, my enemy. Recover. I can afford the luxury. It might have been like this once, if you had come to meet Omnedon instead of Black Omne."

Then he felt the old terrible smile on his face. "But I am well pleased that it was not so. It is my black wolf which is your true opposite, son of certainty. We are better met as enemies than as friends."

"Are we?" Kirk said.

But Omne laughed.

"If you are still my enemy and doing this, you are in for a difficult time. But, curiously enough, I believe you—devious though you are in your right mind. Let's go."

THE COMMANDER hailed the Commander-in-Chief. "It is stalemate," she said to him. "The Doyen will fire on your fleet if you attack the *Enterprise*. I will transport my hostage and his kinsman aboard the *Enterprise* to guarantee that, while I return into the Mouth."

James started to protest that he was going with her, but she silenced him with a look.

"For myself," the Commander said, "I require trial by challenge. The Maelstrom qualifies as a sufficient trial hazard. I will return there with Spock."

"You will confess your treason by going back into the Maelstrom with the Vulcan?" the Commander-in-Chief said.

"I confess nothing," she answered. "My actions are honorable and always were. I will submit only to trial by hazard. It is my right."

The Commander-in-Chief said finally, "It is. I cannot deny you that. But if you do not return, the *Enterprise* will answer for you. Your treason will be confirmed."

"I will return," she said, and switched off.

"I'm going with you," James said.

She shook her head. "As Vulcanoids Mr. Spock and I can stand far more stress in the Vortex. But also, if we do not return, some Kirk must go back to the conference to report on his challenge against Omne—to prevent a split in the Federation, and war."

She saw James absorb it slowly. If they did not return, he would have to become Kirk again, temporarily or even permanently. And alone.

She sent him off with Trevanian and with that thought.

And she watched Scott greet James on the *Enterprise* with the look of seeing that the truth was, finally and irrevocably, true. James put a hand on Scott's shoulder, and one on McCoy's, and led them off with the old look of command.

The Commander headed the ship back into the Vortex with the Vulcan.

# CHAPTER XXXII

OMNE and Kirk climbed through the caves toward the Vortex center.

They turned a corner.

Spock stood in front of them.

Omne felt the Human stiffen, but whether with recognition or mere surprise, Omne couldn't tell.

"Who is that, my lord?" Kirk said.

The Vulcan's eyebrows went up at the question, and higher at the "my lord."

"An excellent question, Jim," Omne said. He was looking into the mouth of a phaser, held by the man whose Captain he had kidnapped into the Vortex—or by the man he had consigned to oblivion in the machine.

Omne reached for the old smile of the wolf. "My compliments," he said. "I could not, of course, check whether you had set some override to release you from the Phoenix machinery in case of accident—or design. It is what *I* would have done."

The Vulcan figure shrugged. "You might equally compliment me on my swift return through the Anomaly."

"Perhaps. In that event, where is the Commander?"

"No one would, in logic, risk more than one person on the other side of the Vortex."

Omne shrugged. "I shall draw my own conclusions. However, I know my own temperament, and yours,

234

very well—in either case. We are more than brothers."

"Then you know that my most logical alternative is to disintegrate you where you stand."

Omne shook his head. "Mr. Spock would see that logic, but he would not finally act on it. *You*, however, might—although in your place, I would be inclined to ask whether I have something you might need."

"Do you?"

Omne nodded. "If you are the Other—which I now suspect—I have your route back. If you are Spock, however, you will probably die here, irrevocably."

Omne felt the Human stir behind him.

"What is it, Jim?" Omne said.

"I don't know, my lord," the Human's voice said in a tone of puzzlement. "Why do you address him as two men? Is he your brother? He does not resemble you."

Omne laughed. "More than you know. Don't trouble yourself, Jim. Stay behind me at all times. All right, my 'brother.' Stalemate again."

The intruder shook his head. "No. You will give me the nepenthe plant."

Omne chuckled. "So we *are* brothers under the skin."

The Other bowed fractionally. Omne knew that the gesture was his own death warrant.

But he shook his head. "You will need the Human as hostage to get off the planet. He has amnesia. It is genuine and serious. In my opinion he needed release from the crushing defeat at my hands and from the knowledge that he could not be sure of his memories even of Spock—since you exist. He found release in forgetfulness. Now he has become dependent on me—perhaps as an anchor to reality. If you killed me now it would send him into a state of shock from which he would not recover—certainly not soon."

The Other shrugged, but Omne knew that shrug. "He is, after all, the enemy," the Other said.

Omne laughed. "Yes. But you will not want to give up the game of galactic confrontation. You will use him to draw Spock here as your ticket out—and perhaps leave Spock here as hostage against Jim and the

Commander, while you force Jim to return to the *Enterprise* with you, use him in your plan—*if* he remains alive and sane . . . "

"My lord," Kirk said from behind Omne, "this man would use me against you or against the one you call Spock?"

"If he could. However—"

Then Omne felt the movement behind him and knew his mistake.

The Human cut away around a rock and out across a stone bridge spanning a chasm.

Omne moved, but not fast enough. He stopped at the end of the bridge, seeing it crumbling and knowing that it would not take his weight in addition to Kirk's. Nor Kirk's for long.

Suddenly the Other was beside Omne.

"My lord," Kirk said, "this enemy of yours will throw me his phaser. I will not have him use it against you. You have said that he needs me."

"Come here!" Omne said. "You owe me obligation."

"I am paying it," Kirk said. "You—whoever you are—throw the phaser."

The bridge was crumbling even more seriously. Omne started to move.

"Damn Spock," the Other said suddenly and shoved Omne aside. In the same instant the Other was out on the bridge. He was lighter than Omne in the Vulcan body. The bridge powdered under his feet but his steps were cat-light.

He reached Kirk and caught him up roughly in an arm, turned and started back.

Omne reached out for him, for Kirk.

With a sound of thunder the bridge cracked from end to end, then dissolved in the center.

The Other ran but it was clear that he would not make it.

For one instant his eyes caught Omne's and for that moment they were the eyes of Spock.

He heaved Kirk to Omne as if the Human were a child.

Then the Vulcan figure went down into the thousand-foot chasm.

Omne felt the Human grow rigid as they both teetered on the edge of the abyss, Omne fighting for balance, finally drawing them in to safety.

He could see horror in the Human's eyes.

Whether Kirk's mind would let him remember Spock consciously or not, Jim Kirk had seen a man wearing the face and body of the Vulcan save his life and fall to his death.

"In that body," Omne said aloud, "the Spock in him became very strong—too strong for his own good. For a moment he was your Vulcan as much as my Other—and he died for you."

The Human could not speak. He sank to his knees and finally the cumulative shock was too much and he sagged, collapsing.

Omne caught him.

Very well. That would make it easier.

Omne roped the Human to him and bit into the nectar-pod of the nepenthe flower.

The implant dead-man switch he had devised long ago worked when triggered by the flattening of brain waves usually produced only by death.

The nepenthe plant simulated that flattening, briefly. Perhaps. It might simply kill him.

However, the result would be much the same. The transporter would home on the dead-man switch and take him. And if necessary, the Phoenix would reconstruct him. Provided that the switch would work through the Vortex, as the animal switches had.

And provided that nothing malfunctioned . . .

Omne noted coldly how deep the fear of death still went even in the face of the Phoenix.

Nevertheless it was necessary to learn to act with that added dimension of capacity.

To go to the wall now it was necessary even to be willing to die. Again . . .

# CHAPTER XXXIII

OMNE woke to find the Human looking down at him.

They were on the transporter platform of the laboratory.

It had worked, and without death.

Omne laughed.

The Human must have awakened first and freed himself. But what could the innocent possibly make of this?

Omne sat up. The effects of the nepenthe drug were very profound, but brief.

"It is all right, Jim. I wear a kind of switch implanted in my head which works on brain waves. If I die, it returns my body here. The nepenthe flower gives the symptoms of death. I used it to bring us back."

The Human nodded. "My lord, it mocks death perfectly. I found you without breath or heartbeat."

Omne nodded. "Necessary. What did you do?"

"I revived you. I owed you one."

Omne blinked. "For what happened in the Vortex world?"

The Human shook his head. "In this galaxy. For Spock."

Omne stood up slowly.

The Human moved back a step and revealed the phaser he held.

"Kirk," Omne said.

Kirk nodded. "Welcome to hell, my lord."

"How long have you known?" Omne said.

"From the beginning." The hazel eyes were chips of cold fire now.

"The moment you woke in the other world?" Omne asked.

"From the beginning," Kirk repeated stonily. "I had you wired." He took another step and rested his free hand on the red switch. "From the moment you whispered about the red switch. I knew. You would trick the Other but not soon enough to avoid exile by the transporter. You would go, but you would be back, if you had to kill yourself. And we could not know what tricks you or your Other had programmed into the computers and the Phoenix." Kirk straightened and somehow looked very tall, like some ancient, implacable royalty. "But I might have left you to that other world and to what you could make of this one. Only—you would have taken Spock." The hazel eyes were very hard. "He would have been bait for us, and he would have kept us all here. We couldn't have attempted the Phoenix ship and the Vortex without Spock. Not successfully. So I substituted myself. And you thought you took me."

"When did you plan the amnesia?"

Kirk smiled icily. "It came to me."

"You played me," Omne said. "You knew what would hook me, and you played me. Every tone, look, word. '*My Lord.*' " Omne heard as if from a distance that his voice had dropped into a low register which warned of a level of rage he had never known or loosed.

"Yes," Kirk said, "exactly. When you came to us first on the *Enterprise*, you wanted that kind of sanction. Our recognition of your greatness. Our acknowledgment of the nobility which had been Omnedon, but also of your whole person, even of the black wolf which was Omne, and of the immortal who would still choose death before defeat. You did not get that sanction. When you saw that we could acknowledge all of that, and yet could not even accept your acknowledgment of what *we* were—you wanted to destroy us. Perhaps your murderous Other was truly born in that moment."

Omne nodded. "He was the true son of the black wolf."

"But creating him did not help you and the need remained in you," Kirk said. "You wanted me to bow and acknowledge you with 'my lord' as the Regent. You wanted it when you became Omnedon for a moment— and I gave it as his due. And you wanted it today. I used it, knowing that."

Omne found himself moving with a slow ferocity which seemed to unfold frame by frame with the brilliant clarity of stop-action destruction.

And in the same stop-action speed he saw Kirk's hand pull the real switch down to the dead-man position. It would trip if Kirk's hand released it.

"No," Kirk said.

Omne stopped.

Kirk nodded. "I have the answer to that, too. I have the answer to you."

"There is no answer to me."

"The fact that you stopped says that there is. The answer to you is—*you.*"

"My Other is dead," Omne said. "He died for you."

"He died," Kirk said as if the memory was a raw wound. "But you have taught me a new meaning for '*is* dead.' " He gestured to the machinery. "I have investigated, and I have programmed this switch to do one of two things. Your Other also wore a dead-man switch. If it functioned, he will be here, recorded by the Phoenix equipment, and ready to return again. I might return him. Two Omnes loose in a world. It is the one thing which can stop you. It *did* stop you. If the Other had not come out on the bridge after me, you would have been defeated by your other self."

Omne stood still. "My Other saved you, but he is also the man who murdered Spock."

Kirk nodded. "Yes, he is."

"You would not dare to set him free. You would

never know whether you were with Spock or with the Other."

"While *you* live in this galaxy," Kirk said, "I would never be certain of that, in any case. You can come in Spock's body—any time. You have taken all certainty from me, and from Spock, as long as there is any Omne loose. But two Omnes would at least occupy each other. It will be justice. It is what you inflicted on the Resident of Razar."

"My Other inflicted that particular misery," Omne said. "I chose my duplicates better. My Other also brewed the war which may already have consumed James, Spock, and the Commander. Why did you let them go?"

The Captain's eyes were vivid with pain. "My ship is there," he said simply. "And—we are the shepherds against the wolves."

Omne nodded with a savage respect. "This day you are the wolf yourself, Captain."

"Yes."

"You have defeated me again—you believe."

"I have."

Omne smiled the wolf smile. "Perhaps. I told you that your wolf would come to me, in silence and alone. It did. What if *I* were playing a double game? Did you really think that I wanted to take *Spock?*"

The Human looked startled for a moment, considering the possibilities. "You might have expected me to get him away from you. You could not have expected me to pretend the amnesia."

"No," Omne said. "I considered that theory but rejected it. My mistake. You had the strength which could take even defeat. It has troubled you. But your answer is not retreat. It is victory."

Kirk looked at Omne and the Captain's eyes for once accepted that tribute. "It has troubled me, as nothing else has in my life," Kirk acknowledged. "I had to go against you again. I did. And I have, ultimately, won. I will be all right now. Even the link burnout was probably caused as much by my unconscious resistance as by anything else. I wanted to meet you—alone. It was, doubtless, not 'logical.' But it was right."

Omne nodded. "Yes. But you have lost. You cannot win by loosing a worse wolf. Why have you not killed me?"

Kirk looked at him bleakly. "I did still owe you. Perhaps I still do. And you were helpless and in my power because you had trusted my lie. I would not have had you die without knowing the truth. But now—" he gestured with the phaser. "I would do it if you charged me. You are unarmed, but dangerous. But I am reluctant to kill you, because of what I have owed you in lives dear to me." He paused, then added with effort, "And—because you are what you are."

Omne inclined his head. It was perhaps the tribute he had sought, or as much of it as he would never get from this man. "I am still the wolf," Omne said, "still the outlaw with the hell-busted ideal or two, and I will still trouble the galaxy if you let me."

"I know that."

"Stalemate, Captain. I know for a fact that you would not loose my Other. You would not risk Spock."

Omne started to move slowly against the phaser.

But Kirk's hand started to release the switch. "I said 'one of two things.'"

Omne stopped.

"When this drops," Kirk said, "it will release your Other. Or it will release *yourself*. Your exact self— another Omne with your body to the molecule, and your memories, to this day."

Omne understood then. It was what he had feared. But he had not expected Kirk to see it.

Kirk nodded. "One learns to use the logic of the Phoenix. The emanations of the mind which you record with the Phoenix equipment radiate not only at death but at the moment of ultimate fear of death, as they did with me in the beginning and with Spock when he nearly died with you. They would have radiated when the nepenthe drug shut down your brain, and you could not be certain whether it was sleep or death. And the

dead-man relay brought the emanations here, too."
Kirk nodded toward the machinery. "You are stored in
here, too. You, Omne, the original, full, complete, including this day, my lord—to that last moment in the
cave."

Omne felt his jaw set, but he did not let his eyes re-
flect what he felt. "If so, you would not dare to loose
that, either. Still less than my Other."

Kirk shook his head. "Don't count on it. Two Omnes
are less dangerous than one. You would have to occupy
yourselves with each other. Your complete self would
be even more dangerous to you than the Other was.
This Omne would have the memories which you denied
to the Other and the body which is the complete equal
of your own. Stalemate. A combat which might itself
last a thousand years."

"More dangerous to you, too," Omne said. "Bluff."

"No, while the wolves tear out each other's throats,
the shepherds will have—at least—a breathing spell.
They can use it to put the galaxy back together. And if
one of you survives, he would still have to come after
me alone. *If* he could get off this planet. No, my lord. It
is a thing I can do, and with ease. It is—justice."

Omne felt the irony touch his mouth. "Perhaps it is,
Captain. Hoist by my own Phoenix. It is fitting. I have
done it to you. But I gave you James. If you could undo
it, Captain, all I have done to you and yours—if you
could stand at the morning of the Phoenix and have me
choose someone else for the trial, and never touch any
of you—never create James, or defeat you—would you
choose that?"

"No," Kirk said.

Omne laughed. "Then for what do you wish to punish me?"

"For all of it," Kirk said implacably. "I would not
wish you on anyone else." Then he said more slowly,
"And in truth, I would not have missed the test of my
steel against yours. You are still the giant. One day we
will tame immortality, and even your new triumph of
medical regeneration. You will have given us that lead.

And for that, if I am able, I will see that the galaxy remembers the man who was born Omnedon. But in any case, *I* will remember Omne."

"You speak as of the dead, Captain. I still live."

"Yes." Kirk drew himself up. "There will be death enough in the galaxy if your plans succeed. It is no defense of freedom to arrange war. But there is no known law by which I can arrest you. And you have spared Spock and Trevanian; you have shielded me with your body, more than once. Your trick against your Other broke the deadlock and set the others free to stop the war. Doubtless you did all of that for your own purposes. But you did it. Very well. I will spare your life. But for the peace of the galaxy, I cannot let you go."

"It is a dilemma," Omne said.

Kirk smiled. "No. The solution for a dilemma is to take it by the horns. There is a time-honored remedy which can be given a new dimension," He gestured toward the transporter positions where Omne still stood. "The world we have come from will make a very suitable St. Helena."

Omne raised an eyebrow. "Even granting the historical comparison, do you not mean Elba?"

"Napoleon returned from exile to Elba," Kirk said. "That is what I mean," Omne said silkenly.

"No," Kirk said firmly. "His second exile to St. Helena was final. He died there. You have ample ability to live in your own world of exile. But you will not return. The computer yields the information that the dead-man implant switch functions only one time without computer reset. The Vortex is otherwise impenetrable from the other side. There is no one to come after you."

Omne did not let his expression waver. "No one to come after me? Not even you, my enemy?"

Kirk did not look happy. "No. Not even me," he said. "You know the legend of the Flying Dutchman was that he was condemned to sail the seas and wander forever until someone was willing to die for him. For myself, if it were only our own two swords which were crossed, I might even risk it, for the sake of what you

were, and are, and could be. And for immortality, for
your new regeneration process which would mean even
an end to suffering from disease, injury. It would be the
end of life as we know it, the end of all customs based
on the inevitability of death and suffering. It is the debate we had. Have I, have you, has anyone the right to
decide that for the galaxy? But it would be the beginning of something new, something we can hardly envi-
sion—a galaxy freed from the shadow of death. Have I
the right to decide *against* that? To consign you to St.
Helena and your greatest discoveries to oblivion? There
will be no time for us to stay here and no chance to
come back. I suspect that the Anomaly is closing completely from the traffic."

"Yes," Omne said. "You will not be able to come
back. If you close the door on me, you are closing the
door on immortality for the galaxy. Are you the son of
moral certainty enough for that? Is that the mass murder of billions? Does anything I have done or would do
compare to *that*? Have you that right?"

"I don't know whether I have the right," Kirk said.
"I do know that I have the duty to decide. The decision
is in my hands. It always was."

"Yes."

"Was *that* what you wanted? Why you chose me?"

"Perhaps. There was a time when I was the son of
certainty, too."

Their eyes locked and Omne knew that for a moment
Kirk saw the face of Omnedon.

"I once offered you amnesty, on condition of your
word on the peaceful and careful control of immortality," Kirk said. "You said, 'Does the wolf accept amnesty from the lambs?' Will you accept it now from a
wolf?"

For a long moment Omne did not answer. Finally he
chuckled in his throat. "What fine teeth you have, Captain. I tell you, it is a kind of temptation. But what you
do not understand is that what is mine is *mine*—to
keep, use, sell, give away, destroy. That includes immortality. It includes, perhaps, such soul as my kind of

immortal may have. And those things I will not sell, even for my freedom, or to have no other Omne before me. In truth, I will not sell them for my life or immortality. I could give you my word on a lie, Captain, but I have not done that, either, and I do not choose to start."

Kirk nodded. "I didn't think you would." He drew himself up. "Then I have no choice. I give too many hostages to fortune, including a galaxy where billions may die not of age-old causes but of war. Women and children, whole worlds and species—not in years or decades, but *now*. He shook his head. "You told me I would sell my soul and the galaxy for immortality. Yes, that's a temptation. But—no. I will regret it bitterly one day when someone dies whom I cannot lose. And I may question that decision every day of my life. But I cannot turn the wolf loose in the fold. Give me your word."

Omne shook his head. "No."

"Then go now to St. Helena." Kirk indicated the transporter.

"And if I jump you?"

Kirk let the switch close a fraction more. "If I cannot stun you and send you off anyway, the switch will close. And I have programmed an irreversible computer sequence to my personal voice and code. The last Omne will rise momentarily in a sealed chamber which you cannot reach until he is fully awake. Even if I am dead, you cannot stop that, and if I live, I will play you off against each other."

"There will then be two Omnes to greet Spock and the Commander," Omne said.

"Then they will just have to deal with that," Kirk said grimly. "But also, I have set a few surprises for you and your duplicate into the irreversible circuit. No, Omne, you have to go. You know it. I know it. You will believe that you will find a way back, but you will not. Still, you will live, and you will not have to meet yourself or make war on yourself. There is a price for being the alpha male of the galaxy. There cannot be two of you. You can be second to no man. But you will yield to me now, for I am alpha here. It is not by muscle but by mind, and not by my power alone but by yours which I can turn against you. But I hold all of the cards. And you *will* yield."

Kirk glanced at the computer clock from the corner of his eye. It was running a countdown. "You have thirty seconds to decide. Then the sequence becomes irreversible."

Omne straightened. "I do not need them, Captain," he said in the careless tone of royalty. "Neither of us boggles at making decisions of life and death or immortality in a moment. We are still the sons of certainty and one of us, at least, is damned for it. Whether you are damned or not, I do not know. But I have learned from you what I wished to know. I told you on the day of the Phoenix that I wished to possess you, to own the other half of my soul, from a man who did not quit, and would not quit, even against me. I have learned that from you—among other things—and I will not quit against you now. You see, the one thing which would really stop me would be to give you my word."

"Because, of course, you are not a man of honor," Kirk said, letting the irony in his tone make it a tribute now.

"Of course," Omne said. "You are quite right, Captain. I do not wish to share the universe or my memories with another Omne. I might gamble on a fight, but the odds against me when the enemy is myself are too high. Beyond that, the problem of memory is insuperable. There is one Omne."

"Yes," Kirk said.

Omne straightened. "Send me off, Captain. I can afford the luxury. And when your Vulcan does not come for you, you will have to decide whether to bring me back, or spend a thousand years alone."

Kirk's eyes did not flinch. "If it comes to that, I will decide."

Omne laughed. "Meanwhile there is a universe on the other side and I am not without resource. It is Elba."

Kirk's other hand reached for the transporter control. "St. Helena," he said. "The planet on the other side must be closed by the Vortex, too."

Then he pushed the transporter control down firmly as the time sequence ran out. The computer did not announce an irreversible sequence. Kirk said, "Goodbye, Omne."

And as Kirk closed the control Omne saw a Vulcan figure step out from behind Kirk.

Omne tried to lunge, but the transporter was already taking him.

In that moment Omne had room for only one question:

Was it *Spock*, back from the Anomaly?

Or was it Omne's dead Other back from much further, by yet another fail-safe mechanism?

# CHAPTER XXXIV

KIRK saw the expression in Omne's eyes, focused on something behind him, and he turned.

His heart lost some beat and he could not breathe.

God, would there always be the doubt?

"Spock?" he said.

Then the Commander stepped out beside the Vulcan.

"I had thought to find you in some difficulty, Captain," Spock said. "But you appear to have matters well in hand."

Kirk sighed. "You might have come with a little more alacrity, Mr. Spock."

"In fact, we did," the Commander said. "We have been here in time to hear part of the argument. We did not want to joggle your elbow." She inclined her head to him. "Besides, it was worth the price of admission."

Kirk stretched in the navigator's chair of the Phoenix ship. He owned no bone or muscle which did not complain, and none which was not entitled.

"You did not actually set an irrevocable computer sequence?" Spock asked, navigating the ship by main force and lightning calculation. The Vulcan could, of course, do it while talking. Kirk hoped.

"I didn't know how, in the time available," Kirk said. "I set only a count-down clock."

"Then it *was* a bluff?" the Commander asked.

"No. To the best of my knowledge and as far as I

could program it, if I had released the main dead-man switch there would have been two identical Omnes. He was quite right. I could not bring back the Other. The danger to Spock—to all of us, but especially to Spock—was too great."

"And from another Omne it was not?" she said.

Kirk grinned. "Another one of those things which are covered by 'It's the only game in town.' "

"Or—'it comes with the territory'?" she said rather acidly. "You still bear a marked resemblance to one James. *You*, of course, had to take Omne on alone. Not to mention his killer Other."

Kirk sighed. "It seemed like the logical thing to do at the time."

Spock shot him a look, but the Vulcan was fully involved in piloting the Phoenix ship while the Commander sat in the auxiliary control chair to help. She functioned as if she were the Vulcan's other self.

They were both needed. The turbulence was becoming fatal even to the Phoenix ship.

The two Vulcanoids at the controls were putting the ship through impossible slight gaps in the turbulence where the force was merely enough to shake the ship apart slowly, not in an instant.

It was a remarkable performance, and Kirk watched it with something like awe.

What a team these two would have made. No one else could have made this trip.

There would be no exit for Omne.

Omne would not make it back from the other side of the Vortex. But if he did, he would still be trapped on this side of the blasted world.

Kirk felt no joy in that. It was almost as if he had killed Omne again. To consign any man—but especially that man—to total isolation—to St. Helena, forever . . .

Kirk pulled himself back from it. There had been no choice. But he kept getting small, flashing pictures of the giant's saving Spock, himself, the Commander, all of them, at one time or another.

Somewhere under all the layers of Omne's black grief

and rage there was still the man who had been Omnedon.

Kirk could hate Omne for what he had done to them,
fear him for his danger to the galaxy, and he did.

Yet something had gone out of the universe with
Omne's going.

There were not very many giants.

And there was only one who was Omne.


The ship lurched and rolled and the Commander and
Spock fought to bring it back under control. Its atmo-
sphere fins sheared off and took chunks out of its outer
hull.

Even the Phoenix ship's tremendous structural
strength was not holding.

Spock lifted his head. "I calculate that the ship will
disintegrate in the outer reaches of the Vortex."

The Commander turned to look at him steadily. "I
concur."

Suddenly Kirk realized that some silent communication had already passed between the two Vulcanoids—
perhaps a checking of figures.

Kirk realized only then the meaning of the incredible
teamwork he had been seeing. The two were acting as
one. They must have established some link on the way
back in, to be able to get the ship through.

Spock had not been able to link with anyone since
the night of the burnout. But he could now. The Commander must have effected some healing.

"No possibility of error?" Kirk said.

"No, Jim," Spock answered. "We will of course push
it to the limit. One can never speak with complete certainty about favorable random factors—as you and I
have learned in a long history of service together, Captain."

Kirk smiled. "Yes, Mr. Spock. Your famous odds.
And my luck—or our random factors. How many times
have we beaten the odds, Mr. Spock?"

"Many," Spock said. "But there can come a time
when the random factors run out."

Kirk leaned forward and put a hand on each of their shoulders. "If so, we have had favorable random factors for a lifetime." He could feel a kind of light contact between the two flow through him as if he became a conductor. And it touched his own mind easily without disturbance. His own recoil from the burnout was gone, perhaps with the going of Omne, and the agony was gone from the Vulcan's mind. Kirk could sense the Vulcan's rapport with the Commander, and the thought of James in her mind—James, whom they would not reach.

Suddenly Kirk rebelled against dying—when they all lived and were whole and had beaten even the worst which the Phoenix and its creator could throw at them.

He filled the link with that thought: one single *NO!*

'Contact James' he sent to Spock and the Commander by some means he did not know, and in some way it was Kirk who gathered the three of them up to do it. He did not know what he counted on to reach James—the Commander's love, the Vulcan's mental powers and one-time link with James, or Kirk's own resonance with James. But he felt the other two join with him to reach James.

Kirk did not know what James could do from the *Enterprise* if they did reach him, since he could not bring the *Enterprise* into the Anomaly.

Nevertheless, the odds were beaten only by the attitude which, quite literally, would never say die.

It was that, most of all, which Kirk had understood in Omne. And he heard the giant's last word in his mind: Elba.

Kirk watched Spock's hands fight the controls with the same spirit, whatever the Vulcan's logic told him.

And the Commander matched him.

Kirk watched the Phoenix ship breaking up under them, and he reached for James . . .

# CHAPTER XXXV

JAMES watched the picture on the transporter room viewscreen while Scott fought the transporter controls.

"Cross-circuit to B," James ordered.

"Aye," Scott muttered in the tone of an oath.

"God damn it," McCoy swore softly, desperately. There was no Vulcan to tell him that no deity was involved.

The *Enterprise* lurched, shuddered, groaned in the Anomaly field.

On the viewscreen the Phoenix ship came apart slowly in pieces, then exploded.

Figures shimmered like ghosts on the transporter platform. Scott's hands worked and finally James reached across to try an additional cross-circuit he had seen the Vulcan use only once.

Suddenly the figures shimmered more solidly—and then abruptly they were there, shaken and battered bracing each other, half-falling.

"Thank G—" McCoy began and then grinned helplessly at the Vulcan. "Well—'Thank pitchforks and pointed ears.'"

The Vulcan picked himself and the others up with some dignity and lifted one eyebrow. "Not *mine*, in this case, Doctor." He inclined his head toward James' elegant Romulan ears.

James laughed. But he had moved to claim the Commander and was swinging her down from the platform.

She took his face between her hands and in that moment he knew all he needed to know.

The *Enterprise* was swinging back out of its parabolic trajectory into the edge of the Anomaly.

James turned to Kirk. "Mr. Scott and I cooked up a little extra engineering based on what I learned in the Anomaly. However, we're not quite out of the woods. The Varal of Voran has arrived commanding a fighting fleet from the Hegemony. He is empowered by the conference to hear the report of your challenge against Omne, or to secede from the Federation and ally with the Romulan Empire. In that event the Romulan Commander-in-Chief will feel strong enough to turn on the Dovan, and on us."

Kirk went to the viewscreen and called the Varal. In a moment the screen filled with the image of the Varal, and behind him the young boy who had been the Hegarch's grandson. But the boy's eyes did not look vacant now.

"I have defeated your Regent, Omne," Kirk said. "By the terms of the challenge, I require peace and unity. The Federation will, of course, hear complaints and arguments on any and all policies—up to and including the Prime Directive. Meanwhile you will break off negotiations with the Romulans and return to Federation space."

"Is the Regent dead?" the young boy asked, stepping forward to speak with the tone and authority of the old Hegarch.

"No," Kirk said, "but he will not return."

The grandson nodded; he spoke with the decisiveness of the dead Hegarch. The galaxy might wonder how the unfortunate boy had suddenly become competent, but the true answer was not likely to be believed. "Then I shall not require a Regent," he said. "I believe you know why. And you have freed me fom the debt I owed the Regent while he ruled, for a service which he performed. Do not concern yourself. Both parties to the 'merger' which Omne arranged are liberated by it, and both survive. We will discuss the Hegemony's differences with the Federation at leisure, Captain. You have won. I shall guarantee your safe exit. Neither the Romulan fleet nor any other will fire on you without war from me."

Kirk gave another order and the Romulan Commander-in-Chief came on the screen. "The Commander has imformed me of the matter of trial by hazard," Kirk said. "I assume you grant that her innocence is established by her return."

The Commander-in-Chief grimaced. "Whether she is innocent or not, she cannot now be placed in second jeopardy for the trial offense—even if it were now to be proven that she has conspired with all of you. Doubtless she *has*. I cannot touch her. For *this* offense. I will merely advise her to walk carefully. Any further contact with you, I would regard as proof of treason on the face of things. But there will be none. I am sealing the Romulan Neutral Zone and the border again for another hundred years. I give you five of your minutes to get out, or I will fire on your ship and anyone who tries to aid you—including the Hegemony or the Doyen."

The Doyen beamed aboard the *Enterprise*.

Trevanian stepped forward to greet her. He knelt to her and then rose to look into her eyes while she inspected him.

"You took it upon yourself to take on a killer?" she said.

Trevanian sighed. "My lady, I have observed *you* in the matter of friendship." He looked at James and then indicated the Commander. "If you stand with the Commander, I believe the Empire will be in for some changes."

The Doyen looked at James, still in his mask, and at Kirk. "I suspect that the universe has changed," she said. "Commander, if you will join me on my flagship I believe that we have a new order of reality to discuss and a long campaign ahead. Friends?" She extended her hand for the crossed-wrists salute of brothers—or sisters—of the sword. The Commander laughed and answered the gesture. "Friends. Trevanian is yours. But so long as I have my 'hostage,' we will doubtless have many reasons to meet."

She turned and there were other goodbyes to be said.

"We also have reasons to meet," she said to the others, "but there will now be no way for us to meet which the Commander-in-Chief will not watch for evidence that James and I are traitors."

"There has not, in fact, been much time," Spock said, "except in the midst of battle. But then, there never was."

He inclined his head to the Commander and it was formal and Vulcan but James saw that the Vulcan was more at peace than he had been since the morning before the day of the Phoenix.

Spock seemed to know the answer now to the question which the Other had asked James in the cave. "Do you love her?"

James reached to link his hand with the Commander's in the paired-fingers gesture which he now knew was not merely Vulcan but Romulan.

With everything which he had only just begun to learn from her, James reached out to let the promise of what he had told the Other flow through his fingers.

It was the offer to burn his bridges behind him, to commit to the new life, and to her.

'Di'on,' he said silently, and then spoke also aloud in the Vulcan and Romulan origin-words. " 'Parted from me and never parted, always and ever touching, and touched—I await thee.' "

Spock and the Romulans understood, and the translator rendered it for the Humans.

The words of forever.

It would be a new life now, and a new man: A Romulan, to walk forever in the path of a Romulan prince, and to see what a man who had once sworn a starship captain's oath to serve the cause of peace could do to continue that mission in a warrior empire, at the side of a warrior starship commander who had become his future, and his heart.

There was no sound in the transporter room while the Commander looked into James' eyes, perhaps reading in eyes and mind whether he could, in truth, let this door close behind him.

Then very quietly Trevanian stepped forward to stand at James' shoulder.

And James remembered how Spock had said, so many years ago at Vulcan, "It is my right; by tradition the male is accompanied by his closest friends." James looked at Trevanian in recognition, and then beyond him at McCoy and Jim, acknowledging in what way they shared the memory of that moment and were his oldest friends. Finally he looked at Spock. And Spock stepped forward to stand at James' other shoulder.

Parted from me and never—

The Commander was saying it, James realized—aloud, and in his mind, " ' . . . never parted—ever and always touching and touched . . . Zh'james—we meet in the appointed place.' "

For the first time Di'on gave his name the Romulan pronunciation which she had said once would be proper. It was his name now—the private Romulan name which only these witnesses and his most intimate friends would know.

He was still the man who had been James T. Kirk, but he was Kirk no longer. The memories which were his alone diverged widely now and he had learned things which Jim Kirk had not learned. He was Zh'james and he was hers. He belonged to her and to the future they would forge together. It was a measure of how far he had come from being Kirk, for it was a path Jim could not have chosen.

Zh'james reached to open to the deep link with she-who-was-his-w—

Jim Kirk found himself looking at the space where James had been.

There had been no sound, no shimmer, no transition.

James had simply disappeared. In one breath. Suddenly and completely.

The Commander swayed and almost crumpled, as if the shock of separation tore something out of her soul.

Spock caught her shoulders and steadied her, and she lifted her head after a moment to meet the Vulcan's eyes in blunt acknowledgment of the loss.

McCoy swallowed any exclamations and stepped to check the Commander with his medical scanner. Scott swore softly over the tracers.

Trevanian turned suddenly to Kirk. "Then *you* are the original," he said. "I was not certain until now."

"Of *what?*" Kirk said. "What would you know about 'originals'? What did the Other tell you? And—*where is James?*"

"With Omne." Trevanian said.

"How?" the Doyen interjected. "How do you know?"

"The Other," Trevanian said with the look of remembering. "I was dying, and so, perhaps, was he. He told me something of the story of the price of the Phoenix. And he told me that Omne had had his own price for creating immortality. The first creation, the perfect replica, he regarded as his—to keep as a hostage against Spock in the game of galactic confrontation, or merely as evidence of his own handiwork. The technology was not fully developed and needed the power of the Vortex field. But Omne laid the groundwork. When the Phoenix process created James, it keyed in a trigger in his mind-recording, below the level of consciousness, which would reverberate at a frequency tuned to Omne's own mind. Given sufficient power, it would draw him to Omne through the nearest Omne-type transporter. The Other tried to use it to draw James to him when the scoutship was disintegrating in the Vortex—although I did not realize what he was doing at the time. But Omne's own 'reverberation' must have drawn James more strongly. It almost brought him through without the tractor beam."

"But Omne is on the other side of the Vortex," Kirk said quietly.

Trevanian nodded. "The Other said that the Vortex

forces, physical and psionic, amplify the effect enormously. I had not suspected that it could reach this far. And I had not realized the meaning of something else he said—something about the stress of ultimate fear or ultimate commitment acting as a trigger within the replica's mind. James was making an ultimate commitment. And if Omne also was making an ultimate effort to use the 'reverberation' to draw James to him—to make us come back after him—"

"Get me a transporter trace, Mr. Scott," Kirk said.

"Aye," Scott said from the console. "I've been workin'. There's some kind o' trace all right. Straight into the mouth of hell."

"With Omne," Kirk confirmed flatly.

"Or dead." McCoy countered, looking into the roiling Vortex.

Kirk shook his head. "When have we known Omne's 'automatic machinery' or his 'dead-man switches' to fail?"

"This would have been a 'live-man' switch," McCoy said without pleasure.

"Exactly, Doctor." Spock said, reaching over the transporter console to make a further check. "If it was designed by Omne's hand to bring a live man to him, do you doubt that it *would?*"

Spock flipped an intercom switch. "Prepare class-one shuttlecraft," he said.

Kirk shook his head. "Mr. Spock, the Vortex is closed. What is the probability that you could make it in—and out?"

"Zero, Captain," Spock said reluctantly. "There is a minute but finite probability that I could make it *in*."

"No." Kirk said. "I can't spare you, Mr. Spock."

The Commander stepped forward. "Nor is it your right, Mr. Spock. The trust is mine. And I will keep it, and him. If there is a way in, it is mine to take. And your trust is here." She turned to Kirk. "You will take Mr. Spock and your ship out of Romulan space. Your ship has just over one minute to be moving—or it will be fired on by Rovan's fleet. We will have started the

galactic war we swore to stop. Go. Beam me to my ship.
I will take care of my own."

The Doyen nodded. "Not alone," she said, and Trevanian moved to stand with her near the Commander.

"No, not alone," he said. His definitive tone made
the Doyen look at him in some surprise.

Kirk looked at them speculatively, but he had no
time or thought to spare for anything but James and his
ship. Only he could know fully the dangers of that other
side of the Vortex. Could he really consign the man who
was his second self to that exile?

Spock looked up from the console. "I was mistaken,"
he said. "I have now added current figures to Omne's
calculations from the Phoenix ship and from his memories. There is not even a minute probability of making it
in. The Anomaly is now a death trap."

It was a verdict, but Kirk saw no acceptance of the
verdict or the logic in the Vulcan's face. For a moment
Kirk locked eyes with Spock and faced down the primordial Vulcan who would hang the expense, defy the
logic and the odds. Then he watched Spock master that
ancient layer which had little to do with Vulcan logic
and which more than once had sent him into the mouth
of hell against impossible odds.

"James would be the first to order us to leave, you
know," Kirk said.

"I know," Spock said.

"You're not gonna *leave* him?" McCoy protested.

Spock turned to him with the severe look of logic.
"The figures indicate, Leonard, that under present conditions the Vortex will remain closed to our best ships
for some 53.725 years."

"But—that's *forever!*" Scotty said.

"No, Mr. Scott," Spock said, "it is *not* forever—to
an immortal." He was looking into the screen, and Kirk
knew that he was seeing Omne.

"Nor even to a Vulcan, Spock," Kirk said, although,
in truth, he did not see how that helped much. Spock
and the Commander had the Vulcanoid 250-year life
span. But James lived on a different time-scale.

"No," Spock said very deliberately, "nor to a Vulcan."

Kirk knew then that if it took fifty years, there would, after all, be someone at least to go after Omne . . .

"If it's true that immortality, once invented, can be reinvented," Kirk said, "that's a date, Mr. Spock."

Spock turned to look at him. "Once the Phoenix flies, Captain, it cannot be returned to the ashes."

"No, it cannot," the Commander said from the platform. "Nor anything which was born of the Phoenix. I accept your figures, Mr. Spock, but not your finality. If ships cannot reach him, I will find something which can. But that is *my* trust to keep."

"That also I know," Spock said. "There is no one else to whom I would leave it."

Kirk checked the seconds ticking out. Would *he* leave her that trust?

But James had already made that decision. And Kirk also had a trust to keep. He looked at Spock. "Energize," he said.

But the Vulcan was already moving. Spock's eyes found the Commander's and locked with them like a meeting of swords: a salute, a promise, a challenge. They planned on a scale of immortality now—and in the teeth of a time which could run out for them at any moment.

"Keep the trust," Spock said, and sent her off with his own hand.

Kirk, Spock, McCoy and Scott watched the three Romulan figures shimmer out.

It was McCoy who turned first to look into the viewscreen and into the eye of the Vortex, where not even imagination could follow.

But Kirk felt his imagination make the attempt.

Aloud he said only the words which had to be said into the intercom: "Ahead Warp Factor Three, out of Romulan space, *now*."

# EPILOGUE

OMNE rose.

The transporter had deposited him back at the place where his Other had died to save the life of Jim Kirk.

One Human had beaten them both.

Omne picked up the fallen spear he had made and went to take on—Elba.

The last mental effort he had made as the transporter took him had, apparently, not worked. He was alone in this world.

But time was long and memory longer.

Never mourn Black Omne.

The last man on the planet walked alone through a cave.

He heard a step behind him . . .

# ABOUT THE AUTHORS

SONDRA MARSHAK and MYRNA CULBREATH have been a writing team for almost five years since the "Star Trek Connection" brought them together. Sondra Marshak is one of the co-authors of *Star Trek Lives!*, an analysis of what makes the Star Trek phenomenon tick. Myrna Culbreath, founder of the Culbreath Schools in Colorado and editor of *The Fire Bringer*, published an article, "The Spock Premise," whch helped to bring them together and she moved from Colorado Springs to Baton Rouge, Louisiana to join Sondra. They have produced two television specials on Star Trek and are the editors of *Star Trek: The New Voyages* 1 and 2 and authors of *The Price of the Phoenix*, to which *The Fate of the Phoenix* is a sequel, and the forthcoming *Mr. Spock's Guide to the Planet Vulcan*. With co-author William Shatner they have written *Shatner: Where No Man . . .*—"Biography, autobiography, and a report from the revolution." Recently they have worked with Shatner on "Star Traveller," a major multimedia science fiction stage show. Sondra and Myrna have been in great demand as guest speakers at many Star Trek and science fiction conventions. They are currently working on a non-Star Trek science fiction novel, *The Power*, with co-author William Shatner. And, apart from science fiction and Star Trek, Sondra and Myrna are now completing a mainstream novel.

Sondra's background includes a B.A. and M.A. in history, while Myrna has a B.A. in psychology and philosophy. Sondra lives in Baton Rouge with her husband, Alan, a professor of electrical engineering at Louisiana State University; their son, Jerry, 7; her mother, Mrs. Anna Tornheim Hassan; and their German shepherd "Omne," named after the villain in *The Fate of the Phoenix*. Recently, on a trip to California, Jerry Marshak was "discovered" by various show business people and has landed his first job on "Diff'rent Strokes."

# OUT OF THIS WORLD!

That's the only way to describe Bantam's great series c science fiction classics. These space-age thrillers are fille with terror, fancy and adventure and written by America' most renowned writers of science fiction. Welcome to out er space and have a good trip!